DR.
YES

DR YES

BATEMAN

headline

First published in 2010 by
HEADLINE PUBLISHING GROUP

1

Cataloguing in Publication Data is available from the British Library

ISBN 9 780 7553 7859 3 (Hardback)
ISBN 9 780 7553 7860 9 (Trade paperback)

Typeset in Meridien by Palimpsest Book Production Ltd,
Falkirk, Stirlingshire

Printed in the UK by CPI Mackays, Chatham ME5 8TD

For Andrea and Matthew

1

It was the worst of times, it was the worst of times.

Spring was in the air, which was depressing enough, what with pollen, and bees, and bats, but my on/off girlfriend was also making my life miserable because of her pregnancy, which she continued to accuse me of being responsible for, despite repeatedly failing to produce DNA evidence. She whined and she moaned and she criticised. It was all part of a bizarre attempt to make me a better man. Meanwhile she seemed content to pile on the beef. She now had a small double chin, which she blamed on her condition and I blamed on Maltesers. There was clearly no future for us. In other news, the great reading public of Belfast continued to embrace the internet for their purchases rather than No Alibis, this city's finest mystery book-shop, while my part-time criminal investigations, which might have been relied upon to provide a little light relief, had recently taken a sordid turn, leaving a rather unpleasant taste in the mouth, although some of that may have been Pot Noodle.

I will not detain you with the details of the *Case of the Seductive Sweets*, other than to say that it had started out as something which, while undoubtedly distressing for the family, was still apparently quite innocuous, at least until I became involved. A thirteen-year-old boy's life at a local secondary school was being made hell because someone had written this graffiti legend about him on a toilet wall:

Mark Bruce will bum for dolly mixtures.

The school immediately had it removed, but it kept reappearing in different locations. Schools are notorious for either covering things up or seeking internal solutions, but it was taken out of their hands when a local confectionery wholesaler, aware that children had taken to asking for 'a packet of Bruce' rather than dolly mixtures in local shops, and who had cornered the market in this generic brand, grew concerned that lasting and permanent damage might be caused to his business. He was undoubtedly aware of my recent successful history in tracking down graffiti artists, as detailed in the *Case of the Cock-Headed Man* and the *Case of the Fruit on the Flyover*, and so I was engaged to track down the culprit. This was not difficult. Children are notorious little squealers. When just the right amount of pressure was applied, they wasted no time in pointing their grubby little fingers at another thirteen-year-old boy, who, as it turned out, had undertaken his malicious campaign not merely for the purposes of bullying or for reasons of innate badness, but because of jealousy and for revenge. His voice had recently broken, and the affections visited upon him by one of his teachers had rapidly shifted to his higher-pitched classmate. Thus I exposed a thirty-five-year-old geography teacher, metaphorically speaking, and it is safe to say that he will never work in this town again, though he has accepted a position south of the border. However, the confectionery wholesaler was not at all amused by my revelations, fearing that they would be plastered all over the newspapers and internet if the case came to court, thus bringing his confectionery in for further ridicule, and he refused point blank to pay me. In fact, I have my suspicions that he actually helped the teacher flee this jurisdiction. They were, fundamentally, very different people, but like the Japanese and Nazi axis of evil during World War II, at the end of the day they enjoyed a common purpose, in their case, the corruption of children, and I suppose it was inevitable that they should suppress their mutual distrust and dislike in order to further their cause.

On this spring day, with not a sniff of a customer, I sat around the counter with Alison, my expectant girlfriend and seller of bangles, and Jeff, my part-time book-stacker, Amnesty International apologist and conspiracy-theory devotee, debating crime and punishment. The secondary-school paedophile had indeed fled the country one step ahead of the law, but we were trying to decide what would have been an appropriate punishment had he been apprehended in time. We had already dismissed the usual suspects – counselling and chemical castration – and moved on to actual physical violence involving metallic objects that had to be swung.

'A claw hammer,' was Alison's suggestion. She pointed at her forehead, the side of her skull, and her nose, and said, 'Here, here and here.'

I disagreed. There were better hammers. I proposed a sledgehammer, or a jackhammer, or a steam hammer, or a trip hammer, or a ball-peen hammer used in metal work; a gavel would probably be quite appropriate, or a blacksmith's dog-head hammer could certainly do some damage. It really depended what kind of injury you wanted to inflict. I explained that the amount of energy delivered to the target area by the hammer blow is equivalent to one half of the mass of the head times the square of the head's speed at the time of the impact. The formula for this is:

$$E = \frac{mv^2}{2}$$

Alison and Jeff looked at me for a little bit, then Jeff said, 'Anyway, I think a much better punishment would be to glue steaks to him, and then throw him into shark-infested waters.'

'Steak's too expensive,' Alison said admirably

quickly, which boded well for the future. 'You'd be better off with stewing steak,' she said. 'Or mince. Mince is relatively cheap.'

'You might have difficulty actually securing the mince to his body,' Jeff pointed out. 'You would have to keep it in its original packaging, you know, with the Styrofoam base and the cellophane. But then how would the sharks smell it?'

'Some blood would leak out,' said Alison. 'It always leaks out in my fridge.'

'Maybe they wouldn't be attracted to it. Maybe sharks only like human blood. They might not like cow blood. I mean, has a shark ever eaten a cow?'

They both looked at me, the fount of all knowledge.

'They've probably eaten a sea cow,' I said.

'Can you milk a sea cow?' Jeff asked.

'Would the milk be salty?' Alison asked.

'They're not like our cows,' I said, although I suspected they probably knew that. 'They're more like seals.'

'Can you milk a seal?' Jeff asked.

'That's how they feed their young,' I said.

'Once they hatch,' said Alison.

'We're getting off topic here,' I said.

They both nodded.

'Okay,' said Jeff. 'Have we agreed that we can tape a paedophile to a seal and then release him in shark-infested waters?'

Alison pointed out that you would have to catch

the seal first. 'I suppose you could get one from a circus or like a water park. A performing seal. He could keep a ball up with his nose. He could put on a bit of a show to attract the shark, because maybe not enough blood would have trickled out of the mince, and even if it did, it could be carried away by the tides and currents.'

I summed up. 'So we're taping the mince to the paedophile, and taping the paedophile to the seal?' Alison and Jeff both nodded enthusiastically. I smiled. The flaw in their logic was obvious. 'If this is designed to be a punishment for the paedophile, and you've taped the mince to him and secured him to the performing seal and released the performing seal in shark-infested waters, don't you think the paedophile will have drowned long before the shark hears about the performance, watches the show, and then gets to tear both the paedophile and the seal to shreds? Doesn't it seem like an awful lot of trouble to go to if he's going to drown in less than a minute?'

Alison looked rather crestfallen. Jeff was going the same way, but he suddenly brightened. 'You're forgetting – the seal, and the paedophile, they could quite easily be caught in nets.'

'What, by fishermen, you mean? How would that . . . ?'

'No, no, no – Atlanteans.'

'Right. Atlanteans. They would be the . . .'

'People of Atlantis. If the Atlanteans spotted a man taped to a seal, they'd want to rescue him. They'd think we were being quite barbaric, taping mince to a man and securing him to a seal and releasing him in shark-infested waters. They already hate us for pollution and dragnet fishing; this would just reinforce their negative opinions of us.'

'They might have negative opinions,' said Alison. 'It doesn't mean they're going to condone paedophilia.'

'Maybe Atlanteans have no laws against it,' said Jeff. 'Maybe they're quite liberal, like the Dutch. Besides, they wouldn't know he was a paedophile; he's hardly going to confess, even after he's learned Atlantean. He'll probably tell them he was the victim of a travesty of justice, like the Birmingham Six and anybody from Guildford.'

'Is Amnesty International protecting paedophiles now?' I asked.

'No, I'm only making the point that he's not going to tell them what he has or hasn't done.'

'We would have to brief the seal,' said Alison. 'She could tell them.'

'She?'

'Absolutely, you'd need a sex you could depend on. And the Atlanteans have lived underwater so long they probably converse with the sea creatures.'

'Yeah, the way we converse with cows?'

'Land cows?' asked Jeff.

The possibility of a customer to interrupt proceedings was remote, so it could have dragged on for ever. Fortunately it was at precisely this point in our discussion that I was distracted by a figure walking past the

No Alibis front window. In truth I could equally have been distracted by a fly or a dust mite, such was the level of our conversation, but in this instance, even though I only had the briefest glimpse of him, there was something familiar, and yet unfamiliar, about his face, and gait. For several moments I struggled to place him, but then suddenly the penny dropped, the cash register opened, and I was out of the door and after him.

Now, looking back, after all the trouble that followed, I know that I shouldn't have moved a muscle, that I should have let him go, and then I would never have become involved in what became my most difficult and distressing investigation to date, the *Case of the Pearl Necklace*, a case that would ultimately put Jeff's life, my girlfriend's life, her unborn baby's life and, much more importantly, my own life on the line.

2

I have never in my whole life actually physically pursued a case, because any kind of activity requiring increased motor function is something I have to be wary of, but I could hardly help myself. Of course I didn't know it was a case *then*. *Then* it was just a man walking past my window – but what a man! You see, in my field of crime fiction, Augustine Wogan was an enigma, a myth wrapped up in a legend, a barely published novelist and screenwriter who was known to so few that they didn't even qualify as a cult following, it was more like stalking. He was, nevertheless, Belfast's sole contribution to the immortals of the crime-writing genre. His reputation rested on three novels self-published in the late 1970s, novels so tough, so real, so heartbreaking that they blew every other book that tried to deal with what was going on over here right out of the water. Until then, novels about the Troubles had invariably been written by visiting mainland journalists, who perhaps got most of their facts right, but never quite captured the atmosphere or the sarcasm. Augustine Wogan's novels were so on the ball that he was picked up by the RUC and questioned because they thought he had inside information about their shoot-to-kill policy; shot at by the IRA because they believed he had wrung secrets out of a drunken quartermaster; and beaten up by the UVF because they had nothing better to do. He had been forced to flee the country, and although he had returned since, he had never, at least as far as I was aware, settled here again. I occasionally picked up snippets of information about him from other crime-writing aficionados, the latest being that he had been employed to write the screenplay for the next James Bond movie, *Titter of Wit*, but had been fired for drunkenness. There was always a rumour of a new novel, of him being signed up by a big publisher or enthusiastic agent, but nothing ever appeared in print. The books that made up the *Barbed-Wire Love* trilogy were never republished. They are rarer than hen's teeth. I regarded the box of them I kept upstairs as my retirement fund. In those few moments when I saw him pass the shop, I knew that if I could just persuade him to sign them, their value would be instantly quadrupled. They say money is at the root of all evil, but I have to be pragmatic. I am devoted to crime fiction, but I am also devoted to eating, and Augustine Wogan was just the meal ticket I was looking for.

By the time I caught up with him, I was gasping for breath. It was only twenty yards, but if God had intended me to be a long-distance athlete, he wouldn't have given me a collapsed lung and rickets.

'Mr Wogan?'

He stopped, he turned. It was indisputably Augustine Wogan, though he had dropped a hundred pounds and lost several chins since we had last spoken. He was gaunt now; he looked twenty years older when it should only have been five; he wore a long, thin beard and clasped a leather briefcase to his chest with a defiance that made him look as if he'd taken a job amongst the Hasidic Jew diamond-sellers of Antwerp and run off with the merchandise.

'What?'

Irritated, distracted, paranoid.

That's just me, so it's always nice to meet a brother in self-harm. You can tell. It's in the eyes. I'm good with eyes. I had recently been unmasked as a charlatan by the Support Group for People Depressed Because They Have Been Rejected by their Cornea Transplants. I kept telling them that I was seeing ghostly images of murder victims during those brief weeks before rejection set in, and that the dead man's eyes I wore were those of a killer. But they refused to believe me, mostly because the paperwork showed they had belonged to a traffic warden from Sion Mills. It was a small group, but torn by power struggles. Not so much a case of the blind leading the blind as the hazy leading the indistinct. As it turned out, in the land of the blind, the one-eyed man truly was king, and he had me out on my arse.

'What do you *want*?'

I had drifted. I shook myself. 'Mr Wogan, it's me . . .' I turned and pointed back at the shop. 'From No Alibis? You did a reading about five years ago?'

'What of it?'

He was glaring at me.

'Sorry – I didn't realise you were in a rush.'

'Why not? Wasn't I *rushing*?'

'Yes, you were, but . . .'

'What do you *want*?'

'I was hoping you might sign some—'

He was all set to growl something else at me, and I was all set to sink to a new, lower level of grovel, when there was a little *ping* off to his left, nothing more than the tiniest piece of gravel rebounding off a car windscreen, but by his reaction, ducking down and scurrying towards me for protection, you would have thought, and he clearly did, that someone had taken a shot at him. It was *not* a shot. Or if it was, Action Man was on the loose. But for the purposes of getting what I wanted, I was quite prepared to accept that it *was* a gunshot, and I quickly ushered him towards the safety of Belfast's leading crime emporium.

To their eternal discredit, Alison and Jeff were still discussing the taping of mince to a paedophile and the paedophile to what had now become a dolphin – without apparently noticing that I had left the building. They certainly noticed my return, but only because I was bustling a terrified-looking Rasputin through the door and ordering Alison to get him a chair.

Alison blinked at me.

I next ordered Jeff, who, being an employee, of sorts, was much more compliant.

'Have a seat, have a seat,' I said as Jeff put it in place.

'Thank you . . . thank you . . .'

'Get him a glass of water.'

Alison was looking at me, knowing how rare it was for me to fawn over anyone. Jeff nodded and turned to the kitchen.

'Please, no, don't go to any trouble.' Augustine held up his hand. 'Evian if you have it.'

Jeff hesitated, then looked to me for direction. From behind Augustine I drew a bottle outline in the air, and Jeff got it immediately. We keep a selection of empty designer water bottles in the kitchen for the exclusive use of prima donnas. In his field, Augustine was actually a prima donna, in the best sense of the words, but it didn't mean he could tell branded water from tap. Or as it turned out:

'Fuck! That tastes like fucking shite!' He grabbed the bottle and examined the label. 'Sell by March 1997 – are you trying to fucking kill me as well?'

He let out a cry, and hurled it across the shop, spraying water over a display of books that would shortly boast a sign saying *Water Damage Sale*, though actually I would have increased their price.

Before I could apologise profusely, he held his hand up again and said sorry himself. He was under a lot of pressure. He appreciated us giving him sanctuary. For the first time he nodded around the shop.

'I do remember this place. Yes. Did a very good reading in here, didn't I? What did you call that tit used to own it?'

I cleared my throat. 'I own it now,' I said.

Augustine nodded at Alison. 'This the missus?'

'Working on it,' said Alison.

He turned his gaze upon Jeff, who shrugged and said, 'Jeff – I just do stuff.'

Augustine shook his head. 'Well, nice to meet you all.' He patted his jacket pocket, and produced a long, thick cigar and snipped the end of it with a small guillotine cutter. He was about to light up when Alison said, 'No.'

'No?'

'No.'

'But somebody just tried to kill me.'

'No.'

He looked at me. I gave him my helpless shrug. I was one hundred per cent against smoking, particularly in my shop, but he was *Augustine Fucking Wogan*! Fortunately he didn't try to force it. It was just another thing that was going against him. He looked sadly at the cigar, then slipped it back inside his jacket. He shook his head. He sighed. 'How appropriate,' he said, 'that a crime writer should wash up in a mystery bookshop, here, at the end of it all.'

14

He stared at the ground. His shoulders began to shake. He cried silently. It was terribly sad to see the great man brought so low, and I would have put an arm around him and given him a hug if I wasn't allergic to people. Alison did the twirly finger thing at the side of her head, asking if he was nuts. Jeff did the mobile phone with his fist, for the emergency services, before miming pouncing with a butterfly net. Their reaction to this first encounter with Augustine Wogan was understandable; they did not know who he was, the giant that he was in his field, nor that his signature, applied to a dusty box of books, would help No Alibis get through the doubtlessly lean summer months. They took him at face value – a head-the-ball I'd dragged in off the street.

Alison said as much, pulling me to one side as Augustine continued to sob his eyes out. 'Just what this shop needs – another maniac. How are we going to get rid of him?'

'We aren't. Don't you know who he is? Augustine Wogan? *The Times* named him amongst their One Hundred Masters of Crime Fiction. At number seventeen. The sixteen above him are already dead. The *Daily Telegraph* put him in their top ten Fifty Crime Writers to Read Before You Die, despite the fact that his books have never been picked up by a mainstream publisher and they've all been out of print for twenty years!'

'So?'

I turned to my trusty assistant. 'Jeff – how many

times a week do people come in here asking about Augustine Wogan and how to get hold of his books?'

'Uhm – once?'

'Yes, but it's every week!'

'Uhm – yes, but it's usually the same bloke.'

'That isn't the point! He wrote the *Barbed-Wire Love* trilogy; he's a genius!'

'Well your genius looks mental.' She shook her head. 'Maybe he could be a genius down at Waterstones?'

'Philistine,' I hissed.

I knelt before him. He still had the briefcase pinned to his chest by his elbows. I gingerly prodded a knee. 'Mr Wogan. Augustine. Is there anything I can do to help?'

He rubbed at his eyes with his knuckles. 'Help? I think it's too late for that.'

'Is there somebody I can call for you?'

'It's definitely too late for that.'

'Well, you were rushing somewhere; do you want me to call wherever you were going?'

'No, I don't think that would be a good idea at all. You see . . .' He let out a sigh. He looked from me to Jeff to Alison and back. Then he opened his briefcase and reached inside. He took out a gun. 'I was on my way to kill someone.'

'Oh,' I said.

'Bloody hell,' said Alison.

As Augustine waved the gun listlessly around, Jeff ducked down behind the counter. I stood up, and stepped back.

'Oh, I'm such a bloody fool,' Augustine wailed. 'I have immersed myself in crime fiction for all these years and convinced myself that I know something about crime, about murder and how to do it and get away with it, when the truth is I'm just a ham-fisted, gold-plated old eejit. I was building up a head of steam, and you interrupted me, and now I don't think I have the strength to make another run at him. Thank God you stopped me when you did – divine intervention, that's what it is, that's what it is!'

We were stunned, we were shocked, we didn't know where to look or what to say. He was the legendary Augustine Wogan, but reduced to a sobbing, gun-toting wreck.

Alison already had the phone in her hand.

Jeff was clutching the mallet I keep for protection just beneath the counter.

'While you're here,' I ventured, 'do you think you could sign some books?'

3

Alison was telling me I had to get him out of the shop, that he was clearly brain-damaged, that we shouldn't allow him to say anything else because I was so weak and insipid I was bound to be pulled into something dark and dangerous, and I would drag her in with me. She was pregnant, and that was scary enough. I had told her a million times that I was only interested in little itty-bitty cases, not much more complicated than crosswords or, God help me, Sudoku, but somehow they never quite worked out like that. There were always gunshots, bodies, terror, blood, pine trees or stuffed animals, and we just didn't need it right now; we had to be thinking of little Caspar.

'Just get the gun off him,' she said, 'and if you don't call the police, I will.'

I met her halfway. I removed the gun. He didn't put up a fight. He was a broken man. But I couldn't phone the police. I didn't want my legacy as a book-seller to be that I had put the greatest crime fiction author ever to come out of Belfast behind bars, especially as he hadn't even responded to my request to sign my precious books, and in doing so render them even more precious.

'Look,' I said, showing her the gun, 'he's disarmed, he's not a danger to anyone now. The least we can do is let him talk about it if he wants to. What's the harm in that?'

'You know exactly what the harm is.'

'I swear to God we won't get involved. I've had it with danger, you know that; my blood pressure is worse than yours, and I'm not even pregnant.'

'Your blood pressure is perfectly normal.'

'That's just what they want me to think.'

She glared. I glared back.

She would win, but I was getting better.

Fortunately, or unfortunately, given what was to come, fate, or Augustine, intervened.

'He killed my wife.'

We both turned.

'Who did?' Alison asked.

Augustine shook his head.

Alison said, 'Sure let me get you a wee cup of tea and you can tell us all about it.'

She's unpredictable and contradictory, and I suppose it's part of the reason I love her, albeit in an infinitesimally small way.

The tea boy brought the tea, and then sat there as

if he was somehow entitled to listen in to a deeply personal conversation. I gave him work to do in the stock room, and he made a face, and I made one back, and he was about to respond in kind when Alison gave him one of her looks and he quickly disappeared. I didn't like it. I didn't like that he was more scared of her than he was of me. Or that she thought she could boss him about when she didn't own the shop like I did. I have the deeds. They're secure.

'I'll be mother,' she said, and I didn't much like that either. Augustine nodded gratefully, but made no move for the cup. 'You were saying, your wife?'

'My beautiful Arabella. Oh yes. He killed her all right.'

'Who he?' I asked.

Augustine sighed. 'Do you remember the days when old people looked like old people? Old and stooped and the women pulled tartan shopping trolleys behind them and wore brown tights like bank robbers, but on their fat varicose legs? Whatever happened to those days?'

'Well . . .' Alison began.

'They all want to fight time, don't they? My Arabella was the most beautiful girl in the world, but you could tell her it until you were blue in the face and she still wouldn't believe you. And now, of course, *she* is blue in the face. I'm sixty-two years old. Arabella was sixty. She looked forty-five. But she wanted to be twenty-five again. Oh, the price of vanity!'

'So who do you think killed her?'

Tenacious is my middle name. I had recently changed it from Trouble.

He looked me straight in the eye and said, 'You.'

He paused.

Whether he meant it to be dramatic or not, it was.

Alison looked at me, already prepared to accept that I was guilty.

'You know what it's like for a crime writer like me, don't you?' Augustine eventually continued. 'My name is known, the critics love me, but I haven't made a red cent from my books. I scraped by for a while writing screenplays, but that was twenty years ago. All this time I've been writing; I've a room full of manuscripts, but I've never sent them out, never been happy with them. But all these years, my Arabella has been supporting me. She's from landed folk, inherited money, and we've lived well, but we whittled most of it away travelling. Once the Troubles were over, we talked about coming back here, we looked at houses. Arabella's a social girl, she likes the parties and the theatre and cocktails, so when she came back, she wanted to look her best. That's where he comes in: the Yank, Dr Yes, Dr Chicago, whatever the hell you want to call him.'

The names meant nothing to me, but Alison was on it straight away.

'I know *exactly* who you mean. Dr Yeschenkov; he's yummy, all the girls would have his babies. With the exception of me, obviously.'

I raised my hands, helplessly. 'Will someone elaborate? Please?'

'He's a plastic surgeon,' said Alison. 'He has his own private clinic, he runs a programme called . . .'

'The Million-Dollar Makeover,' said Augustine. 'Nothing would do Arabella but she had to have it.'

'He takes you away for like six weeks . . .'

'He's cut it down to four.'

'He puts you up in a swanky hotel . . .'

'It wasn't that swanky.'

'And he does a whole series of procedures, brings in the top guys in their field . . .'

'So he says.'

'You've seen it on TV: eyes, teeth, tummy, boobs, keeps you away from prying eyes for six weeks . . .'

'Four.'

'And then does a grand reveal, and you look stunning.'

'He's a butcher!' Augustine shook his head. There were tears in his eyes again.

'Did it all go hideously wrong?' I asked, as gently as I could.

Augustine glared at me. 'What do you think?'

'In what way?' Alison asked. There was something about the way she said things that just seemed *nicer*. More sympathetic. I was pretty glad I hadn't voiced my first thought, which was to tell him he should have been wary of anyone offering to make a silk purse from a sow's ear.

'I don't *know*, that's the point. They wouldn't let me near her the whole time . . . and I know that's what you sign up for . . . but I just missed her so much. We tried to speak on the phone every night, but she was tired and in pain and all bandaged up. She sounded miserable. But she was determined to go through with it. I spoke to her on the Wednesday night and she sounded more positive; she had one more procedure to go through, then they'd start taking off the bandages and showing her what they'd done. After that they'd do hair and make-up, new clothes, then I'd be invited up for the big reveal. Except the call never came.'

'Because?' I asked.

'Because buggery to fuck, she was dead, wasn't she?'

'On the operating table?'

'Yes! No! I don't know. They deny it. They say she was fine when she left them, she looked great. Dr Chicago, Dr Yes, Dr Fucking Scissorhands says she signed her cheque, signed herself out and went on her merry way. He says it's a sad fact that sometimes his programme gives women a new lease of life; they want to recreate themselves, start afresh and so they disappear and sometimes they go to extraordinary lengths to cover their tracks.'

'And . . . could she not . . . have?' I asked tentatively, although obviously not tentatively enough, judging by the look Alison gave me.

'No, absolutely not.'

He would have left it at that, but I persevered.

'You're sure? Women are unpredictable, they change with the . . .'

Alison snorted.

'Do you know how I know?' Augustine asked. 'I know she didn't *just disappear* because of the last words she said to me in our final phone call.'

He dropped in that pause again. He was definitely good at the dramatics.

'Yes?' Alison asked, unable to contain herself.

I was expecting something dark and suspicious, some prescient hint that things were *not as they seemed.*

'She said, "I love you, honey bun."'

And just like that, he drew Alison into the trap, and like a fool, I followed.

4

I phoned Alison at three a.m. Obviously, I wasn't sleeping. She answered groggily. 'Brian?'

In days gone by, the presumption that it was her ex-husband might have driven me insaner with jealousy, but I was now well used to her wicked ways. She was like Bennett Marco in Richard Condon's *The Manchurian Candidate*, perfectly normal for ninety-nine per cent of the time, but secretly brainwashed to say something cutting and nasty at a subconscious trigger, in this case her bedside telephone ringing.

She said, 'What? Who is this?'

'Who do you think?'

'Oh. Sorry. Asleep. What?'

'I just wanted to say . . .'

And having learned the art of the dramatic pause from a master, I gave her exactly that.

'What?'

And kept it going.

'*What?*'

And kept it going.

'Oh for fuck—'

'I just wanted to say, if you think we're calling our son Caspar, you've another think coming.'

And then I hung up.

Sometimes it's the little things that give the greatest pleasure.

I never truly sleep, but I do occasionally venture into the half-awake Land of Nod, where I have timeshare. But this night I endured a nightmare about Mother. I had finally consigned her to a pre-funeral home several weeks previously because since her stroke she was just *too much trouble*, but now as I twisted and turned I imagined that she was back in her bedroom at the top of the house. I heard the clump of her footsteps on the floor above, their creak on the stairs as she descended, and then heavy breathing outside my door. I screamed at her to leave me alone, that I hadn't been bad, but I was sorry and would be a better boy. I buried myself under the quilt and prayed for her to go away, and eventually drifted off.

I was up at the first light of dawn, angry for foolishly terrifying myself when I knew all along that the sounds were not born of a feverish nightmare, but were very real, and belonged to the gaunt, red-eyed and destitute author Alison had invited to sleep in my big, empty house without so much as a by-your-leave and who was already sitting at my breakfast table, gorging himself on Rice Krispies. She was so wrong about my house. You're never alone with a personality disorder. And sometimes it's preferable to having an actual, real-life guest, one whose emaciated chest is exposed by a barely tied borrowed dressing gown last worn by my incarcerated mother and who is happily slobbering down the last of the skimmed milk.

I knew why Alison had done it, and I could understand her reasoning. She wanted to help this heartbroken man, and I had the space. In a way I liked the idea of him being there, because I could pump him for information about his writing, and I could engage him in conversation while quietly passing him copies of his exceedingly rare books to sign. But the reality was different. He was barely through the door before he was ordering pizza, and I had to pay for it when it arrived, an outrageous price considering the size of it, the thinness of it, and the fact that everything he had chosen to top it with was liable to set off my allergies. And also, he wolfed it without offering me *any*. He washed it down with Mother's sherry. He must have had two pints of it. In pint glasses. One might argue that he was drowning his sorrows. But he held his drink with the expertise of a professional mourner. When I tried to talk to him about his work, he never quite managed to answer any question I put to him, opting instead to launch into a preamble, then transferring to a tangent before settling on something *completely* irrelevant. I had some very detailed questions to ask about his *Barbed-Wire Love* trilogy. In fact one question alone took me fifteen minutes to deliver. He ought to have been flattered that I was so interested in his work, but he chose instead to roll his eyes, puff on his cigar, which he lit safe in the knowledge that Alison was no longer present, gulp his sherry and then say at the very end, I'm sorry, could you repeat the question? Even my attempts to get him to sign his own books were thwarted. When I produced the box, he marvelled at their pristine condition and then proceeded to bend their spines as he began to read them as if he had never seen them before. I literally had to prise them loose from his fingers and put them away for safe keeping. I was just trying to do some business, and he was being a nightmare. My plan to quadruple my investment disappeared as fast as the pizza.

Only late on, when he was very drunk, did he finally start talking about his lovely Arabella again. He grew tearful. He raged. He accused and pointed the finger of blame. I listened and nodded – that was all he wanted. He was in no mood to discuss the evidence, or lack of it, or for me to dissect his delusions, which is what they undoubtedly were.

'You need more Rice Krispies,' he said.

He didn't need to say. The box was on its side, the remaining dust spilled across the kitchen counter, only some of it drowned by the trail of milk he had left, leading from the counter across the floor to the table.

As I sat opposite him, having Lo-Lo'd a sliver of wholemeal, he crammed another overflowing spoonful into his mouth and spluttered out, 'He has testicles everywhere.'

'Excuse me? Who has testicles . . . ?'

He swallowed down. 'Tentacles, he has tentacles everywhere.'

'Oh. Right. Who? Mr Kellogg?'

'Dr Yes.'

I just went, 'Mmmmm,' and continued eating. I didn't want to go over the same old accusations again. I was already going to have to repeat them to Alison as soon as she arrived. She hadn't been able to join us last night because of a hair appointment.

A hair appointment.

A *hairdo*.

They are such contradictions.

It was the only time she could go, because of work.

I *ask you*.

She let slip that it cost £75.

I bloody ask you.

Like taking food out of Caspar's mouth.

Shit!

She was now brainwashing *me*. Her original suggestion of Rory was bad enough. No child of mine would *ever* be called Caspar.

If indeed he was a child of mine.

I didn't respond to Augustine's tentacles assertion until about an hour later, when he finally emerged from my shower, having used all of the hot water, and came downstairs, still wearing Mother's dressing gown, fruitlessly searching for something to eat while he got dressed. As he picked his way through the fridge, Alison arrived through the back door and greeted him enthusiastically. She had brought three Starbucks frappuccinos with her, which was a nice thought, and out of character.

As Augustine shuffled off clutching his, Alison raised an expectant eyebrow. Actually, *all* of her was expectant. When I didn't respond she said, '*Well?*'

'Well what?'

'The hair?'

'Did you not get it done?'

'You're funny.'

'No, seriously. It doesn't look any different.'

'It's a different colour.'

'I think not.'

'It was blonde, and now it's honey blonde.'

'If you say so.'

'And it's half the length!'

'Are you sure?'

'Yes! I needed something more manageable.'

'Like me?'

'You're funny.'

'So's your face.'

'Just . . . oh! I don't know why I bother.' She sat down at the kitchen table and opened her Starbucks. I joined her. I gave her a long look.

'Seventy-five quid? I don't think I've spent that much on a haircut in my entire life.'

'I rest my case.'

I could have told her the truth, that Mother had been cutting my hair for the past thirty years. It was a simple process, involving a cereal bowl and a flame-thrower. Or I could have explained that my father used to take me to his barber, as fathers do, but at the age of twelve, when my interest in mystery fiction was just starting to take over my life, I stumbled across an ancient reprint of an old penny blood serial called *The String of Pearls*, featuring that urban legend Sweeney Todd, and I refused point blank to go to a barber's after that in case he cut my throat. I was a sensitive kid. Luckily, I grew out of it. Could have told the truth, chose not to.

Alison said, 'So, what's he been saying?'

'Tentacles.'

'As in . . . ?'

'Dr Yeschenkov, his tentacles reach everywhere, apparently, the police especially, which is why they tend to side with him over lovely Arabella. They think she's run off too. They say her credit card was used at a cashpoint in Dublin a week after she checked herself out of her hotel.'

'It could have been stolen.'

'That's what I said. Apparently the police brought Augustine in and showed him CCTV footage the Garda sent up, taken from the bank's camera above the cash-point, of her taking the money out.'

'What'd he say to that?'

'He said it looked like her, but it wasn't her.'

'But he hadn't seen the new-look Arabella.'

'Exactly. But he's convinced.'

'So they told him to bugger off.'

'Yep. He went to the newspapers, weren't inter-ested. He stormed the clinic, mad drunk, thinking that would get the press interested, but all it got him was a night in the clink. He took to standing outside shouting at anyone going in or out. They took out an injunction. Court told him he couldn't go within half a mile of it. So he stands half a mile away, with a megaphone. He's been bombarding them with phone calls and e-mails and ordering coal for them, and pizza, and wreaths and all sorts of shit, generally just being really annoying.'

'And all he wants Dr Yes to do is stand up and admit to killing his wife?'

'That's all.'

'And he has no hard physical evidence at all?'

'He's seen her medical records. The only thing he can say is that she was allergic to penicillin, but it doesn't show on her consent forms.'

'And they say to that?'

'They say it does on the original, and they sent over poor photocopies; they rectified it and sent better copies.'

'And he suspects conspiracy.'

'Obviously.'

Alison took a sip of her coffee. A little bit dribbled down and nestled in her extra chin. She saw me looking at it and wiped it away. I stared at her hand.

She rolled her eyes but lifted one of the napkins that came with the coffee and wiped the back of it. I nodded appreciatively. She balled the napkin and chucked it over her shoulder.

'It doesn't mean he's wrong,' she said. 'We shouldn't underestimate the bond there is between a man and his wife and the instinctive knowledge that brings.'

'Or you could be talking bollocks.'

'All I'm saying is that short of speaking to Arabella herself, Augustine is probably the one other person in the world who knows her best. That last phone call was so full of love . . .'

'According to him.'

'. . . and there was no indication that she was unhappy or planning to take flight. She would have been on a high knowing the big reveal was coming; why would she suddenly disappear?'

'It doesn't matter *why*. There is no evidence of foul play, but there is evidence that she's alive and well and spending her money. She went to Dublin, she probably caught a flight somewhere. Augustine Wogan is an alcoholic, paranoid wastrel; she's had enough of him. All we need to do is get him to sign some books and then get him the hell out of here.'

'You're wrong. He's in love, and he knows something is badly wrong, but nobody will listen to him. His wife is dead and Dr Yes is pulling strings to cover his tracks and get away with murder.'

'God, you're turning into a conspiracy theorist as well! Have you by any chance swallowed Jeff?'

'Not recently.'

'You're funny.'

'So's your face. Look, you've been championing Augustine for years; don't let him down now. I have a feeling about this. And we're his last hope.'

We locked eyes across the table, each of us unaware that Augustine was standing in the doorway, arms folded, immaculately dressed in one of my father's long-mothballed suits, at least until he said, 'Of the two of you, I think I prefer you, princess.'

Alison glowed.

5

Of *course* I backtracked. It is my default mechanism. I assured him I was merely playing devil's advocate, and of course we were going to look into his case. But I had no intention of it. The truth was that the trauma of having him at such close quarters, in my mother's bed and dressing gown, in my father's suit and eating me out of house and home, had somewhat dulled my enthusiasm for persuading him to sign my stash of books. I could just forge it and nobody would be any the wiser. I had already taken pictures of him on my mobile phone while he dozed sherry-drunk in one of my armchairs, with me posing beside him like we were great mates; pinning those above the signed books would be authentication enough, at least for your average mug amateur or lower-level dealer.

I just wanted rid of him. But Alison, who knows a thing or two about eggs and how to exploit them, sat him down at the table and scrambled the only two left in the house. As he shovelled them in, I made faces at her across the table, but she ignored me. When he had finished scoffing them down, he wiped his mouth with the back of his hand. Standards were slipping *everywhere*.

He said, 'Thank you, Alison, that was lovely.' She smiled demurely. 'Now, what are we going to do about my Arabella?'

'Do?' I said.

'We're going to find her, or find out what happened to her,' said Alison. I made a kind of choking sound. 'In our spare time we do investigate certain cases. We've had quite a lot of success. My partner here is a bit of a genius.'

I made another face. She *would not* win me over.

'Well that would be ... *fantastic* ... I've really nowhere else to turn ... but I'm afraid I've nothing to pay you with.'

'That won't be necessary. We don't do it for the money.'

I *grrrrrred*.

'It would mean the world to me. And do you know something?' He was looking at me now. 'Even though I was rather flustered yesterday, I was looking at your shop, and it's really quite wonderful. You obviously have a great love of books and writing. I was wondering if you've ever thought of publishing your own books, you know, limited editions maybe?'

'Done that,' I said. 'There's bugger-all money in it.'

'Really? Because, as it happens, I have a little manuscript sitting around. Maybe we could work something
out, you know, in lieu of payment; you could publish
that?'

The first faint stirrings.

'Yeah, maybe.'

I didn't want to get too excited. Yes, he was criti-
cally acclaimed, but his only known works were more
than twenty years old. If he had written it recently,
it was probably as mad as he was.

'And you should know,' said Alison, at which point
I realised that I'd said it out loud.

I laughed and said, 'Sure we're all a bit mad. What's
the book?'

'Well, you know this *Barbed-Wire Love* trilogy you're
so enamoured of?'

'Yes?'

'There were always actually four parts to it. Because
it was self-published, and it didn't sell at all, I didn't
have enough money to put the fourth one out. So it's
been gathering dust all these years, which I've always
thought was a great pity, because it throws a whole
new light on the rest of it.'

He nodded thoughtfully.

Alison gazed at me across the table, probably
wondering why I appeared to be suffering a stroke.

I wasn't convinced of the wisdom of leaving him in
the house by himself, but it was either that or bring
him with me to No Alibis, and I could do without

that. He was just a stress to have around. And besides, I wanted to dive head first into solving what would become the *Case of the Pearl Necklace*, because in my head I was already formulating ambitious plans for the first publication of *Fire in the Sky*, the fourth book in what was now no longer a trilogy but a *cycle* of novels, and beyond that persuading Augustine to let me reprint the other books as well. I would be acclaimed throughout the mysterious world for not only discovering the unknown fourth book, but also rescuing the original trilogy from obscurity. And if I kept them to limited editions, I could charge an absolute fortune and secure No Alibis' future as well. I was on *such* a high, although part of that may have been down to my extensive list of medication, which I seemed to have taken twice that morning by mistake.

Even Jeff noticed, and he's an idiot. When he brought me the wrong coffee from Starbucks, I did not even shout at him, merely sent him back for the right one. When he returned I told him to man the till, and trusted him with its key, and he smiled as if he was in seventh heaven; when he enquired if he might advise any customers on their choice of book, I said not if he valued his life. But he seemed content with two out of three.

With Jeff busy – well, not busy, but removed – I consulted the internet. It was not so much a case of know your enemy, because I was far from convinced that Dr Yes *was* my enemy, or anyone's, apart from Mother Nature's, but by finding out as much as I could it would at least enable me to talk knowledgeably about him to anyone else I came across in the course of the investigation.

This information was not difficult to find. His whole business was built around his good looks and personality – the perfectly coiffured hair, the permanent tan, the gleaming teeth, the wrinkle-free brow, the buff frame, the suggestion of a six-pack through a thin T-shirt; he was fifty-five years old and looked twenty younger, and you might have said he was a great advert for his youth-giving procedures, save for the fact that apart from diet and exercise, it would have been impossible for him to operate upon himself. Someone else had fixed his teeth or debagged his eyes or pinned back his lugholes. Buying into his image was buying into someone else's handiwork. He was born and bred in Chicago, Illinois, of Ukrainian extraction. I found a Google image of him that appeared to be lifted from his high-school yearbook. He hadn't changed much. Maybe he hadn't needed any of the work done to start with, he just had good genes. He had flown through Brown University and Washington University, and was a board-certified plastic surgeon and celebrated fellow of the American Society of Plastic Surgeons. In the mid-nineties he had married one of his patients, an Irish girl who'd gone to the States for some relatively minor plastic surgery that nevertheless hadn't been available at home; they'd fallen in love, and he'd also spotted a gap in the market. Within six months he'd set up his first clinic in Belfast, bringing a healthy dose of American chutzpah to the advertising of his services, and before very long he was the go-to man for women, and some men, throughout the island who wanted something tucked, trimmed or drained. He'd gone from strength to strength, particularly during the boom years of the Celtic Tiger, when his ultra-expensive but *very* quick multi-part makeovers had proved such a boon to those who felt themselves too fat, too droopy or too old to compete in the hectic Dublin social scene and didn't have time to hang around. Very soon there were competing services in the southern capital, but at least by coming to Belfast you were out of the country and less likely to bump into your social rivals while swathed in weeping bandages that kept your new ears on or screaming blue murder every time you went upstairs because your fresh tits were killing you while they bedded in.

'Why are you looking at pictures of boobies?' Jeff asked, peering over my shoulder.

'It's work,' I said.

I was trying to put myself in Augustine's shoes, even while he was probably trying to put himself in my father's. He loved his wife and she had disappeared. She had undergone a number of relatively minor procedures at a clinic owned and run by Dr Yeschenkov and nobody had seen her since, apart from disputed CCTV footage from a bank cashpoint in Dublin. He had jumped to the conclusion that she had died in the clinic because to him it was the only one that made sense; he could not conceive of her running off to start a new life. He clearly did not know women as well as I did, and I hardly knew them at all. He was too emotionally involved to make a rational judgement on the likelihood of some grand conspiracy swinging into place to cover up his wife's death.

I found a photo of the lovely Arabella on the web. She wasn't that lovely.

6

Contrary to what I might say or do, I was, somewhere in the back of my mind, trying to be a better man for the coming trauma that constituted childbirth. It was okay for Alison; she only had to bear some extra weight and undergo a little straining that would mostly be covered by painkilling injections. She was designed for it. But I certainly wasn't. I was about to go through the kind of upheaval that rid the earth of dinosaurs. I did want to contribute something to the whole process, and part of that was showing her that I was capable of using my initiative without being prompted. She was always in favour of me dealing with a problem by physically confronting it, not seeking a solution through a third party. She knew that I believed that if I looked pathetic enough for long enough, some-body else would do it for me. Now I was going to prove that I could do things off my own bat. I'd gotten on perfectly well before Alison, and I'd continue to get along well after her. It was just this sticky bit in the middle I had to get through.

I lifted the phone. I looked down at the number I'd written on the notepad before me. I punched it in. Although, obviously, what with my brittle bones, I didn't really. I pressed gently. After a few moments a bright, upmarket voice, but with a hint of Eastern Europe, said, 'Good morning, the Yeschenkov Clinic.'

I needed to satisfy myself that Dr Yes wasn't hiding anything. The medical records that had been released to Augustine were still with his last solicitor, who wouldn't release them until he paid his bill. Obviously *I* wasn't going to pay it for him, and the clinic wasn't going to release them to me, a bookshop owner, or issue fresh ones to Augustine, whom they had a restraining order against, so I would have to find out what there was to find out by doing what I did best – I was a criminal proctologist, shining a light into dark places where nobody really likes to look.

'Yes, I'd like to enquire about the possibility of having one of your makeovers.'

'Absolutely, sir. Could I have your name, please?'

'George.'

'George? And your surname?'

'Pelecanos.'

His new novel had just come in, and I had a business and its reputation to protect.

'Like the writer?' she asked, unexpectedly.

'Ahm, yes.'

'I understand *completely*, sir. Many of our clients prefer the cloak of anonymity. Though I should stress that this is just like going to your own doctor; it's absolutely confidential. Perhaps I could take your phone number and . . .'

'I'd prefer if you didn't.'

'Perhaps your e-mail . . .'

'No, she checks them as well. You see, it's to be a surprise for my wife.'

'So it's your wife who will be having the . . . ?'

'No, it's for me, I'm the bog-ugly one.'

'Well, I'm sure you're not. But I understand completely, sir, what a wonderful idea.'

'I just want to come in and have a chat, see what's involved.'

'Yes, sir, absolutely. A consultation with Dr Yeschenkov. Now I'm afraid there is a charge for that. Fully redeemable if you do join our programme.'

'How much would that be?'

'That would be just four hundred and ninety-nine pounds.'

'I mean for the consultation.'

'Yes, sir. Would you like me to check for an appointment?'

I decided to think of it as an investment. 'Yes, absolutely.'

'All right, then! Let me see. How about the twenty-fourth . . .'

'That's too . . .'

'. . . of May. That's the earliest we have. I'm afraid he's a very busy man.'

'So you've, ahm, nothing today, then?'

'No, sir, I'm afraid . . .'

'I could just like pop in and show him my head.'

'I'm sorry, sir, that's impossible.'

'Just a quick once-over; he could give me an estimate.'

'Sir . . .'

'It's kind of urgent. What about tomorrow? I'll be passing your place around lunchtime. I could just jump up and down at his window and he could give me the thumbs-up or the thumbs—'

'Sir! Dr Yeschenkov is not even working tomorrow.'

'Well you would say—'

'Sir, he'll be playing golf and under strict instructions not to be—'

'Well maybe I'll run into him at the club . . .'

'Oh. You're a member at Malone too, sir?'

'Absolutely.'

I was playing her like a glass harp.

'Well that's different. And he does actually do a special rate for fellow members. It's a wonderful club, isn't it, sir? Play there myself, very active ladies' membership. What's your handicap?'

'Calipers,' I said, and hung up.

I'd wrung the information out of her like a hamster in a mangle. Now I could seek out Dr Yes at the golf club and quiz him about Arabella's mysterious disappearance without having to enter his lair or pay that frankly ridiculous fee for a consultation.

The phone rang and I said, 'Hello, No Alibis, Murder is Our Business.'

And the same woman's voice said, 'I'm sorry, we seemed to get cut off. What were you saying about calipers? And you're from No Alibis? I *love* that shop!'

7

Let me explain why I took Pearl, for that was her name, for coffee. First of all, in chatting to her on the phone I realised that although she claimed to be a crime fiction aficionado, she was all at sea when it came to her actual choice of books. She needed help, she needed guidance. For God's sake, she was still reading Patterson! It is my primary function in this difficult world to steer those who are hopelessly lost towards the light. I am a beacon. A saviour of souls. But I'm not a literary snob, not even for my chosen genre. Yes, of course there are heavyweights out there who are very good, but I'm just as much a champion of pulp fiction or dark and witty noir or even grand-motherly cosies, as long as they don't feature animals who actually physically contribute to the solving of a case. It's my job to match the right book to the right reader. Also, and perhaps more importantly, she was

Dr Yeschenkov's gatekeeper, and in meeting her and engaging her in friendly chat I would surely gain an insight not only into him, but also into the circumstances surrounding the disappearance of the lovely Arabella. I had played her once, I would play her again.

She was warm and friendly and fascinated on the phone, and in retrospect, I have to admit, I was a little flattered. Our conversation was continually interrupted, however, by her having to answer calls on her switchboard. In response I also disappeared several times, pretending that I had to deal with a customer.

She said, 'It's lovely talking to you, but impossible!'

'I know,' I said. 'Sorry, a bit hectic here too.' Thankfully she couldn't actually see or hear the tumbleweed. 'Do you know what I should do? I should pick out some books for you. Take a look at them, no obligation to buy.' She laughed. I was *so* good at this. 'Why don't you pop in at lunchtime?'

'I'd love to – but I only get half an hour and that's barely enough for coffee and a sandwich. Actually, I usually go to that Starbucks just near you.'

'Well tell you what, I could pop across with them.'

'Really? Would you do that? That would be *marvellous.*'

I *was* pretty marvellous. 'How will I recognise you?' I asked.

'Don't worry,' she said, 'I'll recognise you. You'll be carrying books. About one?'

'About one.'

'Marvellous. It's a date.'

I have to admit, I got a little glow inside when she said that, although obviously she meant nothing by it.

I was, I suppose, at a slight disadvantage, because I had no idea what she looked like. Not only would I be carrying books, but as a customer of No Alibis she undoubtedly already knew me to see, whereas I forget my customers as soon as they leave, and occasionally while they're still there. It was, however, reasonable to assume she would not look like a dog's dinner, given that she was the first person people would see when they came along to Dr Yeschenkov's clinic for an estimate, and if she looked like she'd been beaten with the ugly stick, potential customers would probably change their minds as soon as they saw her. On the other hand, if she was a real stunner, I would have remembered her being in the shop. What I did know was that she sounded funny and bubbly, had said she wasn't into horror or gore or any of the more explicit authors, but that Christie bored her and she never quite 'got' any of the Scandinavians. Her tastes seemed to quite mirror mine, so selecting what I felt was right for her wasn't a problem. I picked up an Elmore Leonard, a Robert B. Parker, a Pelecanos, for obvious reasons, and, a little out of left field, Graham Greene's *Our Man in Havana*. I fixed my remaining hair and scooted across to Starbucks a little before one, so that I could have exactly the coffee I needed ordered and delivered before she arrived in case she thought I was in any way weird. I work my way through the menu once a month and any deviation leads to chaos and confusion, particularly in the paperwork that scrupulously records my intake. I couldn't afford to have her arrive first and buy me something out of sequence.

I was studying a leaflet about their East African coffee, and how for every one-pound bag of it they were contributing to a global fund for the treatment of those living with Aids on that continent, and thinking how little I cared about that fact, when her now familiar voice said. 'This must be you?'

It was indeed me, and it was indeed her.

And she was the MOST BEAUTIFUL CREATURE ON GOD'S EARTH.

Beaming down at *me*.

She had luxuriously long black hair, a sprinkle of freckles on her pure white cheeks beneath deep-pool green eyes and above a smile dazzling enough to make Mormons jump off cliffs. She was gloriously free of make-up and wore a top that revealed nothing but suggested everything.

I just nodded, stunned, and she put her hand out and said, 'Hi, it's me, Pearl. Pearl, hi.'

Although I am normally loath to shake anyone's hand, I made an exception. She was not the sort of woman that bugs would exist on. They would give her a pass; they would say not much point in hanging around here, she's out of our league.

I said, eventually, 'Let me get you a coffee. What do you fancy . . . ?'

She glanced up at the menu before saying: 'I'll have what you're having.' I ordered. As I waited at the delivery desk, Pearl picked up the books I'd left on the table, and studied their covers, and then flipped them over to read the back. She smiled up at me again. 'Fantastic, fantastic, I can't wait to get into them.'

I smiled back.

I felt glad to have landed on this planet. I returned to the table.

I said, 'Pearl's a lovely name; you don't hear it much these days.'

'Mum always loved it.'

'Mother of Pearl.'

'Usually I get Pearl's a singer.'

'The only other Pearl I know is . . .' And I tapped the Robert B. Parker book. 'Spenser's dog in this . . .'

'Are you comparing me to a dog?'

I laughed. I reddened. I was thinking, if you're a dog, you're the most beautiful dog I've ever seen. She burst into laughter.

'I'll take that as a compliment,' she said.

'Did I say that out loud?'

Under the table, her foot touched mine.

It was just an accident.

We were on our second coffee. I was still on menu. She had listened, fascinated, to my views on the current state of crime fiction, and to assessments of the career of Leonard and the television work of Pelecanos, and to my explanation – but not justification, definitely not justification – for the Greene. The master himself might have dismissed *Our Man* as merely an entertainment, but sometimes authors can be too close to their works. In my humble opinion, it is a much better novel than any of his 'worthies'. I was on top form; she could have listened to me all day, I'm sure, but I was there for a reason. She handed over twenty pounds for the books. I waited while she rifled her handbag for the additional fifteen pence. Once that business was satisfactorily completed, I moved on to the equally pressing reason for my having lured her into my home from home in the first place.

I said, 'I can't believe you've been in the shop before. I'm sure I would have remembered you.'

'Most times there's an older woman working there? To tell you the truth, she was a bit scary. I never stayed long.'

'That would be Mother. She's no longer with us.'

'You mean she's . . . passed on?'

'Not yet. As the Stranglers used to sing, she's "Hanging Around". She's in a home for the very, very annoying. Actually, though, we do have someone in common.'

'Really? Who?'

'Name of Augustine W—'

'Wogan! Oh God, how do you know . . . ?' She

tutted. 'Of course! How silly of me. He's a crime writer. Though I've never read one of his books, and now I'm quite sure I never want to. What a pain in the neck!'

'He is, isn't he? And he's currently eating me out of house and home.'

'He's not! Oh, how awful! How did that happen?'

'Well he came into the shop all ranting and raving, and I kind of felt sorry for him. I'm sure you've gathered how passionate I am about crime fiction, and he is a bit of a legend, so I thought I'd do the old guy a favour seeing as how he was so distressed and had nowhere else to put his head down. Tell you the truth, I wish I'd never bothered.'

'Oh, I don't envy you. I mean, yes, poor man, but honestly, the trouble he's caused! He's been scaring our customers away and I've had to phone every pizza company in Belfast and tell them to stop delivering to us because we haven't ordered any. He's a menace.'

'He's convinced his wife . . .'

'I know! But what does he think we've done with her, buried her under the patio? Honestly! She's a perfectly nice woman, she had her procedures, everything went like clockwork and she looked wonderful. Tell you the God's truth, after being pampered for a few weeks, the prospect of returning to *him* would put me on the first plane to South America as well!'

'You think that's where she is?'

'I've no idea. Though I have to say, there's a lot of sitting around recovering in what we do, and I couldn't help but notice that Arabella – lovely name, don't you think? – was reading a teach-yourself-Portuguese book. Now, what do you think, is that a clue? Brazil, maybe?'

'Or Angola. Or Cape Verde. Or Guinea-Bissau. Or Mozambique. Or Macau. Or East Timor.'

She blinked at me for a little bit, and then said, 'Or Portugal.'

And I said, 'Oh shit,' without really meaning to, because I happened to have glanced up, and there at the counter, just taking delivery of two frappuccinos, one of them undoubtedly for me, was Alison; and in that instant she looked round, and spotted me, and was halfway towards a smile when she realised I wasn't alone. The staggering beauty of the woman I was with seemed to strike her like a metaphorical brick to the face. The humour drained out of her and she just looked shocked and mortified in the same breath, neither of which stopped her from crossing the couple of metres to our table. My mouth dropped open as she glared at me, and I vaguely pointed at Pearl and mumbled something like, 'Alison . . . I wasn't . . . this isn't . . . this is Pearl . . .', and it must have made some sort of sense, because she responded instantly with, 'I don't give a flying fuck, you two-faced fuck face.' And then she flung her coffee at me, and I would have been burned, but Starbucks put their tops on *really* well, so it just hit me in the face, which was like being punched, especially with my brittle bones, and even though it wasn't really sore I let out a little yelp, a learned reaction to the slings and arrows of everyday life, and then Alison was away, storming out the way only an enraged, hormonal and heavily pregnant woman can, even though she was only three months gone.

Pearl said, 'Ooops.'

And I said, 'She works with me.'

'Don't worry,' she said. 'I know who she is. You're thinking about having surgery to make her find you more attractive.' She reached across the table and put a hand on my arm. 'She'll understand once you explain. But listen to me. I've taken a good long look at you. And no amount of surgery could make you look any more attractive.' It sat in the air for what seemed like an eternity, during which my heart sank to the pits of hell. Wasn't she saying that I was the ugliest man on the planet? But then she squeezed my arm, and her touch was so soft. 'I think you're just lovely as you are.' Our eyes met for a perfect moment, and then she moved her hand away. 'It's probably time I got back to work.' She stood and gathered up her books and I wanted to say, stay, just a little bit longer, but before I could she had opened her purse and taken out a business card and set it down and said, 'Why don't you give me a wee call sometime? My mobile's on there too,' and she smiled that smile and walked away.

I watched her go.

Everything had happened so quickly.

When she had slipped from sight, leaving only her

scent and the outline of her bottom on the armchair opposite, I picked up the card she had so recently caressed and read what it said:

THE YESCHENKOV CLINIC
Pearl Knecklass

8

Alison was a jealous, moody cow and I was quite prepared not to speak to her for the rest of her life. We could communicate through our respective solicitors. I wouldn't demand visitation rights with the child even if she produced proof it was mine. Children are overrated. If I wanted to see it, I could stand in her shrubbery at night and watch through the window the way I usually did.

Then I saw her opposite No Alibis, waiting to cross the traffic.

So, another showdown.

She didn't scare me. But mostly to protect my property, I put my hand on the mallet beneath the counter. It used to be a meat cleaver, but that was too dangerous. You could cut someone's head off with a cleaver. With a mallet you would just flatten anything that stuck out, like a nose. I didn't necessarily want to flatten

Alison's nose, but I was prepared to, and just about had the strength, thanks to the steroids I'd been taking for the past ten years. You wouldn't necessarily notice my muscle definition but you could tell by the size of my penis, which had shrunk further. Alison said that size wasn't everything, and I was in a fortunate position to agree with her, particularly when applied to bookshops.

She opened the door and gave me a bright smile and said, 'So how did it go?'

'How did what go?'

'Your meeting.'

'I believe you were there. I believe you threw coffee at me and called me a two-faced fuck face.'

'Ah, I was only putting on an act. You're so easy. Jeff told me where you were and I came across to offer moral support and to take a gander at her, working for a plastic surgeon and all. She's a bit of a beauty, isn't she? Well out of your league.'

It was a double bluff, because I can read people, years of training, and I'd seen the fear on her face and the terror in her eyes at the thought of losing me, and you don't hurl a steaming cup of coffee at someone and hit them in the face with it as an act. You could scald someone.

And she said, 'I couldn't have scalded you with an iced coffee, halfwit.'

And I said, 'Did I say all of that out loud?'

She ran her finger along the counter top, checking for dust, which was just ridiculous. 'She was gorgeous, though, wasn't she? So skinny she only needs one eye. And isn't a girl allowed to be a teensy-weensy bit jealous? After all, you're my man.' I snorted, although, actually, I liked the sound of that. 'So, did you think she was fantastically sexy and lovely?'

'She was all right. It was work.'

'Did she not look a bit pinched?'

'Not that I noticed.'

'Like her skin was tied up behind her neck and all you'd have to do is snip the knot and her whole face would fall into her chest, which, incidentally, appeared to be pointing upwards. A sixteen-year-old would be lucky to pull that one off.'

'I wasn't aware of her pulling anything off.'

'Yeah, you wish.'

I said, 'Is there a point to this conversation, or did you come over to apologise for your appalling behaviour?'

'Apologise for what?'

'Throwing . . . and calling . . . and embarrassing me in front of an informant.'

'That was nothing; you should see me when I'm angry.'

'You're really selling yourself. You're going to end up an old maid.'

'How can I be an old maid when I'm carrying your child?'

'So you say.'

We both sighed.

If I'd had a single customer, he or she would have

been embarrassed by the exchange. Fortunately, I did not. And unfortunately. Times were hard and getting harder; I needed to get on with finding the lovely Arabella and start on my quest to ruthlessly exploit Augustine's back catalogue and treasured fourth instalment. No Alibis needed an injection of cash, and I needed to eat. I had to stop swapping insults with this strange impetuous woman from across the road.

I said, 'Bangles?'

She said, 'I'm on flexi. What did she say about Arabella?'

'Pearl said Arabella was learning Portuguese.'

'Pearl?'

'For that was her name.'

'Your granny's called Pearl.'

'My granny's called Frank, but that's another story.'

'I mean, it's an awful old name. Pearl what?'

'Pearl it's-none-of-your-business.' Nevertheless, I took Pearl's business card out of my pocket and briefly examined it. It still said:

THE YESCHENKOV CLINIC
Pearl Knecklass

I slid it across the counter to Alison. She picked it up and read what it said. Her lips moved silently. They were nice lips. I had kissed them before, and since, and told complete strangers that I had. She looked up at me. There was a glint in her eye.

'You're serious?' she asked.

'Always.'

'I mean, Pearl *Necklace*?'

'Yes. With a K.'

'But nevertheless.'

'Are you feeling some sort of connection to her name because it sounds like jewellery?'

'I'm not feeling any sort of connection to her, and her name doesn't sound like jewellery, it sounds like – you know what it sounds like.'

'I know exactly what it sounds like. A string of pearls. But spelt differently.'

'You know what it sounds like, and it's not that, although spelt differently.'

'I have no idea what you're talking about.'

'You think it's a coincidence that a woman who looks like that has a porn name like that?'

'A porn name?'

'Yes, a porn name.'

'What're you talking about? What's a porn name?'

'Oh for God's sake. A porn name, a porn name. A porn-star name. She has a porn-star name. Pearl *Necklace*, for frig's sake.'

'How is that a porn-star name?'

'How is it not? Pearl Necklace!' She was laughing, and examining me at the same time, and then abruptly she stopped and shook her head and said: 'You honestly have no idea, do you? You know more irrelevant shit than anyone I've ever met, but you don't know anything important.'

'Like a porn-star name?'

'Yes! Man dear, Pearl Necklace! Even with a K. Come here.' She waggled a finger at me, but actually she was the one who moved nearer, leaning over the counter. I thought she wanted a kiss, but her lips diverted to my ear and she whispered to me what a pearl necklace meant in sexual parlance, and then she stood back and raised an eyebrow. 'You're shocked,' she said.

'I am shocked that anyone would want to do something that wasn't directly linked to procreation. Next you'll be telling me that Pussy Galore has nothing to do with the love of cats.'

'Sometimes I don't know whether you're the world's greatest wind-up artist, or you're slightly autistic.'

'I think you know what the answer to that is.'

She sighed again. 'Bloody hell, you're so infuriating. I'm going to Starbucks.'

'You can't.'

'I can't?'

'I'm their best customer. They saw what you did. I had you barred. It was childish and vindictive but I'm afraid it's irrevocable.'

She glared at me, and then rolled her eyes and said, 'Oh *fuck off.*'

She returned from Star ten minutes later, and with the correct coffee, which told me that she paid more attention to my requirements than she ever let on. She said, 'You're such a bullshitter.'

I preferred to think of myself as adept at playing

people. The way I'd played Pearl. Her name was Kneck-lass. That there were hitherto unsuspected sexual connotations was just a coincidence. She probably didn't know herself. She wasn't the sort of girl you sniggered at, for she could melt you with a look. Kneck-lass as a name was probably as common as muck in some godforsaken part of Europe I would never visit. The Czech telephone directory was more than likely crammed with them. It was the equivalent of restaurants in Hong Kong with names like Fuk U. It meant nothing until taken out of context. Bond had enjoyed a run of porn-star names beyond Pussy Galore – Holly Goodhead, Plenty O'Toole, Honey Rider, even Mary Goodnight – but they were fiction; this was uncomfortable fact. And seeing Alison come through the door with the right coffee reminded me how lovely *she* was, and that although I would never admit it, she was right: Pearl was way out of my league. I'd squeezed her for information even while she flirted outrageously with me. I'd played her, and now I could leave her behind. She'd given me a good lead on where the lovely Arabella might be; now it was just a case of turning up some physical evidence of her departure, something that Augustine couldn't possible argue with.

'Like a bank statement,' said Alison.

'Obviously,' I said.

'Showing that she bought a one-way ticket to Rio.'

'Ditto.'

'But he must have thought of that. The police must have checked.'

'Who knows that they did? Maybe she paid cash. Maybe she used a card and the statement didn't come in for a month afterwards. Augustine's life has been chaotic ever since she ran off. We just need to get him to focus, show us the paperwork; it must be sent somewhere even if they have been living like a couple of gypsies. I'm good with paperwork, you know that.'

'Yes I do.'

'The Resistance – in fact all sides in any war going back to Peloponnesian times – relied on facts, information, patterns and codes.'

'Yes, they did. You accountants are so damn sexy.'

'You're the pregnant one. And I'm not an accountant. I'm like a forensic analyser.'

'Of paperwork.'

'What I'm saying is, we need to ask Augustine to show us what he has.'

'We?'

'He likes you. You can wind him round your little finger.'

'Like Pearl with you.'

'I just don't want to antagonise him. I don't want to jeopardise . . .'

'The Holy Grail.'

'Exactly.'

She gave me a look. 'Where would you be without me?' she asked.

Happier was the obvious answer, but for once I

kept it to myself. I was learning a little self-control. I needed her, for now, but nobody is indispensable.

After work, we took the Mystery Machine back to my place, though, technically, while she clung by her fingernails to this mortal coil, it was still Mother's.

We went in, and smelled food, and alcohol, and called his name, but he didn't respond.

We went upstairs, and we stood at his door and called again, and he still didn't reply.

'He's flown the coop,' I said.

'He wouldn't, not without saying,' said Alison, so, for the second time in her life, she entered Mother's bedroom.

And for the second time, she screamed.

9

It is a little-known fact that the lyrics to 'Suicide is Painless', the hit song featured over the titles of Robert Altman's classic 1970 film *MASH*, were actually written by the director's fourteen-year-old son Mike. I'm not sure how he did his research, but judging from the state of my mother's bedroom, and the fact that Augustine Wogan had blown his brains out in it, and that the photograph of my late father that hung on the wall behind where he had carried out said act was now adorned with one of his bloody ears, I would have said that no matter how brief a passage of time there was between him pulling the trigger and actually departing this mortal coil, suicide was *pretty fucking painful*.

Alison was in some state, but there wasn't much I could do about that beyond patting her back. I find outbursts of emotion uncomfortable, and I was too busy hyperventilating myself to be of much use to anyone. Alison was in fact the first to calm down, and phone the ambulance, which I would have told her was obviously a complete waste of time if I could have gotten the words out.

We waited downstairs for them to arrive. We had spent less than twenty seconds in the room. It was eighteen seconds too long. I do not like to look at the dead, because that is the image you carry with you of that person for the rest of your life. I had just seen one of the greatest crime writers of his generation with most of his head missing. He had been sitting in the chair by the window that Mother used to sit in to spy on the neighbours. He had a bottle of whiskey by his side, a partially smoked cigar between his fingers, a cereal bowl he'd been using as an ashtray on the arm of his chair, and a newspaper at his feet. There was blood all over the wall and in a thick pool on the wooden floor around him. I was wondering if it would stain. I was wondering if he had done it deliberately to annoy me, or to cheat No Alibis out of its financial windfall. I was wondering what this would do to my reputation. I was wondering if I would no longer be widely revered as the owner of the finest mystery bookshop in Ireland, but known as the bookshop owner damned by the fact that he had been the final host of the legendary Augustine Wogan. I knew how these things went. Even if every fact came out, they would be ignored in favour of innuendo and rumour. I would be blamed for somehow causing his death. His suicide would migrate from Mother's bedroom to the bookshop itself. He would have killed himself because of the pressures of being an author, depressed because he hadn't been published in twenty years despite the critical plaudits. Indeed, because he'd blown his head off, conspiracy theorists would speculate that he wasn't dead at all, that he had staged it to feed his well-known desire for obscurity.

'You're quite the shit magnet, aren't you?'

That was DI Robinson's opening line. He had made minor contributions to the solving of several of my cases, but had also often been more of a hindrance than a help. He claimed to be a fan of crime fiction and regularly bought rare first editions from me, but I still wasn't convinced. There was something about him. A book never seemed to be an end in itself. There were always accompanying questions. Some might have mistaken it for mere conversation, but I know people too well. He was never off duty. Never relaxed. Although he was relatively so, here in the environment where he was clearly most at home, an interview room at Lisburn Road police station. I'd been told by the police at the scene to call in and make a statement at my own convenience, which would have been never, if Alison hadn't insisted. She was waiting outside to make hers. It was normal procedure for suicides, although made less normal by the method Augustine had chosen. A simple overdose would have sufficed, or he could have suffocated himself with a plastic bag, or jumped out of a window, but the mere fact of using a gun elevated it enough to have someone like DI Robinson involved.

He told me to sit; he told me he was taping the interview, but to read nothing into that, it was merely more efficient than laboriously typing everything I said. It would be rendered into print by computer software, then checked, corrected and signed by me.

He said, 'Shame, he was a great writer.'

'You've read him?'

'I've read *of* him. Everyone seems to agree. What did you think?'

'He *was* a great writer.'

'How'd he end up with you?'

'He turned up in the shop; he was homeless, needed somewhere to stay, least I could do.'

He studied me. I knew what he was thinking. It seemed out of character for me to be accommodating. And it was. I know what I'm like. There's no sugar on my almonds. But there was no reason for Robinson to know about my plan to get rich, or at least eat, on the back of Augustine Wogan's past and future glories.

'Did he seem depressed?'

'Depressed. Paranoid.'

'In what sense?'

'In the sense that he thought someone was trying to kill him; in the sense that his wife had run off but he thought she'd been murdered.'

DI Robinson studied me some more. He clasped his hands. 'And she wasn't murdered?'

'Not that I'm aware of.'

'Because I know what you're like, and your investigations. The problem is that whenever you get involved in something, the body count tends to mount. Like I say, shit magnet.'

'I don't think that's very fair.'

'It seems that every time I run into you, my paperwork multiplies tenfold.'

'You should avoid running into me.'

'I would, but there always seems to be a gun involved, and that tends to be my line.'

'He shot himself in the head.'

'That's not what concerns me. It's more the gun, like where he got it from, him being in your house, and you having a history with them. Did you give it to him?'

'No, of course not.'

'Of course not.'

'Why would I give him a gun? That's just stupid.'

'Were you aware that he had a gun?'

'Sort of.'

'Sort of.'

'He kind of had one.'

'Kind of had one.'

'He had one in his briefcase. He took it out in the shop and I disarmed him.'

Robinson snorted. 'You disarmed him?'

'Yes.'

'Why did he take it out in the shop?'

'He was all fired up about his wife being missing, thought they'd murdered her at this clinic.'

'I heard about that. It was all bollocks.'

'Yes, it was. But he'd convinced himself.'

'You didn't think to tell us? That he had a gun, that he was threatening murder?'

'I disarmed him, so he didn't have a gun, and he was no longer threatening murder. He was upset; I didn't think it would help to call you lot.'

'Us lot?' Robinson shook his head. 'So what did you do with the gun?'

'I hid it.'

'Where?'

'In the house.'

'In the house where you took him?'

'Yes.'

'Did he see you hide it?'

'No, that would defeat the purpose.'

'But he knew you had it, and that you must have hidden it in the house, and then you left him alone in said house for an extended period of time, even though you knew he was paranoid and depressed. You didn't think there was a fair to middlin' chance he might have gone looking for it?'

'No.'

'No, that would be too sensible.'

'What's that supposed to mean?'

'Whatever you want it to.'

He got up and left the room. He came back in. He had a see-through plastic bag in his hands, which he set down on the table. 'There's a lot more I need to look into. I want to know how he came by the gun;

they're not supposed to be easy to get any more, not round here. But in the meantime, these are his personal possessions. For the moment you seem to be the closest he has to a next of kin; you may hold on to them until we can track down his wife, wherever the hell she is.'

'Brazil,' I said.

His eyes lingered on the bag. I don't know why he didn't just come out and say it: *I think there's something odd about this and I want you to look into it.* Why else would he give me Augustine's personal possessions, so quickly? A hospital might, if there was no relative present, because they have a high turnover. But the police? They let cases fester for years, and they hold on to possible evidence for ever.

Or, I was misreading him, and he didn't think there was anything suspicious at all and the quicker he could write Augustine off the better.

There was never a right answer to anything, just more questions.

It was life, and life was such.

DI Robinson nodded at the bag and its contents.

'Looks kind of sad,' he said.

I nodded too, but I was thinking that inanimate objects can't actually be sad.

He tutted, which made me think that I'd said it out loud.

The forensics people had to do their stuff. They had to photograph and scrape. Since things had turned peaceful in Belfast they didn't have much to do, so they took their time. It was a couple of days before they gave us the all-clear to bring the cleaners in so that Mother's bedroom could be turned back into something approaching habitable. When the cleaners were packing up to leave they said that they thought they'd 'gotten most of it', which wasn't very re-assuring. I didn't want to be tidying one day and pull back a chair to find Augustine's other ear.

As far as I could tell, they'd done a good job. There was a definite reddish tinge to the wallpaper, but it was actually a slight improvement on its previous nico-tine hue. The wooden floors were stain-free and the actual chair where he'd shot himself was, amazingly, looking as good as new.

Alison and I stood in the middle of the room. The sun was coming through the window, but there were no dust motes to be caught in its rays, which appeared perfectly pure and life-giving. I stayed well out of them. Alison couldn't take her eyes off the chair.

She said, 'He was such a nice man.'

I grunted.

She said, 'Don't blame yourself.'

'I wasn't.'

'Well just in case you were, just in case you were thinking you shouldn't have left the gun in the house and Augustine by himself, it wasn't your fault; you didn't actually put the gun to his head and shoot him, no matter what Robinson thinks.'

'He said that?'

'Yes, he did. But we all know what he is.' She gave the international sign for wanking. 'And all this time Arabella is probably cavorting around Rio with some toyboy and hasn't a clue. God, it didn't even make the local news, let alone CNN.'

As far as anywhere other than the mysterious world was concerned, he was just another suicide. Despite having been feted in his lifetime by *The Times* and the *Daily Telegraph*, there had been no obituaries, no contact from reporters wanting to know the circumstances under which he had died. He was an obscure writer in a largely ignored genre. Maybe there was stuff on the internet about it, but I didn't check. I was off Augustine Wogan. He had promised me big things, and backed out. His whole life, in fact, was about unfulfilled promise.

Alison said, 'Will I throw this out?'

She was holding the blood-spattered *Irish Times* that Augustine appeared to have been reading prior to his death and which the cleaners had folded and set to one side.

I nodded. It was a grisly memento of the great man, and might conceivably have fetched something on eBay, but it clearly showed my pissedoffness with Augustine that I wasn't even prepared to check.

Alison crossed to a pedal bin by the door and deposited the paper. She turned back and asked if I wanted to go to her place for something to eat, because it just didn't feel right cooking here in the house with Augustine so recently dead. I nodded. I was hungry, plus he'd eaten everything and I hadn't had the wherewithal to restock. She was just asking me what I fancied, when she stopped mid-sentence and turned back to the bin. She retrieved the newspaper. She stared down at it. Her lips moved silently. Then she said, 'Bloody hell.' Followed swiftly by, 'Bloody bloody hell.'

She looked up and gave a disbelieving shake of her head before holding the paper out to me.

I took it, but reluctantly. Augustine's blood.

I held it at arm's length.

There was a headline that said *Dublin planners accused of corruption.*

She read my lips and said, 'No, the photo, look at the picture.'

I studied it, although there wasn't much studying involved. A beaming man with a glamorous woman on his arm. The caption said: *Celebrated surgeon to the stars Dr Igor Yeschenkov pictured at the opening of the Xianth Art Gallery in Upper Leeson Street with socialite Arabella Wogan.*

My eyes flitted up to Alison.

The truth, staring up at us.

Augustine had read these words, and seen her face, and remembered her saying, 'Love you, honey bun,' and then he had blown his own head off.

10

We ate in a Chinese restaurant on Great Victoria Street. I managed to get through it without an allergic reaction to anything, which I suppose was progress of some sort. Alison kept talking about Augustine as if she actually knew him, like he was her father-in-law, or older cousin, or like someone you grew up calling an uncle but actually he was just a friend of your parents, a little too much of a friend, a friend whom you actually suspected of having an affair with your mother except your poor sad father never knew, and who had gone to his grave taking all the details of his sordid affair with him, save for your mother locked up in a high-security nursing home, and she would deny it until she was in the ground as well because she liked to masquerade as pious when in fact she ranted and raved in her sleep and it was pretty clear that she had had a voracious sexual appetite. Alison hadn't known Augustine personally any better than I did, but my advantage was that at least I knew him through his work, and was aware that he was a giant in his field, even though he was well camouflaged in that field.

At the end of the night I dropped Alison home, and she invited me in. I said no, I'd things to think about, and she said that I thought too much, which was just ridiculous. The case was gone, Augustine was gone, my reputation in the mysterious world was probably gone, plus I needed to find money to redecorate Mother's bedroom.

I stayed up thinking about Augustine. I hadn't slept properly since the 1970s, but from the night Mother was dragged kicking and screaming to her nursing home, it had been easier to come by. This night I didn't even attempt it. I sat at the kitchen table, drinking Coke, eating Twix. Before me was the transparent plastic bag containing his personal effects. I have perfect control of my emotions, so I wasn't particularly angry, more annoyed: he had a wife, the lovely Arabella, who should by rights be picking over the contents of this bag, and getting teary, but instead she was somewhere in Dublin, having it off with the sleek Dr Yeschenkov. She had killed him. And as a reward she would inherit the rights to all of his books, published or not. She was not only currently shafting Dr Yes; she had also shafted her husband and the future prosperity of No Alibis.

Poor Augustine – to feel so deeply about anyone

that you would want to end your own life. I would never understand it. If I was horrendously betrayed the way he was, the worst I would consider was a paper cut. Although given my haemophilia, that might well be the end of me anyway. Perhaps if I'd found him with the gun raised to his head, I could have talked him out of it. I could have assured him that there were plenty more fish in the sea. Actually, having seen a documentary recently, I understand that technically there aren't plenty more fish in the sea, although that depends on your definition of 'plenty', and 'more', and possibly 'fish'. Or maybe I couldn't have. His head was screwed up. He had thought he was happily married; his wife had gone into Dr Yeschenkov's clinic, fallen for his plastic smile and youthful vigour, and unceremoniously dumped him. I knew the police had tried to contact her, without success, but I suspected she knew all about it and was deliberately lying low, knowing she had been the cause of his death. I wondered if she would have the gall to turn up at his funeral. No other family members had come forward. Alison and I might well be the only mourners. Perhaps afterwards, having no one else to give it to, the crematorium would present the urn to us. I could create a little shrine to him in the shop. Fans from all over the world might travel to pay their respects. I could put it in the store room at the back, with a little curtain, and charge entrance. Perhaps, over time, Augustine's shrine would pay me back for all the trouble he had caused, the food he had eaten, the drink he had guzzled, the redecoration charges he had run up with his bloody last act, and the hope he had extinguished by pulling that trigger.

I opened the bag and emptied the contents on to the kitchen table. Augustine's actual clothes had been retained by the police for routine forensic examination. I knew for a fact that if they looked for it they would find alien DNA upon them – they were after all my father's: his suit, his shirt, even his socks. They had remained mothballed in my mother's room all these years, her own little shrine to him, until Augustine had borrowed them. What was now spread out before me were the poignant little reminders of his daily routines, as much the essence of the man as his writings: his wallet, his loose change, a torn cinema ticket, an old-fashioned handkerchief, his mobile phone, his cigar cutter, even the cigar he had started to smoke. There was an unopened packet of sugar from a café, a slightly furry Polo mint. I opened his wallet: a twenty-pound note, two credit cards, one for Lloyds Bank in England, and an expired one from a bank in Cyprus. A folded bill from the Europa Hotel in Belfast showing two nights' accommodation preceding his appearance outside No Alibis, a bar receipt from the same location showing that he'd drunk six pints of beer. He had a kidney donor card, which, given his apparent alcohol intake, would have been no use to anyone, a laminated card for a library in Scotland, a business card for a solicitor in Belfast, and one for the Yeschenkov Clinic, which, like mine, bore Pearl Knecklass's name. I flicked it back and forth between my fingers. It wasn't beyond possibility that Augustine had organised it all for his wife, knowing she was depressed about her fading looks, and had retained the card so that he could phone up and ask how she was getting on.

There was a small pocket at the back of the wallet containing a crumpled, yellowed clipping from *The Times*. It was Augustine's entry in their One Hundred Masters of Crime Fiction supplement. I had had him on his pedestal for so long that I had ignored the truth of his writing career – he was a failure. Of course it depended, like the fish, how you defined failure. If just writing well was enough, then he wasn't one. But he was self-published. He was out of print. Outside of devoted aficionados of the genre he was completely unrecognised. He had no *career*. He had started out the way nearly all writers do, and I'd seen it a hundred times – amateurs transformed into gibbering wrecks by actually being published; what once they'd done for fun ruined for ever by the burden of expectation, the hope of sales and good reviews and riches, hobbyists turned authors made bitter by the knowledge that they'd missed their main chance. I'd met grown men who were only saved from complete insanity by the fact that they were the twenty-third best-selling crime writer in Lithuania. But because Augustine had been local to me, because he had impacted on me, I had elevated him above the morass of writers who are good for a couple of books and then fade back into richly deserved obscurity; because he had been a flickering candle in the darkness of a troubled Belfast, I had exaggerated his worth and impact. He was a failure, and he'd taken the coward's way out. If he was remembered at all, it would be for blowing his head off in a house belonging to the owner of No Alibis, who, actually, was much better known in the crime-writing community than he ever would be.

I was the star all along.

I was the one who should be sitting back content at what I had achieved. I should have been the one puffing on a cigar, not bloody Augustine Wogan. *Oooooh, my wife's disappeared, she must obviously have been murdered, it couldn't be that I'm just a disaster and she's had enough of me.* I picked up his cigar and held it up. I would obviously not put it in my mouth; his spit was probably still upon it. But I quite happily mimed it. I lifted the cigar cutter and pretended to cut off the end; I pretended to puff upon it, and then sat back, like the satisfied, successful champion of crime fiction that I was, and waxed lyrical to an imaginary audience about the greats of the genre, Americans mostly, with a sprinkling of English and French, no mention at all for the Scandinavians, obviously, and certainly not for a loser like Augustine Wogan, except to mention that he had blown his head off in my own shop, driven mad by the success of what he incorrectly perceived to be less talented authors than himself.

Much as cigarettes distress me, I have never minded the smell of a cigar. My father smoked them, although always from the cheaper end of the market, usually Woolworth's, and he always had a lingering whiff of them about him. Mother smoked them as well, but that's another story. *This* one smelled richer, more exotic. The lovely Arabella had money, so it was more than likely hand-rolled in Cuba or Brazil rather than mass-produced on an industrial estate in Reading. Perhaps as soon as Augustine saw the picture of her with Dr Yes he knew it was the end of the line, that quality cigars were a thing of the past. Although in that case, why not savour the whole thing, rather than blow his head off after just a couple of puffs? Maybe this wasn't the last of his expensive cigars, but the first of a lesser brand, a bitter taste of how life was to be post-Arabella.

Maybe. Maybe. Maybe.

I'm a terrible one for having to know things, but it's what I do and am. I set the cigar down and went upstairs. Although No Alibis is crammed with tens of thousands of crime books, and there are many more thousands here in the house, I also keep my *other* books here, books I have accumulated over the years to feed my endless quest for knowledge or, indeed, trivia. It is a large house, with seven bedrooms. Mother, having in recent years largely been confined to her room at the top, hadn't really noticed the extent to which I had quietly been filling every available inch with my collection; not on shelves, because I couldn't afford them, but in teetering piles or sagging cardboard boxes. Even when she did pass a remark, it was more along the lines of 'Why don't you use the fucking internet like everyone else, you little shit?' rather than a concern about the fact that I was transforming her house into my own private library. She never would understand books. 'They're a fucking fire hazard!' she yelled more than once, oblivious to the fact that on four out of any five nights I had to remove a burning cigarette from her lips after she nodded off and on more than one occasion had to put her head out with a fire extinguisher.

It took me until dawn, but I found what I was looking for at the bottom of a box that was second in a pile of three sitting in the first-floor bathroom. It was *A History of Post-Revolution Havana Cigars*, an expensive illustrated coffee-table tome that I'd picked up for a tenner in a second-hand bookshop a couple of years before. I didn't know for sure that Augustine's cigar was from Cuba, but I suspected. I lugged the book downstairs and sat at the kitchen table. It was such a large volume that the cigars illustrated within were nearly all life-size, so I was able to fairly easily compare and contrast. I established that it was indeed Cuban in origin, and while being from the hugely popular Montecristo line, was in fact a rarer sub-brand, an Edmundo, named after the hero of Alexander Dumas' *The Count of Monte Cristo*, Edmond Dantes.

So, I knew.

Which begs the question – so what?

Reader, I was born suspicious; I have man's intuition, if you will. When I feel uncomfortable about something, there is generally a reason for it. Admittedly, I am *generally* uncomfortable, and have been since I landed on this planet. My ill health, my allergies, my profound mental problems, they all contribute to my state of never quite being relaxed or settled. *Big* things annoy me, but I can't really control them. The smaller things I can do something about, even if it's just the gaining of knowledge so that I can say I found out. I now knew about Augustine's cigar. But I still wasn't happy. There was something nagging at me.

Two hours later, agitated, excited, worried, slightly creeped out but stunned and impressed by my own remarkably analytical thought processes, I called Alison.

'Brian?' she asked groggily. I remained silent. She very quickly reconsidered. 'No, there's only one idiot would call me at ... six fucking forty-five in the morning. What is it? Has somebody died?'

'Augustine.'

'Yes, I believe I know that.'

'Augustine. I don't think he killed himself.'

She cleared her throat. I could hear her shuffling, sitting up in bed, a lamp clicking on. She said, 'Well, he did a pretty good impression of it.' She sighed. 'You haven't been to bed, have you?' I retained a diplomatic silence. 'Jesus God, man, how do you do it? Well? You may as well spit it out.'

'Okay,' I said. And then fell quiet, because I hadn't quite worked out how to put it into words. 'Well. It's like this. I was researching the cigar he was smoking just before he died . . .'

'Lord preserve us.'

'It was a Cuban, Edmundo . . .'

'Yeah, I was just thinking that.'

'. . . but it's not about the cigar.'

'Thank God for—'

'It's about the cigar cutter.'

'The what?'

'The cutter. You have to cut off the end of the cigar before you can smoke it.'

She sighed. 'Yes.'

'Yes. You saw Augustine use his in the shop, and it was amongst his personal possessions returned to me by DI Robinson.'

'Yes.'

'The problem is, the cut in the cigar Augustine was smoking before he died does not match the shape that should be made by the cutter he uses.'

'Should I be phoning the papers to hold their front pages?'

'Listen to me. There are three basic types of cigar cutter: guillotine – sometimes called straight cut – punch cut or V-cut. Augustine used a straight cut; it's the most common. The entire cap is cut and the maximum amount of smoke is allowed out. With me?'

'Yes.'

'The cigar he was smoking before he died was

V-cut. There was a wedge cut out of it rather than completely removing the cap. Some smokers prefer it because it penetrates deeper into the filler inside the cigar. Do you see where I'm going?'

'If only . . .'

'Alison, if he sat down, took a puff of his last cigar, and then shot himself, and the cigar was found still in his hand, and you saw the size of the gun, then it would have been extremely hard to do all that one-handed. But not impossible. What *is* impossible is for him to inflict a V-cut with a guillotine cutter. He didn't have a V-cut cutter. Now do you see?'

'Nope. I'm sure this is all fascinating to you, but I have to get up in an hour to throw up because you got me pregnant, and then I have to go to work. And besides, he could have cut it before he even got to your house, using a V-cut cutter, another one he has . . . Oh, I don't even know why I'm talking . . .'

'Alison, no cigar smoker is going to cut in advance. The cap keeps the cigar fresh and cutting it is almost a ceremonial act. He could not have cut the cigar in that fashion, in that room, without using a V-cutter. Therefore he had to borrow one. Therefore there was somebody else in the room with him. I think he had help.'

'Like an assisted suicide?'

'No, like a murder.'

There was a long pause before Alison responded with: 'Do you remember the moon landings?'

'Yes.'

'God, you're old.'

'*What?*'

'Do you remember what Neil Armstrong said, one small step, et cetera?'

'Yes.'

'Well I think you've just taken a leap that is even bigger, you frickin' head case.'

And then she hung up on me.

11

I am a puller of threads. It is the nature of me. Alison maintains that I sometimes destroy perfectly good metaphorical jumpers by completely unravelling them, when all that was wrong with them in the first place was the loose thread. Loose threads are not a crime, she maintains. But she is wrong. Loose threads are an indication of a crime and if you have to pull them until the metaphorical jumper, or civilisation itself, falls to pieces, then one must do so. I have a moral obligation. And also, it's fascinating.

To say that I was distracted by my cigar-cutting discovery would be an understatement. I could not stop thinking about it. Jeff noticed straight away. We had customers in the shop, for once, and when they asked their pathetic, needy questions, I just looked at them and pointed them vaguely in the right direction where normally I would have been full of salient advice or haughty condescension. Jeff tried to step up to the plate by offering his opinions, but they were those of an idiot and the customers soon left. Yet I didn't chastise him.

Augustine, murdered in my mother's bedroom.

Yes, it was a huge leap from suicide to murder based on the shape of a hole in the end of a cigar, but the cut was impossible. That single fact altered everything.

'Penny for them?'

I looked up, surprised, my hand already seeking the mallet. But it was only Alison. The bell, which played the theme from *The Rockford Files* every time the door opened, must have sounded, but I'd heard nothing.

'Oh. You. Just thinking about the great cow uprising.'

'What great cow uprising?'

'Exactly. They are a secretive herd, but poised and ready to strike.'

She shook her head, set a Starbucks on the counter for me and said, 'I just thought I'd pop over and thank you.'

'For what?'

'For waking me up, and then keeping me awake thinking about you and your bloody cigar thingy for the little time I had left before I had to throw up.'

'I detect that your thanks have a basis in sarcasm.'

'No shite, Sherlock.' But she was smiling, and the coffee was the correct coffee. She was definitely getting better, although she still had a long way to go and an ulterior motive. Everybody does. It did not take long to manifest itself. 'I was thinking about your cigar thingy, and I suppose there's a remote possibility that you could be right.' I raised an eyebrow. 'Just remember, pally, I was the one wanted this case in the first place; you were the one who wanted to get rid of him because he was too much of a hassle to have around. I always knew there was something suspicious about this, and it's you who're just coming round to my way of thinking.'

'If you say so.'

'I do. So, any further along?'

I shrugged.

She sighed. 'Okay. Here's what *I'm* thinking. It's your fault.'

'Good start.'

'I'm thinking that Augustine was at your house, and the only people who knew he was at your house were you, me, Jeff and your beloved Pearl.'

'Pearl?'

'Listen, I've been around, I'm a girl, I know what you guys are like. Pearl is gorgeous and she played you like a fiddle.'

'That's bollocks. I played *her* like a fiddle. In fact I played her like a string quartet, with a bassoon and a trombone thrown in.'

'Uhuh. How, exactly?'

'I found out she was interested in crime fiction, I lured her to Starbucks, I plied her with coffee and found out all about Arabella, and the fact that she was learning Portugese and was bound for Brazil or Portugal or Cape Verde.'

'Uhuh. The same Arabella who turns out to be Dr Yes's new girlfriend?'

'We don't know that . . .'

'They looked pretty bloody chummy in that photo, and she isn't, you may have noted, *in* Brazil.'

'She may be by now.'

'Uhuh. Let's look at it another way. *Pearl* lured *you* to Starbucks. Dazzled by her great beauty, you told her all about Augustine, particularly the fact that he was living in your house.'

'What're you saying, that *Pearl* killed him?'

'Possibly.'

'That's just ridiculous. *I* called *her*, remember? *I* brought up Augustine, not Pearl.' Alison mimed playing a fiddle. 'You're not funny,' I said, 'you're just jealous.'

'That's right. Or, wait a minute – yes, that's bollocks. Oh, think about it! You brought Augustine into the shop, laughing at him behind his back because he thought he was being shot at. Well what if he really was? What if they *were* trying to kill him because he keeps asking awkward questions about Arabella? What if whoever it was saw him come in and put two and two together, because you haven't been backward about getting publicity for your investigations, and deserved or not, you're getting a reputation for solving crimes, and so he, she or they thought they better find out what you were up to.'

'But *I* called *them*.'

'Exactly. They were expecting it; you merely confirmed that you were investigating them. Augustine had gone to ground, but they knew you could lead them to him. You told Pearl, and a few hours later he was dead.'

'And you're always complaining about Jeff and his lunatic conspiracy theories? You're the one quoting Neil Armstrong and giant leaps for mankind.'

Alison raised her coffee cup and tapped it against mine. 'The thing is, Mystery Man, Neil Armstrong *did* make a giant leap for mankind.'

The fundamental flaw in her analysis of Augustine's murder was the fact that Arabella was still alive, and therefore there was no reason to kill him. Why would they murder someone just because he was annoying? All businesses attract paranoid weirdos from time to time, but those businesses rarely concoct complicated plans to rub them out. If that was the case, I would have been dead years ago.

But the fact remained that he *was* dead, and murdered, and someone had done it, someone who had entered my house and splattered his brains all over my walls.

It would have been too easy to say, *This time it's personal*. In truth it was a wee bit personal, even if that doesn't have quite the same ring to it. I wasn't intent on blazing a trail of violence across the city chasing the killer, and the truth is that Mother's room had needed redecorating anyway. I was, at best, mildly annoyed. Intrigued. Someone had not only tracked Augustine down to my house, but had gone to the trouble of making it look like a suicide, and done a sufficiently good job of it to throw the police off the scent. The question was *why*? Yes, Pearl *could* have given his location away. Yes, Dr Yeschenkov *might* have ordered the hit. But how likely was either scenario? Since being dumped by Arabella, Augustine had been penniless and drunk. Surely it was much more likely that he had other enemies? He had gotten hold of a gun, and how else would you do that but by rubbing up against lowlifes? Or, severed from Arabella's money, perhaps he'd taken truck with loan sharks and couldn't pay it back. People who didn't accept IOUs but settled debts the old-fashioned way. It could even have been a random murder. Or the killer *hadn't been looking for him at all*. What if *I* was the intended victim? In fact that was *much* more likely. I had made many enemies through my investigations – not to mention the Christmas Club. I was the scourge of the criminal underworld. Rubbing me made a lot more sense.

'Did anyone ever tell you you've a very high opinion of yourself?' Alison asked, and by so asking I became aware that I had said at least some of that out loud. I just gave her the kind of pitying look I reserve for my least favoured customers, those who just come in to use the toilet or to fold back the covers of the books while sheltering from the rain.

She shrugged it off and said, 'Look, I'm with you on this. He's been murdered; now we have to work out who did it, and why.'

'*We?*'

She sighed. 'Yes, *we.*'

'But you're . . .'

'Yes, I'm with child. I'm not *disabled.*'

'Well I think the jury's still out on that one.'

She fixed me with a look, and I fixed her with one, even though I knew there could only be one winner, what with my malfunctioning tear ducts.

She said, 'Look, we've dealt with murders before . . .'

'Not out of choice.'

'. . . and the way you're getting on it's almost like you're blasé about it. Augustine was murdered in your mother's house; you should be fired up, you should be like a bloodhound on the trail of whoever did it.'

'I am.'

'Well, forgive me, it's difficult to tell. But if you're in, then I'm in, and we can crack this one. It could be your greatest case yet, and I want to be there with you.'

'Even in your condition.'

'I am one hundred per cent committed to solving this. I feel like I owe it to him. He trusted me.'

'Okay.'

'*Okay?*'

'Okay, we'll solve it then.'

'Together?'

'Together.'

'Brilliant! Okay! Gotta run.'

'You what?'

'Hello? I do have a job, unlike you.'

She was already halfway to the door.

'I thought you were one hundred per cent committed?'

She paused, and thought about that for the briefest moment. 'I may have exaggerated,' she said.

She winked, pulled the door open and went out. As she passed across the front window she gave me a little wave and blew a kiss. I ignored *that* and pointed at myself. I cupped my hands and shouted, 'At least he can depend on me. *I'm* one hundred per cent committed!'

'You should be!' she yelled back.

She'd barely disappeared from view before Jeff appeared at my elbow.

'*I* offer one hundred and *ten* per cent commitment,' he said.

'That's good to know. There are boxes upstairs that need unpacking.'

'That's not what I meant,' he said.

'I know,' I replied. As he turned away I said, 'Jeff?'

He stopped and gave me a hopeful look. I take a particular delight in dashing such hopes. He's a student, and worse, a member of Amnesty International, and worse still, a budding poet, so he should get used to disappointment. 'Jeff, you heard what we were talking about there?'

'Kind of.'

'Kind of all of?'

He nodded. 'I couldn't help it.'

'Well, you know the way we were debating who might have let slip that Augustine was staying in my house, and Alison thinks it's Pearl only because she's devastatingly attractive . . . ?'

'Yes?'

'It wasn't you, was it? Because you've ratted us out before.'

'No it wasn't, and I didn't, and I wouldn't.'

I gave him the Death Stare. For some reason I can do it with him for considerably longer than I can do it with Alison. Perhaps it is because she is a reincarnation of the Gorgon.

'I swear to God,' said Jeff.

His cheeks had coloured somewhat, and he quickly turned and hurried back up the stairs, ostensibly to finish unpacking the books. But he knew that I would be watching him. And I knew that he knew that I would be watching him, and he knew that I knew that he knew that I would be watching him. I didn't believe for one moment that he had actually told anyone. He had merely flushed the flush of the innocent man accused, but it is good to keep the staff on their toes.

12

Let me explain why I took Pearl for coffee again.

What had hurt me most was Alison's assertion that Pearl had somehow played me, rather than the other way round. It hurt because, on reflection, I realised that there was a remote chance that there could be some infinitesimal grain of truth in what she had said. I didn't want to give Alison the satisfaction of being right, but I did wish to address the previously unrealised possibility that there was a microscopic flaw in my professional armour and/or personality. *If* Pearl had played me, she had played a player, and now this player would play her better than she had played me in the first leg. And this time I would play her away from home, where away goals counted double. Playing her on unfamiliar territory would take me out of my comfort zone, sharpen my Spider sense and, most importantly, make it less likely that we would be interrupted by a jealous girlfriend wielding coffee.

I phoned her at the Yeschenkov clinic and said, 'There's a brilliant new Bernie Rhodenbarr I think you should read, and by the by, did you hear about Augustine Wogan?'

'Yes, I did! My God, how terrible! I love Bernie Rhodenbarr's books!'

And just like that, I had exposed her as a fraud. Now it was important to press home the advantage.

'Listen, I'm up your way shortly; can I buy you a coffee? I can tell you all the grisly details.'

'I'm not sure I can . . .'

'Did you see your boss in the paper with Arabella?'

'Yes I *did*. Would you believe it?'

'She's not off to Brazil yet, then?'

'I think she is, I think that picture was from the night she went . . .'

'That's unfortunate.'

'Why?'

'The funeral, of course. And when the police couldn't track her down, they gave me his personal effects. I really wanted to hand them over to her; I feel a bit odd having them around. His diary, a lot of e-mails Arabella sent him I'm sure she'd like back even if she has dumped him.'

I had baited the trap anew.

'You know something, maybe I could sneak out for ten minutes. There's a café just round the corner? Singing Kettle? And will you bring the Block?'

'Yes, of course.'

I put the phone down. She was smart, that was for sure. In the midst of our conversation she must have Googled Bernie Rhodenbarr and realised her mistake: that he was a character, not an author. Alternatively, her familiarity with crime fiction was such that she had understood exactly what I had meant when I mentioned Rhodenbarr instead of Block. You can read so much into so little, and I generally do, but one thing *was* clear: once I had mentioned Augustine's fictional diary and Arabella's makey-uppy e-mails, she had very quickly changed her tune about going for coffee. Or, she had genuinely changed her mind, because she fancied a bit of gossip or found me irresistible, just as Alison did. You can read so much into so little, and I generally do, repeatedly.

The Singing Kettle was just around the corner, at least to a normal person with functional legs, but I made it there with time to spare and just a few stops for my inhaler and an energy-giving lick of a Twix. It was an old-fashioned café with a common name which appeared to be family-run. The most exotic thing on the menu was a German biscuit. I have a lot of time for German biscuits, not only because they are nice, but because they are living evidence that political correctness does not always win out. Although not *actually* living, or the public health inspectors would need to get involved. A German biscuit is, ostensibly, two biscuits with jam in between them, and white water icing on top, usually decorated with a glacé cherry. It is derived from the Austrian Linzer Torte or Linzer biscuit, which was more generally known in the UK as a German biscuit until the First World War came along and the PC brigade insisted on renaming it the Empire biscuit with the same flag-waving hysteria that later saw sauerkraut renamed Liberty cabbage and French fries rechristened Freedom fries. That is, except in Northern Ireland, where Empire biscuit had an even greater political connotation, and so it remained, defiantly, a German biscuit here, the locals even preferring that name while the Nazis were bombing the hell out of them during the Second World War.

I explained all of this to Pearl within moments of her sitting down, and she blinked at me for a while and said, 'Actually, I might have a Paris bun.'

That was a whole different barrel of fish and one I chose not to climb into. I bought her one without passing comment, and a coffee for each of us, although obviously I didn't touch mine, having sworn a blood allegiance to Starbucks. I was to Starbucks what the Knights Templar were or are to the Holy Grail: champion and protector.

I passed the Block across as she took her first sip, and she immediately put her cup down and examined it with apparent excitement, opening the front cover and starting to read the synopsis and then quickly changing her mind and closing it and setting it down and running her hands over the back of the book as if it was silk, which it was, in a way. 'I shouldn't read that bit, it always gives the plot away,' she said.

She was beautiful. She had a little crumb of bun in the corner of her mouth, and I just wanted to reach across and lick it off. I mean, pick it off. She saw me looking, I'm sure, for her tongue flicked out, touched the crumb, seemed to play with it for an eternity, and then drew it back across her scarlet lips and into the warm cavern of her voluptuous mouth.

'So, that writer, my God, in your own house!'

'It wasn't pretty. How'd you find out? I don't think it made the news.'

'Kind of roundabout. Our legal people phoned and told us, something to do with the restraining order we had against him being rendered null and void. I mean, he was a pain in the arse, but what a thing to do.'

'To do?'

'Kill himself!'

'Well, that hasn't been established.'

'Really? You mean, like an accident?'

'Posssibly. Or murder.'

I fixed her with my look.

I'm not sure that she noticed.

But she did move forward, leaning on the table between us, exposing the wonderful craftsmanship that goes into a brassiere. Or, not to put too fine a point on it, an over-shoulder boulder-holder.

'*Seriously?* Who would do that? Why? What do the police say?'

'I really don't know.'

'Someone must have said something.'

I gave a little shrug. Sometimes less is more. Her eyes widened. She sat back. Her mouth opened. It closed again. She sat forward, close enough for me to know that despite the bra she wasn't making mountains out of molehills, near enough for her to whisper, and for me to catch the mix of mouthwash, coffee and Paris bun on her breath: 'My God . . . I know what you're doing, I read about you on the net: you're investigating this, aren't you? That's what you do. You think he was murdered; you're the only one who does, and you're determined to prove it.'

I gave an even littler shrug. Lesserer was morerer.

Her hand went to her mouth. 'That's . . . fantastic . . . All the stuff you know about crime, you put it to good use. I read that in an interview you gave. Do you, you know, have like a crime-fighting partner?'

'No,' I said.

'I'd love to be your partner.'

'Okay,' I said.

Just in case you get the impression that she was playing me again, that I was under the sway of her hypnotic eyes and perfectly high cheekbones and luxuriant Harmony hair, it was in fact the other way round. I had drip-fed her information and sucked her in. In order to be my partner she would have to divulge everything she knew about Arabella and her time at the clinic; she would be able to find out from Dr Yes exactly where Arabella was going and why. While there clearly couldn't be anything to Augustine's claims that she had died in the clinic, maybe he had unwittingly stumbled on something else, some darker secret that had required his liquidation. By letting Pearl think she was my partner, I would actually be gaining an inside track on the case.

She seemed genuinely excited. She moved from sitting opposite to pulling her chair round beside me. Our shoulders touched as she looked into my eyes. 'Where do we start?' she purred. 'Or have you started already? What have you found out? You have his diaries and e-mails; can I see them? Sorry, tell me if I'm being too forward. I'm just so excited, my job is so dull and this is . . . oh!'

'It's fine, don't worry about it. Yes, of course you can see them. I just don't have them with me.'

'Brilliant! What else do you know? Why do you think he was murdered?'

'Let me turn that around – why do *you* think he was murdered?'

'I didn't say I thought he was murdered.'

'But you're very keen to help me investigate; you must have some reason for thinking that he might have been.'

'Well, no, not really. But you clearly do, and I'm just anxious to help. It's very exciting. Why do *you* think he might have been murdered?'

'I have an open mind. But I think it might be connected to your clinic.'

'*Really?* Why?'

'Because he was so convinced that Arabella died there, and he was kicking up such a fuss . . .'

'But she didn't die, she's alive and kicking.'

'You know that for sure?'

'I saw the same photograph you did.'

'But you didn't speak to her?'

'No, but Dr Yeschenkov did; they bumped into each other at that exhibition in Dublin. He was furious because the caption sort of encouraged you to read between the lines, and I know his wife wasn't happy. Normally she goes with him to all his social events, but she couldn't go to that one.'

'You talked to him about it?'

'Just in passing. He was saying guess who I saw in Dublin, and she was in great form, very pleased with the clinic, her treatment, the result. She was going to Brazil, all excited about it.'

'Definitely Brazil.'

'Definitely. I think so. It's what he said.'

'And she didn't say anything about dumping her husband?'

'If she did, he didn't say.'

'Do you think there's something going on between them?'

'No, definitely not.'

'Definitely?'

'She's much older. She looks fifty per cent better now than when she came to us, but she still isn't exactly . . . well, she has an unusual look one would hesitate to call beautiful. Dr Yeschenkov goes for youth and beauty.'

'Has he ever gone for you?'

There was not even a hint of colour to her porcelain skin as she said, 'You're very blunt.'

'It's the nature of the business. Bookselling, I mean.'

'He's not my type,' she said, and her eyes held mine, and I didn't need a reader of eye language to tell me what she was implying. She broke it off and played with the crumbs of her bun. Her eyes flitted up again. 'So that's all I know. You must know something else to make you think what you think?'

Ninety-eight per cent of me wanted to tell her about the cigar cutter. It was a perfect illustration of how clever I was. But that minuscule two per cent was tougher than it had any right to be. It took a very strong grip on my throat and wouldn't let the words out. I had a name for that two per cent.

Alison.

I had a vision of her striking me across the nose with a hard-backed book and calling me a tit for even considering giving up the only fact we had. So despite this almost overwhelming inclination to reveal everything, I nevertheless gave a slight shake of my head.

Pearl said, 'We're partners, but you're playing your cards very close to your chest.'

'And you're playing your chest very close to your cards.'

And it was at this very moment that her spell over me was broken, because her natural reaction was to furrow her brow in bafflement, but she couldn't because it had been so heavily Botoxed. Her eyes moved up, but the corrugation that should have rippled across her forehead failed to materialise. There was no movement in it at all, and I suddenly knew that all of her was just as fake, that she was an actress and a bewitcher of men's souls, a landlocked siren who had employed flattery, innuendo and lipstick to try and suck me into her clutches, but I had resisted, and triumphed, as I always do.

13

I had established that Pearl was attempting to play
me, but beyond that her motives remained unclear.
She could just be curious. She could be seeking to
protect the reputation of her employer. She could be
a femme fatale. She looked like a femme fatale, she
got on like a femme fatale, she had the suggestive
name of a femme fatale, although that might have
been just as fake as her serene forehead and impressive chest. I myself had not noticed that she had a
fake chest, but Alison had nailed it at once. 'Anyone
whose waist is that skinny should not have tits that
big,' she said. 'That girl,' she said, 'gets paid in kind.'
It was a fair point. If you worked in a fruit shop, you
would expect to get the occasional free pear.

Deep down I knew that I had been foolish. Because
of Pearl's beauty I had allowed myself to believe that
meeting her was vital to the case, whereas it was only

vital to my ego. The actual solving of Augustine's murder would require a very different but much more obvious approach. I would examine the detritus of his life, the minutiae of his existence, and I would re-create his world, and in doing so I would uncover fresh evidence that would lead me to the man or woman who had killed him. I did not doubt it. I have a certain pedigree in this line of work, and when women don't get in my way, I am usually very quick and efficient at bringing a case to a satisfactory conclusion. I have been aided in this by my obsession with and addiction to crime fiction. Those tens of thousands of novels have been my education, in a way that my very short attendance at the nearby Queen's University was not. Being asked to leave that seat of learning might have held someone else back, but not I. Being accused of what I was accused of might have driven others into hiding, but not I. I hasten to add that nothing was ever proven, in a court of law. In a way it was a blessing in disguise – I might easily have followed a different career path, perhaps into academia, or joined the Royal Canadian Mounted Police or become a mercenary, but no, my immediate removal in handcuffs from halls of residence was fortuitous in that it caused me to focus on what I really wanted to do, and that was to open my own mystery bookshop, and the tenacity with which I pursued that dream has been the making of me. Not only do I now operate the finest mystery bookstore in Belfast, but my investigative talents are second to none. I am practically the fourth emergency service.

The depressing detail of Augustine's last days was here in the shop: the receipts, the business and credit cards, the invoices and ticket stubs. They were a story in themselves, and all I was looking for was the plot. I started with the bill from the Europa Hotel. He had stayed there for the two nights preceding his appearance outside No Alibis. The great thing about the phone or e-mails is that you don't have to appear in person. You can be as impressive as your word power allows, you can give yourself whatever fancy title you want and nobody questions you, whereas if I turned up at the front desk of the Europa and said I wanted to know what they had on Augustine Wogan they'd tell me to take a run and jump. On the phone my wonderful facility for creating believable characters and personas served me well. I became Donald West-lake, the executor of Augustine Wogan's estate. I had a bill the hotel had issued; I wanted to know if his account had been settled and if not whom I should send the cheque to, and incidentally, did he leave anything behind, because anything he left belonged to said estate. I had a notion that Augustine had fled from the hotel without settling, and I was entirely correct. He had indeed left items behind, but the hotel manager assured me that they were only articles of clothing, toiletries and the suitcase they had once fitted into. I then explained that we were having some difficulty tracking his movements prior to his unfortunate demise, and asked if an itemised record of his phone calls could be made available. The manager said yes, of course, and where should he send it, and I told him I wanted it in a hurry so if he didn't mind I would arrange to have it biked round. On hanging up, I immediately dispatched Jeff to retrieve it. He said, 'But I don't have a bike.'

This is the calibre of my staff.

While he was gone, I turned to my occasionally loyal database of customers. They had become more communicative in recent weeks, now that my annual bombardment of e-mails beseeching them to join the No Alibis Christmas Club had lessened somewhat – a breather, really, before the campaign started anew in July – and had been sharing with me their piss-poor insights and opinions on recent crime fiction and boring me rigid with the sad facts of their personal lives. I had been doing my best to act the genial host, but it is such a chore. Sometimes when I just can't handle their cheeriness any more I tell them all to f-off, and they laugh as if I'm having a joke, but I'm really not. However, at that moment my relations with them were relatively good, so it was precisely the right time to ask for a favour, and as an added incentive I offered a signed copy of Eric Ambler's *The Mask of Dimitrios* – albeit signed by Jehovah's Vengeance Grisham – to anyone who either worked in the travel industry or knew someone they could lean on who did.

As I waited for that e-mail to circulate, I studied the blood-spotted newspaper featuring the photograph of

Dr Yeschenkov with the lovely Arabella taken at the Xianth art gallery in Dublin.

The paper was published on the day Augustine was murdered, but while there was an implicit suggestion that the picture had been taken the night before, it wasn't actually stated. I checked the gallery's website and discovered that the launch had actually been three days prior to its coverage in the paper. They were showcasing a further seven photographs taken at the opening. One of them featured Dr Yeschenkov, but there were no others of Arabella. Working on the theory that Dubliners couldn't tell one Belfast accent from another, I phoned the gallery and asked to speak to the owner. I introduced myself as Dan Starkey, the editor of *Belfast Confidential*, a local magazine that had started out as a champion of hard news but had recently re-imagined itself into a web-based scandal sheet, and explained that we were interested in running something on Dr Yeschenkov's visit to Xianth, and on the basis that I didn't name my source, and the understanding that he never talked about clients, he said ask away.

'Well, did he buy anything?'

'He bought a Corcoran. Ex-prisoner, IRA I believe, but hot stuff.'

'How much?'

'That's private.'

'Ball-park?'

'You wouldn't get much change out of a ten-grand note.'

'Would you get any change out of a nine-thousand-pound note?'

'None.'

'What about out of a nine-thousand-nine-hundred-and-forty-pound note?'

'About a tenner.'

'What sort of a painting?'

'It's called *Fields, Trees and Bushes outside Lisburn*.'

'Uhuh.'

'It's really quite wonderful; it features a wildebeest . . .'

'What's he like, Dr Yeschenkov, regular client?'

'Occasional rather than regular. He has a good eye.'

'What's he like?'

'Charming, rich.'

'And the lady who was with him on the night?'

'Mrs Yeschenkov was unable to attend.'

'But there was a photograph of him in . . .'

'Yes. I saw that. He wasn't happy.'

'He looked happy.'

'He always does, it's the teeth.'

'He complained?'

'Yes. It gave the impression he was with that woman. I think his wife didn't like it or something.'

'Is that why it's not on your website?'

'No – we took the ones on our website. The one in the paper must have been taken by the *Irish Times* themselves.'

'This woman, Arabella Wogan, what did you make of her?'

'Can't say that I spoke to her. In fact, that picture in the paper is the first time I laid eyes on her. It said she was a socialite, but I've never heard of her.'

'You must have invited her to the opening?'

'Nope. I mean, she was probably someone's plus-one. We were chock-a-block so there were a lot of people I never got to meet. I just know I didn't speak to her and she certainly didn't buy anything.'

When I hung up, having promised to give the gallery a glowing mention, I took another look at the newspaper photo. Their smiles looked slightly forced, but only in the way that most posed photographs do. Their shoulders were touching. His left arm was hidden, giving the impression that it was around her, but it might only have been his way of holding a glass of wine out of shot. Perhaps he didn't believe it was a good idea for a surgeon to be seen drinking in public; all those droopy-faced potential clients wouldn't want to have to worry about a shaky hand. At the base of the picture, just above the caption, there was a single line of black type: *Photo – Liam Benson.*

Still working according to my thread theory, I pulled this one as well. I called the *Irish Times* and asked to be put through to their photographic department. I asked for Liam Benson, but was told there was no one of that name on staff. I used the Dan Starkey cover story again, but this time said I wanted a copy of the Xianth photo to use in our next issue. A hassled-sounding manager called Donny said that wouldn't be possible because Liam was a freelance photographer and the copyright belonged to him. I asked where I could contact Liam and he said, 'He's from your neck of the woods, not mine, but I'm not his fucking agent.'

He hung up. I was not unduly miffed. I had met Irish people before. Many of them spoke like this.

I typed Liam Benson's name into Google and was rewarded with a link to his website. He was *Liam Benson, freelance photographer – news, corporate and public relations.*

Under his list of satisfied public relations clients: The Yeschenkov Clinic.

14

I was mulling over the significance of this, and trying to decide if there was any, when Jeff cycled past the window. When I say he cycled, he was actually miming cycling, much in the manner of the Knights of the Round Table pretending to ride horses in *Monty Python and the Holy Grail* and using coconuts to replicate the sound of hooves. *They* were quite funny. Jeff just looked like a prick. He lacked coconuts. I was thinking about what he could have used to achieve the desired sound effect but the only satisfactory answer I could come up with was a bike.

Jeff came in and I said, 'Any problems?'

He grinned. 'None whatsoever.' He put an envelope on the counter and I took out Augustine's phone records. 'I asked them if he'd had any visitors they were aware of, anything suspicious.'

'Did I ask you to ask them that?'

'No. I was using my initiative.'

'I've warned you about that. You think of it as initiative; I think of it as you blundering into what is none of your business.' He looked at me, and I looked at him. After a while I said, 'Well?'

'Well what?'

'Did he have any visitors?'

'Not telling.'

I sighed. I studied the list of calls.

Jeff said, 'No.'

He'd made six calls. They were all to the same number. I called it. It was the Forum International Hotel on Bedford Street. It isn't far from No Alibis. Not much in central Belfast is. You could skim a stone to it. *You* could; I couldn't, what with my wasting muscles and arthritic wrists. The Forum is a converted linen mill. Five stars. Not cheap. The calls lasted for between seven and thirty-five minutes. I'd a fair idea whom he was calling. I asked for the manager and did my executor-of-the-will routine and confirmed that yes indeed, Mrs Arabella Wogan had been a guest for four weeks and that there was no need to worry about the bill as the hotel had an arrangement with Yeschenkov and all accounts were settled directly with the clinic. I explained that we were having trouble tracking the lovely Arabella down and asked if he or his staff had spoken to her about her future plans. He said he hadn't, but asked for a moment so that he could speak to his staff. He was very efficient. Five stars will sometimes get you that. He came back on and said that her departure was via their express check-out service, which was really just dropping the keys in a box, so nobody had actually seen her leave, but it was understood that she was catching an early flight and had travelled to Dublin in the late evening. He wasn't sure *how* it was understood. I said it would be helpful if I could get Arabella's itemised phone records and he said absolutely, where should I send them, and I said I needed them quite quickly, is it okay if I have them biked round? He was most accommodating. I told Jeff to get back on his imaginary bike and warned him about using his initiative.

I glanced across the road and saw Alison, in behind her counter, selling bangles, and slightly overweight, even at this distance. She was hard work, but probably just about worth the effort. I hoped when the baby came out it had none of my ailments and all of her looks, minus the chins. But it should have my smarts. I would read him *Emil and the Detectives* in the crib. He could play with a pair of plastic handcuffs in a way that Alison had thus far refused to. He would inherit No Alibis, if there was still a No Alibis to inherit. This thought returned me to my work. It is amazing what you can get done when you apply yourself. I called Liam Benson and identified myself as Dan Starkey and said I was looking for a copy of the photo from the show at the Xianth gallery, and he said, 'You don't sound like Dan Starkey,' and I hung up. It was an abject lesson in the dangers of getting too cocky.

A few moments later the phone rang, but I was

wise to that one. I allowed it to go to answer machine, and then regretted it immediately, for he would know who I was, and where I was. His message however was: 'Sorry, must have got a wrong . . .' And then he hung up. But maybe somewhere, further down the line, he would remember, or make a connection, or mention it to someone who would.

I sat and thought about what it meant, Liam Benson being employed by the Yeschenkov Clinic. It was too much of a coincidence that he should just happen to travel to Dublin and end up photographing Dr Yes at the gallery. He must surely have been there at the doctor's request; it was therefore unlikely that the photograph had been submitted to the *Irish Times* without the doctor's knowledge and approval. Why then had he complained to the gallery about the photo, if he had known they hadn't taken it and had himself actually paid someone to be there for that purpose? Was he laying down some kind of a smokescreen? Or had he miscalculated – what he thought of as handy PR had backfired when his wife had seen him with Arabella and he had been forced to act aggrieved to cover his tracks? More importantly, did it have anything to do with Augustine's murder?

Not obviously.

I checked my e-mails and found that one of my idiot customers had finally admitted to having a dead-end job in a travel agent's. I asked him to see if he could find out if Arabella Wogan had booked and taken a flight out of Dublin, and gave him the day after the Xianth gallery event as the most likely, but to check further ahead as well. He came back to me in twenty minutes and confirmed that Arabella had been booked on a flight the next day to Rio de Janeiro via Paris. It was a one-way ticket. He had no means of checking if she had actually travelled. That wasn't particularly satisfactory, so I responded with something sarcastic and clicked off. A proper 3-D customer wasted another twenty minutes of my time asking for my advice on a book for his fifteen-year-old daughter; wasted only because my insights were roundly ignored. I knew exactly what he was doing: he was using my expertise to select the correct book, and then he would leave without buying it and make his way down to Waterstones where he would get it cheaper. I gave him the international sign for wanking as he passed the shop window, but he misinterpreted and waved cheerily back.

As one clot disappeared, another reappeared, reprising his pathetic attempt to entertain me with his invisible bike-riding routine. When he rested the invisible bike against the window and entered the shop, I made him go back out and move it so that the handlebars wouldn't make a mark on the glass. He did it too, which I thought *was* quite funny. Then he put another envelope on the desk and smiled. I took out Arabella's phone records and read down the list. She'd made many more calls, including half a dozen to a number I recognised as the Europa Hotel's, but others I would need to check out. As I studied them Jeff stood there, still smiling, and I said, 'What?' and he kept grinning and I gave an exasperated sigh and said, 'You did it again, didn't you?' He nodded. 'I'm about to tell you off for using your initiative again, yet you're standing there happy as a pig in shite, so obviously my telling-off is going to be completely pointless because you think you've discovered something relevant, so you may as well tell me now, though even if it turns out to be useful, it doesn't change my basic instruction not to try to use your initiative, because just because you've lucked upon something this time, it doesn't mean you will again, and generally you just waste everyone's time and complicate matters and get me or the shop or my investigations into trouble, so please don't do it again, understood?'

'I'm only trying to help.'

'Just tell me.'

'Well, I went into the hotel; it's a lovely big place, they've really done a—'

'Just the relevant bits, please.'

'Okay. All right. I spoke to the guy you spoke to, and he was just putting the phone records in the envelope when I asked him if Arabella had had many visitors, and he said yes she had, but that was normal, because she was with the clinic and they're always sending round nurses or doctors or fashion designers to check on or consult with their patients, or clients as they call them. And he was clearly in the mood for a natter, because he said you wouldn't believe some of the mess our people have to clean up in those rooms, and I said like what, and he said well they've all had their operations and the like, there's always blood-soaked bandages and syringes and medication left behind; the clinic people are supposed to take it all with them but they push them really hard so they're rushing from room to room or to a different hotel, and they end up forgetting to tidy, or sometimes it's the patients themselves, they've had their procedures and they're all bandaged up for a reason, but they can't resist taking a wee peek but it's too soon, so they bleed all over the sheets.'

'I'm waiting for the big reveal,' I said.

'It's coming. I asked him if there was anything like that in Arabella's room, excessive bleeding, some kind of an emergency, and he said no. I asked if anything had been left behind like medication or syringes and he said no, not that he was aware of, but he could check with the Museum.'

'The . . .'

'I know. The Museum. It's what they call a cupboard they have in their staff room; it's a display of all the unusual things that guests leave behind in their rooms. They either forget about them entirely or are too embarrassed to claim them back once they realise they've left them behind, or the hotel has no forwarding address for them. He said a lot of them were of a sexual nature – vibrators, dildos, even a blow-up doll. There was also jewellery, a complete wedding dress, intimate photographs, the complete works of William Shakespeare, a stuffed monkey, a map of Liberia, a lucky rabbi's foot . . .'

'Rabbi?'

'I may have misheard . . . a sizeable chunk of a coral reef, a signed photograph of Lou Reed . . .'

'I get the picture. Christ, it's like *The Generation Game*.'

'. . . and finally there was what they discovered under a sofa in Arabella's room and which has only just made its debut on display in the Museum, but which they have passed on to me, to give to you, to give to her, because they had no forwarding address.' Jeff slipped his hand into the pocket of his combat jacket. 'Are you ready?'

'Yes.'

'Sure?'

'*Yes.*'

'Then without further delay, I present to you, straight from the room of Arabella Wogan, wife of the late Augustine Wogan . . .'

'Will you just show me the fucking thing?'

So he did. He set it on the counter. It was small and shiny. It was made of stainless steel and brushed chrome. It was a V-shaped cigar cutter.

15

While I waited for Alison to arrive, having called her in a state of great excitement, I took a Valium, and then another, and then a third. It was important to be settled, because foaming at the mouth is not conducive to good teamwork.

I do, literally, foam. Once, memorably, when I tried to commit suicide by swallowing four Ariel washing machine tablets.

The source of my excitement sat glinting on the counter. I believe it was glinting because of the angelic, self-satisfied glow that was coming off Jeff.

'So you must be feeling pretty proud of yourself,' I said.

'I am. Using my initiative. The boy done good.'

'Yes, you did. I'm proud of you. But you know what they say.'

'What do they say?'

'Pride comes before a fall.'

'But you were the one expressing pride. You said you were proud of me.'

'That's not the point I'm trying to make.'

'Well then you should express yourself more clearly.'

He was hurt, I could tell. He was annoyed. He thought I was raining on his parade. He was incorrect. Or if I was, it was a mild sprinkle. In fact I withdraw that. *Sprinkle* is an American word for light rain, and I despise it. When we say it, we say it is *spitting*. I was spitting on his parade. Spitting is a much better word. It is less mild and fluffy. Spitting is God's way of teasing us. *I might let it rain, I might not, it's entirely up to me because I am God. I'm sitting up here with my big white fluffy beard and I have the power to make it rain, or the power to make it sunny. Here's a little bit just to confuse you. You'll look out the window and say it's spitting outside, I wonder if I'll need an umbrella, or will it stop and the sun come out, and then I might need a parasol. A gamp, a brolly or a bumbershoot. I enjoy playing with you, I revel in toying with your expectations; that is my role, my joy, my raison d'être, and yes I invented French as well, just to confuse you further.*

'You're presupposing the existence of God,' said Jeff, 'but either way, I accept your apology.'

I blinked at him for a little bit.

'All right, Columbo, you lucked into something. For the moment it's just a thing, it contributes nothing. So take your best shot. What's the significance of this V-shaped cigar cutter, what does it tell us about our case?'

I fixed him with my look.

'It tells us that whoever murdered Augustine also murdered Arabella.'

'Does it?'

'Yes.'

'Explain.'

'You said Augustine couldn't have cut his cigar with the cutter he had, so there had to be someone else in the room with him, which shifted the case from suicide to murder. Finding a V-shape cutter in Arabella's room, and presuming that she herself does not smoke cigars, suggests that the killer also paid her a visit.'

'But surely we have been arguing all along that Arabella died either on the operating table or post-operative, and that is why there's a cover-up, and they felt the need to dispatch Augustine because he was trying to expose them. Why then would the killer need to be in Arabella's room *prior* to Augustine being killed, or at all?'

'Perhaps maybe . . .'

'Never start a sentence with perhaps maybe.'

'Perhaps Dr Yes was present in her hotel room when she died, and was so distraught that he had to light a cigar to calm himself down. He inadvertently dropped it and—'

'Ha-ha!'

'Excuse me?'

'Excuse *moi*!'

'You what?'

'The flaw in your logic is . . . ?'

'That . . . Dr Yes, being a surgeon, probably doesn't smoke?'

'That if he dropped it in Arabella's hotel room, how then could he cut Augustine's cigar at a *later* date?'

'He had a second one. A back-up. A reserve. God knows he's rich enough. Or there was a second killer who also smoked cigars, and who also favoured the V-cut.'

I took a deep breath. I drummed my fingers on the counter. I studied the V-cut.

It was time to take a step back.

I had learned to my cost in the *Case of the Cock-Headed Man* that sometimes the McGuffin is more than a McGuffin; that an ingenious plot device is occasionally more than just a device, but the entire plot. I was also, crucially, aware of the weight of ten thousand volumes of crime fiction upon my shoulders, aware that it was at points in the plot *exactly like this* that less talented authors completely lost their way by piling improbability upon improbability, by making ludicrous and nonsensical connections between events designed only to reinforce the perception that their leading character, their detective or PI, has astonishing insights that lesser mortals couldn't hope to match. It was important to remain grounded in reality.

There is no greater barometer of reality than Agatha. She may be old-fashioned, she may no longer sell in vast quantities, she may indeed be dead, but she is or was indisputably the doyenne of crime fiction authors, and it is laughable to suggest that any member of the present generation, many of whom write as if they're having a knees-up in an abattoir, is even fit to suck the mud off the hem of her voluminous skirts. Crime fiction is largely created according to a series of templates, which, like the tectonic plates that make up the surface of the earth, do not always sit evenly together, and occasionally clash, causing earthquakes and volcanic eruptions, but there is no disputing that despite their sometimes huge differences in style and subject matter, crime writers generally live and die according to the template that Agatha laid down. She is the source of the Nile.

Agatha understood that it was important to stop a book mid-course and go, hold up, I'm in danger of confusing not only the reader, but myself; here, let's pull the old emergency cord and bring this hurtling express to a halt, let's review the evidence as it stands so that everyone is absolutely clear as to what is going on, who the characters are, and what they are all up to at any particular time. Chandler and Hammett might have cornered the market in fruity phrases, but they rarely thought to pull that cord themselves, leaving generations of fans capable of quoting individual lines but absolutely lost when asked to explain who did what to who and when or *how the fuck* it could all possibly work.

Jeff was looking at me. 'You say all that,' he said, 'but I think there's a simpler way of looking at it. Basically what we're doing is playing Cluedo. Think of all the man hours you'd have saved if you just studied

Cluedo rather than wasting time on those ten ... thousand ... books.'

He had to finish what he was saying, but he could tell by the way what little colour I had was draining from my face that he had crossed the line. He had disrespected me, the shop and the genre. He had dished me.

'Jeff, you don't know what the bloody hell you're talking about. Cluedo? Cluedo! I should stick your fricking Cluedo up your arse, sideways.'

'I was only—'

'And follow it with a dagger, a candlestick, a revolver, a lead pipe, a spanner and a ... and a ...'

'Rope,' said Jeff. 'I'm sorry, I didn't mean to ...'

'Cluedo was devised by a man named Pratt in 1944.'

'I only meant ...'

'Do you know what he did for a living?'

'I don't ...'

'He was a solicitor's clerk and a *part-time clown.*'

'I didn't know ...'

'Which funnily enough is exactly what you are.'

'I've never worked in a solic—'

'You're a prat and a clown! And do you know how I know Mr Pratt the part-time clown designed Cluedo in 1944?'

'Did you look it up on the—'

'I read it in a fucking book, you halfwit!'

I turned and swiped the first book that came to hand off the shelf behind me, the shelf I used for special orders. I don't have much strength in my muscles, due to my wasting disease, but I summoned up enough to hurl it at him, and it caught him just above the eye, and he stumbled backwards into the *Buy one and get one at exactly the same price* table, scattering the books, upsetting the table and ending up lying amongst them on the floor. But only for a moment. He immediately jumped to his feet. There was blood streaming down the side of his face.

'Jeff, I . . .'

'Did anyone ever tell you you were fucking mental?'

He bolted for the door before I could give him a truthful answer. He yanked it open, and stormed out, with the theme from the *Rockford Files* failing to soothe his tortured and bleeding brow *at all*.

Immediately overcome with worry and concern, I hurried across to the overturned table and carefully righted it. The books, thank God, were not damaged, that is, apart for the one Jeff had assaulted with his forehead. The blood on the cover could easily be wiped off, but it had also soaked into the pages themselves, staining them for ever. I turned it over. It was a rare copy of Jim Thompson's *Pop. 1280*.

It was a sign.

16

No, *literally* a sign. The population announcement and road sign design on the cover of my 1964 signed first edition of his *noir* classic. Albeit signed by I'm a Zebra Grisham.

It would be a mistake to say that there were any other parallels between Jim Thompson and Augustine Wogan beyond the fact that they were both dead. Although none of the American's books were in print when he exited this mortal coil in 1977 either, he had in fact experienced much success earlier in his career (the Steve McQueen movie *The Getaway* was based on his novel), before his eventual decline into alcoholism. In recent years his books have experienced quite a revival. The French in particular have embraced him, with the director Bertrand Tavernier turning *Pop. 1280* into the acclaimed *Coup de Torchon* in 1981. There's nothing like a set of subtitles to improve one's cultural standing. Augustine, on the other hand, was never successful in the first place and thus couldn't qualify for a revival. Discovery, perhaps. But if he was ever to grace the shelves of any bookstore beyond my own it would probably only be because of the public interest aroused by my unmasking of his murderer.

I am like the sun. The planets align around me. Some are gas giants. Like the vision coming through the shop doorway.

'Was that Jeff I saw running away with blood on his face?' Alison asked.

'He had an accident,' I said. 'Paper cut.'

'To his head?'

'He was showing off.'

'He's a buck eejit. Is that it?' She was nodding down at the V-shape. 'It was a stroke of luck you asking if the hotel had a museum.'

'Luck, genius, it's a fine line.'

'So what are we thinking this means?'

'What are *you* thinking it means?'

She smiled. 'I'm not playing that game.'

'What game?'

'Where you ridicule my ideas, or steal them for your own. Why don't you tell me what you're thinking, Mystery Man?'

'I'm thinking you have a very poor opinion of me. But if you insist.'

It was like the sun being asked to prove why it is the dominant force in the solar system, despite it being so fricking obvious.

I moved the V-cutter to the centre of the counter and began to slowly rotate it. The best sunlight a spring day in Belfast could manage barely raised a glint from its shiny surface. As it turned I began to summarise what we knew of the circumstances surrounding the disappearance of Arabella Wogan and the death of her husband. How she had checked in to the Yeschenkov Clinic, and either died as a result of the procedures she underwent or blossomed because of them, having a brief affair with Dr Yes himself before skipping the country. Augustine was convinced she was dead, and that the clinic was covering it up to such an extent that they had taken legal action to warn him off, and then, finally, when he would not desist, he had been found murdered, by person or persons unknown, for reason or reasons unknown.

Alison put her hand on mine, stopping the revolution of the V-cut. She said, 'Stop turning that, it's annoying. And stop telling me stuff I already know. I'm not stupid, I have the capacity to retain information. Tell me what you actually think is going on.'

'No.'

In truth, I surprised myself.

'No?'

'Yes.'

'Yes?'

'Yes, no, I'm not going to say.'

'You have to say. We're partners.'

I let that one stand.

'What I mean is – we don't have enough information yet for me to form an opinion, and an uninformed one will just lead us down too many blind alleys. Let's find out more. Do you know something, Alison? I've read ten thousand crime novels . . .'

'This year alone. Are we going to get into the McGuffin thing again? Because it didn't work out too well last time.'

'No, not at all. In fact, I'm not talking specifics at all, I'm looking at the bigger picture, what we're doing here. What it all boils down to is nothing more than a big grown-up game of Cluedo. Who did what to who, where and what with. It's all guesswork. We need to get away from punts in the dark and establish the facts, then I, we, can sit down and work out the truth.'

She was smiling at me.

'What?'

'You know something, kiddo? I do believe you're getting older and wiser. You're going to make a wonderful dad, in spite of yourself. Once we get the visitation rights sorted out.'

But she was still smiling.

I don't know why. I had no intention of visiting at all.

'Or.'

'Or?'

She lifted the cigar cutter. 'One could argue that you haven't a baldy notion what's going on, and that this V-cutter—'

'What do you mean, baldy notion?'

'Excuse me?'

'Baldy. There's no need. Receding is—'

'Would you get over yourself and stop taking everything personally, you twit. You don't get it, do you? You phoned me up in a state of great excitement about the V-cutter, not because you wanted to involve me, but to show off, to boast about the fact that you'd discovered this supposedly crucial piece of evidence. You didn't even think about what I could bring to the table . . .'

'What can you bring to the . . .'

'. . . even though I work in an *effing* jewellery store that sells these *effing* things. Even though I . . .'

'I'm not a child, you can say fucking if you . . .'

'. . . make part of my living being able to talk knowledgeably about these fucking things . . .'

'. . . want to, though that said, it's not very ladylike and I wouldn't suggest speaking like that in front of . . .'

'. . . and I at least know that I only have to flip the fucking thing over to find the hallmark, which not only tells us the type of metal, but who made it . . .'

'. . . the children . . .'

'. . . and when they made it, and look at this, the serial number, which will allow us to track down where it was sold. I have my fucking uses, Mystery Man, and did you say *children*?'

'Slip of the tongue.'

'You're usually pretty precise about what you say.'

I was looking at her and thinking, my God, with your knowledge of bangles and whatnot, you actually have a use after all, which gave me a brief moment of elation, but this rapidly collapsed into a resigned depression, because the likelihood of me having to call again on such expertise in the future was on the anorexic side of slim, which meant that at her very moment of triumph she had actually rendered herself useless, like a wasp dying after it has stung, although she hadn't stung, but only provided me with some technical information I could quite easily have looked up in a book.

'In this instance, I was not.'

She was still smiling. Sometimes I want to wipe that stupid grin off her face. With a big mallet. Just keep hitting her right in the mouth with it until her teeth are flying all over the shop, embedding themselves in the walls.

Alison picked up the V-cutter. From her pocket she produced a magnifying glass. She had come prepared. It was a jeweller's magnifying glass. Compact. Not like the big Sherlock Holmes one I kept under the counter. I had never had the nerve to take it out of its box, at least after that first time. I had ordered it over the internet in my initial flush of excitement after solving the *Case of the Musical Jews*. When Jeff saw it he couldn't stop laughing. I told him I was thinking of increasing the stock of crime-fiction-related merchandising we kept in the store, a move I had long contemplated but bravely resisted. But he knew. Jeff knew, and even when he stopped laughing, he smirked, and even when he stopped smirking, it was in his eyes. Alison wasn't the first person in my immediate circle whom I had contemplated battering with a mallet.

'Well?'

'Hold your horses.' And then, after another ten seconds, 'Mmmm. Not as straightforward as I thought.'

'In what . . .'

'Lemme go check across the road.' She lifted the V-cutter. 'Back in five.'

'Could you . . . you know, just leave the V-cutter here?'

'Why? Do you think I'll lose it?'

'No. Of course not. But you know . . .'

'Oh, right. It's a crucial piece of evidence, and what if I trip outside the shop and it falls down a drain? Or I drop it crossing the road and a lorry flattens it and renders the serial number indistinct.'

'I just . . .'

'Do you want me to sign for it? That's what they'd do at the cop shop if they were checking out evidence for expert evaluation. Better still, why don't I just make a note of the serial number, and then maybe if you have some tracing paper I could make a tracing of the hallmark, and maybe a pencil drawing of it from several different angles, or maybe if you have CAD software I can render a 3D impression of the fucking thing?'

'Why don't you just take it with you?'

'Good idea. I will.' She grabbed it and stormed to the door. 'Back in five,' she snapped, and then added, 'Arse.'

She wasn't smiling now.

Chalk one up to me.

17

She was gone longer than five. More like seven and a half. Her ledger was soon going to require a second volume. I would have killed the time reading, or further investigating and probably solving the case at hand, but I was distracted by a phone call. They are rarer than hen's teeth and my business is in a constant state of peril, so I was more or less obliged to answer. With the benefit of caller ID flashing up, I was able to at least establish that it wasn't Liam Benson calling back, so I was happy to pick up. Not happy, given that it meant some kind of interaction with a human being, or possibly a dolphin, but resigned.

I said, 'Hello, No Alibis, murder is our business, in a strictly nonliteral sense.'

A woman's voice said, 'I'll give you bloody murder.'

And ordinarily this would have caused me to slam down the receiver and hide under the counter, but as it happened, I recognised her voice. I said, 'What has she done now?'

It was Mrs Collins, the owner of the Sunny Delight nursing home where I had sequestered Mother. Although physically she was falling to bits, and mentally she was as mad as a bag of spiders, Mother had always expressed a horror of and revulsion for such establishments, and had made me swear on a bible that I would never send her to one. She believed in God as much as I did, so she must have known it was meaningless. She would also have guessed that my absolute denial that she was going into Sunny Delight because of her deteriorating condition was complete bollocks, and instead chose to accept my justification for her 'temporary' removal from her own home: that she was actually going into hiding as part of the witness protection programme she was being obliged to join because of her involvement in the *Case of the Cock-Headed Man*. She had demanded to know why I wasn't also part of the scheme and I'd told her that I could look after myself, which had caused her to snort, and Alison also, listening in the background. But the thing was, as long as Mother could convince herself that she was part of such a scheme, then she was happy enough to go. She was finally self-aware enough to know that she wasn't capable of looking after herself any more. And that I couldn't be bothered.

However, her capacity for causing mayhem did not diminish with her change in circumstances. Calls from Mrs Collins were a weekly, occasionally daily, occurrence.

'I can hardly bring myself to tell you what she's done.'

'I'm sure it can't be that bad.'

'Well you'd be wrong. It is important that our patients are not . . . upset. That means that the television programmes they are allowed to watch in the communal area have to be monitored, and where we believe them to be inappropriate, then the channel must be changed.'

'I understand.'

'Well your mother does not. *The Exorcist*, you will also agree, is not suitable afternoon viewing.'

'How did . . . ?'

'Sky Horror Movies. She coerced the pin number out of one of our young nurses.'

'My mother . . .'

'I had to switch it off. Your mother showed her displeasure by . . .'

'Yes?'

'By . . .'

'Uhuh?'

'Oh I can't even bring myself to say it.'

'Please just say it.'

'She . . . lowered her . . .'

'Her . . . ?'

'She took down her . . .'

'She took down what?'

'She lowered her . . . and then she . . . in the middle of the . . .'

'She what what and a what what?'

'She had a . . . *shit* on the lounge carpet!'

'*Oh*. God. I'm sorry, I . . .'

'And that was bad enough.'

'There's more?'

'We have all types of residents here. We are not easily shocked. Many of them no longer have control of their faculties. Your mother, despite her stroke, is *not one of them*. It isn't just that she *did* it.'

'It isn't?'

'It was the look of triumph on her face *while* she did it. That's what got me the most. The pure, unadulterated pleasure she took from her disgusting act of defiance.'

That's my ma.

'Well,' I said, 'I'm really dreadfully sorry. It can't have been very pleasant, to observe or to clean up.'

'Don't worry on that front; we have Filipinos for that. I just . . . don't know what to do with her.'

'Have you tried sedation?'

She laughed. I did not.

'To be serious for one moment, I really am at the end of my tether. I simply cannot condone or allow this type of behaviour.'

She paused. I waited. She kept with the pause.

'What are you saying?'

'I'm saying we have decided to institute a three strikes and you're out policy. You may consider this a verbal warning. If she gets to number two . . .'

'Number two . . . ?'

'Please, if there's a second offence, then you will receive a written warning. If it happens again after that, then we will have to ask you to remove her from the home. Is that understood?'

I sighed. 'Yes. Okay. I'll come and have a word with her. I'll make sure it won't happen again.'

Neither of us, obviously, believed *that*.

18

Alison came steaming through the door just as I hung up. She was smiling again.

'How clever am I?' she asked.

There was a simple answer to that. But I contented myself with a simple 'Well that remains to be seen.'

She put the V-cutter back on the counter and said, 'See, not a scratch on it.'

'I'm not sure if that constitutes clever. Careful, maybe.'

'Oh shut up and listen. I know you don't have a very high opinion of me ...'

'I never ...'

'... but I know my stuff, and I knew that wasn't a UK hallmark. It's really only us, the Dutch and the Swiss who go in for hallmarking anyway, and America, where this baby's from, don't give a toss.'

'America? Do you ... ?'

'They may not hallmark, but they leave what we call a maker's mark. See this . . . ?'

She pointed to something on the cutter.

'No.'

'*There.*'

'Sorry, no. Not with my eyesight.'

'Well get out your thingamajig.'

'Excuse me?'

'Your Sherlock Holmes spyglass.'

'What on earth are you talking about?'

'Jeff told me all about it. Get it out and have a look. It's a clue.'

'I haven't a *clue* what you're talking about. And Jeff's a notorious liar and fabricator. He said you were a two-faced cow.'

Her eyes narrowed. 'And what did you say?'

'I'm allergic to cows. And therefore you can't be one. A cow.'

'Right. I'm not getting into this. Just look and learn. This manufacturer uses a particular symbol to represent the year it was made. What you would be seeing if you had the gumption to take out your little toy is the image of a small bugle. *That* tells us that this was manufactured in 2005 by the Palio company out of Providence, Rhode Island. And *this* . . . super-minuscule number obviously allows them to keep track of their products, which allows *me* to e-mail them and ask where this was purchased, which I did, and they responded . . .'

'You did this in seven and a half minutes?'

'No, five. Two and a half were getting there and back. Impressed?'

'No, I was wondering why so long.'

She gave me a sarcastic smile and said, 'There's like an international fraternity of jewellers; we help each other.'

'The fellowship of the rings.'

She ignored me. She slapped a piece of paper on to the counter. 'So now it's over to you. Here. This is the cell phone number for Joe's Cigars. As far as I can determine, it's basically a cart set up beside the valet parking entrance for Caesar's Palace in Las Vegas. That's where your V-cut was purchased.'

'Vegas?'

'Vegas.'

'And what do you want me to do, phone some *cart* and ask if it, he or she remembers selling someone a V-cut at some point in time, in Vegas, where everyone smokes cigars?'

'Yes. That's the number. I even included the international code. The point is, according to the serial number, the V-cut was delivered to Joe's within the past six weeks. It was a special order. Joe ordered just one, not a box of them. You and I know that Vegas is all about high rollers, high stakes, big cigars. Joe must sell a lot of V-cutters. So why order just one? Most cutters cost five or ten dollars; this one cost Joe fifty dollars wholesale. Makes you think he's bringing it in for someone, and that if you press the right buttons, like the ones on your phone, he might tell you who it was.'

'Why don't you do it? You're on a winning streak.'

'Because you're the boss, you're *the man*, it's your job.'

'I don't like phones and I don't like people, and what if I can't get rid of him? Have you any idea how expensive international calls are, especially to a mobile phone?'

Alison folded her arms. She tapped her fingers on the counter.

I said, 'Okay, damn your eyes, I'll call him. But could you go and stand over there?'

'Why?'

'I don't like being looked at or listened to while I make a call.'

'What if I have something relevant to contribute?'

I raised an eyebrow. She shook her head and crossed the shop, although not far enough. Nevertheless I moved to the phone and tapped in the numbers. I turned my back to her while I waited for an answer. The dialling tone switched to an international pulse.

It was answered with a 'Hey.'

'Hello, can I speak to Joe?'

'Joe dead.'

It was, even given my line of work – bookselling – totally unexpected.

'I . . . I . . . I . . . Oh. I'm very sorry. Ahm. My sincere condolences. How did he . . . ?'

'He shot.'

My eyes flitted up to Alison's. She had moved closer,

stealthily, while my back was turned. My heart rate was up. My shirt was sticking to my back *already*. I shook my head at her. She mouthed, '*What?*' I mimed putting a gun to my head and shooting.

'That's . . . *terrible* . . . What happened?' I asked.

'He owed money, he shot. It's Vegas.'

'When . . . when was this?'

'Nineteen fifty-six. We over it now.'

'Nineteen . . . ! Oh – I misunderstood.'

'Hey, everyone asks for Joe, no Joe since fifties. Been my family since 'sixty-two, me here since 'eighty-seven. Everyone call me Joe 'cos it say Joe above my head. I don't mind. Every day I'm Joe, go home, I'm not Joe. I'm Manuel Gerardo Ramiro Alfonzo Aurelio Enrique Zapata Quetzalcoatl. Most people find it easier just call me Joe. What I do for you?'

'Well, my name is Donald, Donald Westlake,' I said, for I have a business and its reputation to protect. 'I'm a police officer, I'm calling from ah, Scotland Yard in London, England.'

'I heard of that. What the problem?'

'We're trying to trace the owner of a V-cut cigar cutter, to do with a big case, a murder case. Traced it as far as you, wondering if you could help us. There are obviously official channels we could go through, but sometimes it's easier to get it straight from the horse's head. Mouth.'

'Yeah, sure, okay, do what I can. V-cut you say? Sell a lot of V-cut, not sure I . . .'

'This one was probably a special order, expensive,

you brought it in in the past few weeks, I have the serial number here.'

'Special order? Okay. Gimme that number.'

I gave him the number. He said he needed five minutes, could I hold on? I said no, I'd call back.

During the five minutes, the only word exchanged between Alison and me was 'Cheapskate.' She was the one who said it. There were a thousand words I could have fired back. She wouldn't have understood the half of them. Instead, I gave her the fingers. She gave them back.

She was the mother of my child. For now.

I called Joe. He said, 'How I know you are who you say you are?'

I said, 'Well, you don't. Except I am, and I will swear to that on my mother's grave.'

'Shit, how I know she ain't still alive?'

'Well, you don't. But I wouldn't lie about my mother; you Mexicans can relate to that.'

Alison rolled her eyes at me. I rolled them back. She reached across and put us on speakerphone.

Joe said, '*You Mexicans*? What the fuck are you, Scottish?'

'Aye.'

'*You Mexicans.* You got no jurisdiction here, I don't got to tell you nothing about Buddy Wailer!'

'Buddy Wailer?'

'That's right, you heard, way over there in Scotland, in your stupid-ass kilts. Buddy Wailer, you don't want to get involved with Buddy Wailer.'

'Joe, listen to me.'

'I ain't Joe.'

'Well listen to me, Manuel Gerardo Ramiro Alfonzo Aurelio Enrique Zapata Quetzalcoatl.'

'How'd you do that?'

'Do what?'

'Remember my name. Nobody remember my name.'

'Names are important. It's my job, Manuel.'

There was static on the line for half a minute. No, that's a lie, with digital lines there isn't really static. There was nothing for thirty seconds. Then he said: 'Okay, what you want to know?'

'This Buddy Wailer? He bought the V-cut?'

'He a collector, he a regular here. Sure, I order for him.'

'What can you tell me about him?'

There was another long pause. Longer.

'Manuel?'

'I tell you this about Buddy Wailer, and this all. He tall, real tall. He thin, real thin. He never say much, he nice to me, but my friend, one time my friend, works in the hotel, was in Buddy Wailer's room, delivers something, towels maybe. Buddy not in the room, he leaves them in the bathroom, he come out, sees like gift box, hatbox, on the bed. My friend, he curious, high-roller room, what this guy Buddy got in the box, 'spensive gift for some girl? He open the box. You know what in the box?'

'No. What?'

'A head. A head in the box. My man, he scream,

and he get outta there, and he tell no one, no one but me, and not till he drunk.'

'Why didn't he inform the . . . ?'

''Cos he scared. He tell the police, maybe he get to be hero for half an hour, and then they send him back cross the border or worse, plus he scared shitless Buddy Wailer come lookin' for him, and next thing, *his* head in a box. Me? I curious. I talk to people, I ask the questions, this guy with a head in the box, and I find out he does whacks, that's what he does, he does whacks and he thinks it funny to keep their heads in a gift box. That sick? Or that scary? Buddy Wailer, tall, thin, head in a box Buddy Wailer, he creep me out. He does whacks, that's what he do, his job, he whacks people and that scares the crap outta me.'

Manuel Gerardo Ramiro Alfonzo Aurelio Enrique Zapata Quetzalcoatl hung up.

I looked at Alison, and she looked at me, and in a rare moment of unity we said, 'Fuck!' together.

19

'Well,' I said, 'that's the end of that case.'

'Absolutely,' said Alison.

'I'm never even thinking about Augustine Wogan again.'

'And I don't give a ripe fig if Arabella is pushing up daisies or taking it up the arse from some toyboy in Rio.'

'I don't care if I never see Pearl Knecklass's ample bosoms again.'

'Sugar tits can bugger off.'

'I'm quite happy selling my books. There's not a big living in it, but there's enough for me and my family.'

'And I'll still bring in a little extra from the jewellery, though I do intend to be a full-time mum. I can work from home, I can do like costume jewellery parties. It doesn't have to be jewellery either. It can be Avon or Kleeneze or sex aids. On the whole I prefer sex aids. Metaphorically speaking.'

We leant on the counter, facing each other.

'Whacks,' I said.

'Whacks,' she said.

'Soon as he said whacks, I knew it was over, we don't need that.'

'Not with little Orinoco on the way.'

'Not with little Bulgaria on the way.'

'Not with little Tobermory on the way.'

'Not with little Bungo on the way.'

'Not with little Wellington on the way.'

Alison's eyes narrowed. So did mine.

She said, 'Are you done?'

'Nope.'

'You are done. You're bluffing.'

'You forget, I have total recall.'

'Why are we talking Wombles when we should be talking whacks?'

'Because I'd rather talk Wombles than whacks. No one was ever killed by a Womble, though they did murder a few songs.'

'Madame Cholet,' said Alison, raising her fist triumphantly.

'Madame Cholet,' I agreed. 'And also?'

'There is no other.'

'Tomsk,' I said.

'Damn, you're good. When civilisation crumbles and anarchy prevails, your knowledge of 1970s children's television programmes will surely see us through.'

'Was there a television version? I was talking about the books by Elisabeth Beresford. The first one appeared in 1968 and subsequently—'

'Let's get back to the whacks, and what we're going to do. This is serious.'

'Of course it's serious. But I thought we'd decided what we were going to do.'

'No, we discussed it, we didn't decide. I'm not sure if we *can* just drop it. I don't know why anyone would ever need a can of worms – maybe it has something to do with fishing – but we seem to have opened it. They, whoever *they* are, must know that we've been looking into this, which would appear to me to make us fair game if they're still in the market for whacks. And maybe we should stop saying whacks.'

'What would you prefer? Execute? Assassinate? Just plain murder is as good as any. We need to walk away. We don't need this. We need to let them know that we've dropped it.'

'So how do we do that, an advert in *Whack Weekly*?'

'We let it be known. I slip it to Pearl.'

'Metaphorically speaking.'

'Sorry?'

'Never mind. What if it's not Pearl?'

'Then we tell Dr Yes himself.'

'And how do you do that without getting us deeper in the shit? He'll be worried that we know something and are just holding off, intending to blackmail him later. He might still say, let's play safe and whack them. He'll phone up Buddy Wailer in Vegas and say, I have another job for you, those pesky amateur detectives need whacked.'

'I wouldn't say we were amateur.'

'You wouldn't? I don't mean amateur as in crap, I mean amateur as in it isn't our primary way of making a living. We're like Nick and Nora Charles.'

I looked at her. I beamed. 'You know Nick and Nora?'

'Doesn't everyone?'

'No, my dear, everyone doesn't.'

'We *are* meant for each other. We could call him Asta.'

'A dog name rather than a Womble name? I think you might have stumbled on to something. Ah, *The Thin Man*. When crime was crime, and the killer just killed people; he didn't worry about making a suit out of their skin.'

'Simpler times,' agreed Alison.

'Except who said Buddy was in Vegas? Who says he's not down the road bunked up in a hotel, waiting for orders? It's only a couple of days since Augustine was offed. Maybe Vegas is too hot for him anyway; maybe he's moved over to this side of the Atlantic. Maybe the exchange rate is better. *Certainly* the exchange rate is better. There's no VAT on books, and there's certainly none on murder.'

I sighed. I rubbed at my head. I had the beginnings of a migraine. I'd had the beginnings of a migraine since 1973. Sometimes it developed. Sometimes it didn't. It could go one way. Or it could go the other. Stress didn't help, but I lived in a perpetual state of it. Mostly it was caused by the state of the independent bookshop business. Then it was the internet. Lately it had been downloads. Buddy Wailer was added stress. I didn't need it. I couldn't do anything about piratical downloads, but I could do something about Buddy Wailer.

We drummed our respective fingers.

Alison said, 'You know what we're coming to?'

'Pretty much.'

'Far from walking away from this, we need to walk towards it, and quicker.'

'We need to solve it before it solves us.'

'We need to find Buddy Wailer, connect him to Dr Yes, and connect Dr Yes to Augustine, and all before Buddy Wailer whacks us.'

'We don't know that he's looking for us.'

'We don't know that he isn't.'

We nodded.

'No time to waste,' I said.

'I'm on flexi. I'm all yours. You have a plan?'

'I have a plan.'

'Do you want to put it up before the committee?'

'Nope.'

'Good. I like a man who knows what he's doing.'

'Uhuh.'

'Uhuh what?'

'I'm waiting for something sarcastic. Or caustic. Like, I like a man who knows what he's doing, and when I meet him I'll let you know.'

'You have a very low opinion of me.'

'And vice versa.'

We sneered. But there was a hidden smile behind them.

'We're a perfect match,' said Alison. 'Lead on, Nick.'

'After you, Nora.'

'Where are we going?' she asked.

'Starbucks is as good a place to start as any.'

'Thought so.'

Halfway up the road I said, 'I'm not naming our baby after a dog.'

'Damn right,' said Alison.

20

The plan wasn't a hugely complicated one. The Mystery Machine, the No Alibis van, with its chalk outline of a body on the side and *Murder is Our Business* to go with it, was hardly appropriate for staking out the premises of Liam Benson, *freelance photographer – news, corporate and public relations.* We were instead settled in Alison's red Volkswagon Beetle. Liam had a smallish office on the corner of a newly built unit in a business park in the Titanic Quarter. Belfast had about sixteen of these quarters, which was good for the city but bad for anyone still grappling with the fundamental basics of maths.

The unit and surrounding business park was busy enough that we could sit in the car park and keep an eye on the comings and goings from his office without being noticed, except there wasn't much in the way of comings, or goings. We saw Liam Benson – his picture was right there on his website – returning from lunch, unlocking the door and going in. Over the next hour we saw him passing a window a couple of times, but mostly he was out of sight. He didn't appear to have any staff.

Alison asked three times what we were doing besides watching a building, and I told her truthfully that we were there to talk to Liam. But my loins needed to be girded. And I had to catch my medication at the right time. Too soon after cramming it all into my mouth and washing it down with Vitolink and I'd be buzzing; too long after swallowing and I'd be dozing. That's not to mention the suppositories. They're difficult to take at the best of times, let alone while sitting in a tiny car with a pregnant woman watching you. They're roughly the same size as artillery shells. And quite often they have the same effect.

Alison said, 'I'm going to get you off all that shit, and soon.'

'Good luck with that,' I said.

She didn't know the *half* of it.

Then we saw her. Pearl Knecklass, going into his office, and Liam Benson at the door, letting her in. Her heels alone would have gotten her to base camp on Everest. Her tartan skirt rode just north of decent.

'Walks like a hooker,' said Alison.

'Walks like an Egyptian,' I said.

We both hummed it for a bit, and did the hand movements. We were still dancing when Pearl emerged five minutes later. She climbed into a Porsche on the far side of the car park and reversed out of her space at speed. Her tyres squealed as she took off. When she hit the road, she also hit a speed bump, at speed. She was in a hurry, or a bad mood, or both. It was time to speak to Liam.

We tried to open the door to his office, but it was locked. We rang the bell. His face appeared. He had a goatee beard and small brown eyes. His hair was receding and he'd a ponytail at the back. Men with ponytails should be shot. He wore a black suit with a white shirt, open at the neck.

He said, 'Sorry, I'm closed for lunch.'

He was nervous, sweaty.

Alison said, 'We were looking at your website, think we need some PR, some good photos; we were up at our wholesalers – we're in jewellery – realised you were just around the corner, thought we'd call on the off chance.'

'Well, really, you need an appointment.'

I nodded and turned away.

Alison said, 'Excuse me?' to him.

He said, 'Excuse me, what?'

'Is this how you treat potential clients? Are you so fabulously wealthy in this time of recession that you can turn valuable business away just so that you can eat your lunch? Here we are on your very doorstep, no hard selling to be done, ready to be impressed, money to spend and you're just giving us the brush-off? Well if you ask me, you don't deserve to—'

He jerked the door open fully and cut in with:

'You're absolutely right, it was unbelievably rude of me, I don't know what I was thinking of . . . Please, please come in . . .'

Before I could move forward, Alison said, 'I'm not sure I want to now.'

'Really, I do apologise . . . Let me show you what I can do, please . . .'

'I don't think I'm in the mood any more.'

'And it goes without saying I can offer you a discount for your inconvenience. Right away. Ten per cent.'

'Try twenty.'

He smiled. So did Alison.

'Fifteen.'

'Okay. You have a deal. Now all you have to do is impress us.'

Alison winked at me as she stepped through the door. She thought she was very clever. But she wasn't half as clever as I was. I hadn't even opened my mouth, and I was already on the inside. One hundred per cent less effort, for the same result. Who's clever now, you tubby cow?

The offices were modern, spacious and minimalist. There were framed black and white photographs, one on each wall: sports stars caught in action, yachts battling massive waves, an injured civilian in rubble.

'Take these?' Alison asked.

'Sure did.'

'They're very good. But they're news photographs. We're looking for something more commercial, something that sells a product.'

'Not a problem. I have a number of business and corporate clients who demand exactly that. You're in the jewellery business? Whereabouts?'

'Botanic Avenue,' said Alison. I sighed. 'We're part of a group. You do group discount as well?'

'I'm sure we can work something out. Botanic? Whereabouts? I'm up and down there all the time.'

'Up near the top. Or the bottom, depending on which way you're coming.'

'Think I know where you mean. There's a book-shop just across the road? No . . . something . . . ?'

'Alibis,' said Alison, helpfully.

'Yeah. Funnily enough, I'd a wrong number for there earlier on. Small world, eh? Ever been in there? Wandered in one day a few months back, there's this old bag behind the counter scared the life out of me.'

'She's gone,' said Alison.

'She was one horrible-looking individual.'

'Retired,' said Alison.

'She'd had like a stroke or something and was all drooly out of her mouth and she could barely speak. Frightening.'

I hated the old gorgon, but she was *my* old gorgon. One more word from him, and he'd be in my ledger.

'Accused me of shoplifting. And then said I flashed her. One mad old bitch.' He turned suddenly to look at me. 'And what have you got to do with it?'

'The bookshop?'

He looked at me. Funny.

'The jewellery business. You're very quiet.'

'I'm the silent partner.'

He studied me.

'Silent but deadly,' said Alison. 'I do all the talking, but when it comes to the deal, he takes no prisoners.'

'Better than you? I'll remember that.'

'Or I could be bluffing,' said Alison. 'Anyhoo, like I was saying, we were looking at your website; you list some of your satisfied clients. Would they back you up if I called them?'

'Back me up? You're very suspicious.'

'These days you have to be. We've been ripped off before.'

'By a photographer?'

'Jewellery thieves, but who's to know? So we could call them?'

'Yes, of course.'

'What about those ones with the foreign name . . . ?' She looked at me. 'Which ones were they?'

'The Yessomething Clinic.'

'The Yessomething Clinic, they were the only ones we'd heard of. What do you do for them?'

'Yes*chenkov*. PR work. The other companies are probably more representative of what I—'

'They do all that nippy-tucky stuff, don't they? Do you do, like, before and after shots?'

Liam shifted uncomfortably. 'To tell you the truth, I can't really tell you what I do for them. They're extremely private. Everyone who works for them has to sign a confidentiality agreement.'

'Why?' I asked. 'What have they got to hide?'

He studied me anew. 'Hide? Nothing. But they have a lot of famous clients, and they don't necessarily want that information out there. Privacy is a big thing in the plastic-surgery business. It's also part of their express makeover service that they provide before and after shots for their clients, and, also, between you and me, for insurance purposes in case the clients aren't happy and they decide to sue.'

'Does that happen often?' I asked.

'Not that I'm aware of.'

'Met anyone really famous?' Alison asked.

'I'm sorry, I can't say.'

'Can't say or won't say?' I asked.

'I'm sorry?'

'It's only between us. It might swing the deal your way.'

'You haven't even seen my portfolio.'

'If you're good enough for Dr Yes,' said Alison, 'you're good enough for us. Go on, who have you seen? Someone famous who looks like a Martian with her make-up off?'

'Look I'd love to, but I can't. They're really serious about it. In fact, I just had one of their directors in here about ten minutes ago scooping up my last job. They don't even let me keep the digital negatives.'

Pearl. A *director* of the company. I gave Alison a nod. It was a prearranged signal. Time to ramp things up.

'You ever do any work for Buddy Wailer?'

Liam's mouth dropped open slightly, and his cheeks reddened.

'How do you know Buddy Wailer?'

'How do you think we know him?' Alison asked.

'How do I . . . ?' He was confused. We had turned the tables. And half a dozen chairs. 'I don't . . . I mean . . . I told you I signed a . . . I can't talk about Buddy Wailer.'

'Can't or won't?' I asked.

'What? How do you know about him anyway? What's it got to do with jewell . . . What's with all these questions anyway? You know something? It is lunchtime, and you don't have an appointment, and I don't like being quizzed . . .'

'We can do it here, or we can do it down at the station,' said Alison.

Whatever had caused his cheeks to colour up now made it drain away.

'You're . . . ?'

'No, but it's where we're headed if we don't get the right answers.' She looked so soft and malleable, yet she could be as hard as nails. 'If I were you, I'd spill the beans while you still can.'

'Yeah,' I added.

He looked at me. He looked at Alison. He said, 'What the fuck are you playing at?'

'Not playing,' I said. 'You were at the Xianth gallery in Dublin with Dr Yeschenkov and Arabella Wogan.'

'I . . . no, that wasn't . . .'

'We want to know about Buddy Wailer,' said Alison.

'And the whacks,' I said.

'Who *the fuck* are you?'

'We are employed by the estate of Augustine Wogan,' said Alison.

'And the late Arabella Wogan,' I added.

'*Fucking hell!*' His hand reached back and flicked nervously at his ponytail. 'I . . . look, okay, I don't know who the hell you are, maybe you're just doing your job, but there's nothing I can tell you. They've warned me, and frankly they're scarier than you are. You want to know about Buddy or any of that whack shit, you have to ask the clinic. It has nothing to do with me, I was only doing my job . . .'

'What job, what were you doing?'

'I can't tell you! I just take pictures, that's all I do, anything else is . . . I can't talk, okay? I signed up; they pay me, take it up with them. Now I think you'd better go. Please.'

He strode across to the door. He held it open, his knuckles white, and didn't look at us as we moved towards it.

Alison went through first. I stopped in the doorway. I took out my wallet and selected a business card. I held it out to him. He showed no inclination to take it. So I tried to tuck it into the breast pocket of his jacket, but it was one of those ones with the pocket already stitched closed. Forcing it open ruins the shape of the jacket. I knew it for a fact. I had half a dozen of them at home. Every time I cut the stitches I thought the result would be different. It never was. But I would never give up trying. I thought about pushing the card into the top of his jumper, or slipping it behind his ear, but they were both a little overfamiliar, so I just showed it to him and then let it flutter to the floor.

I said, 'You're up to your neck in this, Liam, but it may not be too late. If there's anything you want to tell us, you know where to call.'

'I haven't, and I won't.'

'Your funeral,' I said.

As we walked to the car, Alison said, 'You hear that?'

'I heard that. What did you hear?'

'He didn't deny that Arabella was dead.'

'That's what I heard too.'

'Quick thinking, slipping her in like that.'

'That's what I do.'

'But we're out in the open now, we've announced ourselves. If there was any doubt before, there's none now: we're in this and there's no going back.'

'No going back,' I agreed. 'Sometimes you've just gotta stand up and be counted.'

Alison had her keys out, but stopped at the driver's door without opening it. She looked across the canvas roof at me.

'You gave him *my* business card, didn't you?'

'Absolutely,' I said.

21

There was a limit to how much flexitime Alison could take from her jeweller's. It was spring, and the minds of young lovers were turning to engagement rings, so demand was high, which meant all hands on deck. I walked her back to her shop. At the door, she avoided what must have been an overwhelming temptation to kiss me. Instead she said, 'Be careful,' and I said I was always careful, and she said she didn't mean with money, and I said oh.

I opened up No Alibis and took up my position behind the counter. I checked my e-mail. None of my customers had anything of value to tell me, but plenty of guff about their personal lives. I took advantage of the quiet to sit on my stool and read. I had moved on to Joseph Wambaugh's satirical take on the LAPD, *The Choirboys*. It seemed at one point in the 1970s that Wambaugh might become a major voice in crime fiction. The book was a popular success at the time, and it undoubtedly has its moments, but on the whole it has not aged well. It is a poor man's *MASH* without the saving grace of having been turned into a decent film, just an instantly forgettable one. Although he continues to publish, Wambaugh has pretty much sunk without trace, and in so doing has proved conclusively that there is no sustainable market for crime fiction with a sense of humour.

I was reading, but also thinking about Liam Benson and how frightened he had been, and what our next move should be. I had suggested that Arabella was dead, and he had not contradicted it. It would be a mistake to take that as one hundred per cent proof that she was indeed dead – he might easily have misheard, or not even heard at all, given how discombobulated he was by our revelations – but if I had to put a number on it, based upon my past experience of how people react in similar situations and my intuition and unsurpassed knowledge of crime fiction, I calculated that there was an eighty per cent probability that Liam believed Arabella Wogan was dead. Or possibly seventy-six per cent. Or maybe seventy-three per cent. Or in all likelihood, seventy-one per cent. Or maybe sixty-nine. Guessing is an inexact science.

At just after three, two customers came into the shop. I did my best to hold off on singing 'Hallelujah' at the top of my voice, despite the fact that this constituted the No Alibis equivalent of a gold rush. If

I was lucky, three or four times a day, a solitary individual would enter and begin to peruse the books; half the time, he or she was sheltering from the rain, or working up to asking if they could use the toilet, or if I had change for the parking metre, or if I was interested in Scientology, or believed in elves, but two at the same time was unheard of; it was like capturing a breeding pair, if they hadn't both been men.

My elation, of course, was short-lived.

They were roughly of the same height and build: about six foot and wide. Hair short and cropped. One with a stud in his ear. The other with a spider's-web tattoo on his hand. I saw this when he reached up and lifted a book down from the shelf and showed it to me. It was John Ross Macdonald's Lew Archer novel, *The Drowning Pool*. 'Is this any good?' he asked.

'It's a classic,' I said. 'That particular copy is interesting because although his real name was Kenneth Miller, he wrote under the pseudonym of John Ross Macdonald, at least until another young writer, John D. Macdonald, started having some success, so to avoid confusion he dropped the John out of Ross Macdonald, and was Ross for the rest of his life. This is one of the rare copies with John Ross still on the front, that's why it's worth so—'

'Seventeen-fifty? Fucking hell.'

Spider-web had opened the cover and spotted where I'd written the price in pencil on the title page. He tore the page out and crumpled it up. Then he dropped the book to the floor.

It was at this point that I suspected something was amiss.

Spider-web took down another book. He held it up to me. 'Is this much crack?'

It was *Now Try the Morgue* by Elleston Trevor.

I said, 'It's one of his early books . . . he's better known as Adam Hall . . . You know, *The . . . The Quiller Memorandum . . .'*

He already had the title page out and balled and chucked. The book followed it.

He took down a third title.

I sensed a pattern emerging.

I said, 'Gentlemen, I don't believe you're book collectors.'

The other guy, the one who so far seemed pleasant and harmless, immediately mimicked me. *'I don't believe you're book collectors,'* he said, making it all high-pitched and tremulous. He wasn't very good. My voice isn't high-pitched at all. He quickly added a much more manly 'Fucking right!'

The two of them then began to tumble the books off the shelves. Dozens of them. And soon, hundreds.

I sat where I was. Eventually they would tire themselves out, or grow bored. Beneath the counter there was a mallet, a machete, a butcher's knife, a set of Ninja nunchucks and a Sherlock Holmes spyglass. As I took them out, one by one, first Spider-web then his companion noticed, and stopped.

It was a calculated gamble. They were thinking

bookshop owner, bound to be, well, bookish, weedy and weak. I was all of those things. But they weren't to know that. I could equally have been stereotyping them as well; just because they looked and behaved like thugs, it didn't mean that they weren't nuclear physicists or capable of reasoned argument and compromise. But what they did was out of my control; for the moment all I could do was screw with their preconceptions of me. I did have a panic button, but the police had come round and disconnected it because Mother pressed it every time the door opened. There was another button that could close all of the shutters in *seconds*, but of course that would only trap me in with them. Of all the weapons at my disposal, the Sherlock Holmes spyglass was the only one I was capable of handling. It wasn't a conventional weapon, but given Saharan sunlight I could quite easily have focused its beams through the lens and started a small fire, and from that I could have made a flaming torch to thrust at them, like an angry villager confronted by Frankenstein's monster. Unfortunately, Saharan sun was sadly lacking in Belfast. If it came to it, I would be reduced to throwing the spyglass at them.

They *literally* nudged each other.

Spider-web said, 'Rolo, them's nunchucks.'

'What the fuck are you doing with nunchucks?'

'Come closer and I'll show you.'

They *literally* exchanged glances.

Rolo said, 'We were told you sold books.'

'I do sell books.'

'We were told you were a wanky dweeb boy we could blow over.'

'I am. Although I'm also the Irish featherweight champion at nunchucks.'

'You?' said Spider-web. 'At nunchucks?'

'You don't look like the Irish champion at anything,' said Rolo.

'Neither does your face.'

I have a tendency to hyperventilate, particularly when I see a cow, but I was controlling myself rather well. It was because I was in a tight corner. In a tight corner the wheat gets sorted from the chaff, metaphorically speaking, as I am allergic to both. I had promised Alison that I would try and stand on my own two bunioned feet, and now I was about to do it. I would rise like a cake from the floury gloop in an oven. I would fall back on my chosen specialist subject: my wit and intellect. It was all I had. If I even attempted to use the weapons, I would just make a tit of myself. They would take them off me like a rattle off a baby, and kill me, or worse.

They did not appear to have any weapons of their own. They were just big, and muscled.

'If this is about the Christmas Club,' I said, 'it's not me, it's the Chinese economy.'

'It's not about the fucking Christmas Club.'

'Good. Because the Chinese economy is fine. What is it . . . that you want, then?'

'What do you think we want, dipstick?'

'I don't really . . .'

'You've been poking your nose in,' said Spider-web.

'And we're here to make you stop,' said Rolo.

'By pushing a few books off the shelf? They're only books.'

I almost choked, saying it. They were my children. They had thrown *my children* on the floor. They had ripped pages from them. They *would not get away with it*. A complaint would be lodged. They would be in my ledger. But for now, all I wanted to do was get them away from my children. If they concentrated on me, then my children would be fine.

'How about we push *you* off a shelf?' Rolo asked.

'You'd have to get me up there first.'

They took it as a challenge. They advanced.

I said, 'I've only twenty-two pounds in the till.'

'It's not about the money,' said Rolo.

'Although we will take it,' added Spider-web.

'It's about teaching you a lesson, you four-eyed little shit.'

I picked up the machete. Rolo took it out of my hand and threw it across the shop. It imbedded itself in a colourful reproduction of the front cover of *Black Mask* magazine from June 1926, photocopied and taped to the wall rather than framed and glass-fronted, because framers are notorious rip-off merchants, along with insurance agents, farmers, bricklayers, carpet-fitters and clowns. Spider-web swept the remaining weapons off the counter with his hand.

'Violence,' I said, 'is the last resort of the scoundrel.'

'Shut the fuck up,' said Rolo.

He grabbed me by the shirt and pulled me across the counter until his face was no more than an inch from mine.

'I should pull your eyeballs out and stuff them up your nose,' he hissed.

'Okay,' I said.

'Okay? What the fuck do you mean, okay?'

'Do your worst. You big fucking bullies.'

Rolo was looking suitably perplexed. Then he slapped me hard across the face. Slapping in movies looks quite effeminate. It's what hot-blooded men used to do to calm irrational women down, before political correctness drove it from the screen; now they shoot them and make lampshades out of their bingo wings. In what passed for my real life, it *hurt*. He caught me across the ear as well, and for fully thirty seconds I could hear the tide coming in on Strangford Lough. But it was a foolish act on his part. It told me everything I needed to know.

These were two hard men. Their accents, their tattoos and piercings told me what side of the tracks they came from. These were not men who normally *slapped*. They had been told to slap me around, and taken whoever had told them at their word. They had been told to cause some damage, but not to go too far. They were here to intimidate me. They were heavyweights being told to behave like pixieweights. I was in no danger.

Spider-web said, 'Who're you calling a fucking pixie?' and head-butted me, expertly, on the bridge of the nose. As I fell, the blood already exploding out of my face, I was regretting, not for the first time, saying something out loud that I had presumed to be merely thought.

I hit the ground. My skull felt like it had caved in. I lay there clutching my nose as the blood squirted out between my fingers.

'I have you now,' I cried. 'I have you now . . . !'

'What the fuck are you talking about, you limp little . . .'

'I'm a haemophiliac! You were only meant to give me a scare, but now you've busticated my nose and it won't stop bleeding until there's no blood left! You've killed me! You're going down for this! You . . . you . . . fucking philistines!'

'What the fuck is he talking about?' Spider-web asked.

'How the fuck do I know? What's a fucking homophiliac?'

'*Haemo* . . .' I whimpered. 'Get me a towel . . . get me a towel!'

Spider-web looked at Rolo, who hesitated before nodding.

'Where . . . ?'

'In the kitchen . . . back there!'

Spider-web hurried through the shop. Rolo crouched and helped me up into a sitting position.

'That's a real thing 'n' all, isn't it? It's like being a

bleeder. My cousin had that: every time I gave her a dead leg for a laugh, they'd have to call the ambulance. Killed her in the end. I mean, not the bleeding; the ambulance crashed, going too fast, ran a red light and smashed through someone's front room. But yeah, she had to wear one of those things around her neck like a silver locket thing to say she was a bleeder in case she was ever brought in unconscious, but you're not wearing one, so how do I know you're really a . . .'

'I'm . . . allergic to silver . . .'

Spider-web returned with the towel. He handed it to me and I pressed it to my crushed nose.

'Thanks,' I said.

'No problem. Rolo, what do we do now?'

'Whattya mean?'

'Well if he's going to bleed to death, maybe we should skedaddle.'

'And just leave him?'

'Yeah, why not? Someone'll sort him out.'

'We've been watching this place. There's about four hours between customers; he'll be bled dry before someone comes through the door.'

'Well should we give him a lift to the hospital or something?'

'We can't leave the car back with blood on it; it's my mum's, there's like cream seats, they'll stain something awful.'

'We could buy some Stain Devil, wouldn't that . . . ?'

'Nah, you'd have to get the seats out of the car

and into the washing machine; how's that going to work?'

I said, 'I'll be fine. Just go, you've delivered your message.'

'Are you sure?' Rolo asked. 'No hard feelings? It's just what we do, same as you do what you do. We all gotta earn a living.'

It was a *very* awkward situation. Particularly when they made me a cup of tea, and I asked for it stronger, and hotter. We sat around sipping it while they debated their next move. And after a bit it just felt as if I was getting on with them well enough to pursue my enquiries.

'If you don't mind me asking,' I said, 'what do they pay you for doing something like this?'

Rolo looked at Spider-web. Spider-web shrugged. 'Sixty quid,' he said.

'Each?'

They both looked a bit sheepish.

'Between you?'

'They chipped in for the petrol,' said Spider-web. 'But I know what you're thinking. Thirty quid. It's a bit rubbish, isn't it?'

'It's the market,' said Rolo, 'it's saturated. The recession, everyone's trying to make a buck. Do you think I want to be doing this? Do you think I want to be threatening and scaring and intimidating and breaking knees? Do you think that's what I dreamt of when I was a kid?'

'I did,' said Spider-web.

'Yeah, well you're a fucking numbskull. How's the nose?'

'Sore,' I said.

'You want I can snap it back into place?'

'No, it's okay.'

'It's no problem.'

'Really. I'm fine.'

It was funny, looking at him, this bruiser hulk, so recently having vandalised my shop and supported the vandalism of my face, standing there, looking concerned and talking wistfully of unrealised dreams. I hadn't really felt fear, mostly because of my anger about what they were doing to my books.

I said, 'What *did* you dream of? When you were a kid.'

'Me?' Rolo looked thoughtful. 'Well, you know, I was a kid. Stupid stuff. Astronaut. But I never got my quallie. Didn't really finish school. Had a kid real young; he's eighteen now, going the same way as me. It's a fucking shame, no jobs for anyone.'

'You never think of . . . you know, retraining, back to school?'

'Nah. Too old for that shit now.'

'Do you ever read? Books?'

'Nah.'

'What about movies?'

'Yeah, of course. Used to be in the movie business.'

'Really?'

'Yeah, we'd do pirate copies down the markets, but

that's all gone to shit now as well, everyone down-loading.'

'But you watch them?'

'Sure. Who doesn't?'.

'Well, you know, books are just like movies, except they're movies only you can see. In your head. That's what makes them so fantastic. They just make life seem a little better. Take you out of yourself. You meet people and listen to them chat, you encounter beau-tiful women and watch them being seduced, you see terrible crimes and learn how they're solved.'

Spider-web said, 'What the fuck are we listening to this shite for? We should get outta here.'

Rolo kept looking at me. Then he said: 'We deliv-ered the message, we slapped him around, went a bit too far maybe. Where are we going now?'

'I dunno. I've a donkey riding at three; go down the bookie's check on that.'

'Well it's not three yet. Tell you what, we'll give you a hand putting the books back up.'

Spider-web stared at him. 'What the fuck?'

'Sure what's the harm?'

'Fuck sake. You do what you want, I'm goin' outside for a fag.'

Spider-web shook his head and walked out of the shop. Rolo shrugged. He nodded down at me. 'Sure you sit where you are, I'll sort these out. Will I just put them anywhere or do they need to be in some kind of order?'

The answer to that was *much* too complicated – but

it was too early in our relationship to get into that particular bag of spiders. So I just said, 'Anywhere would be great.'

And so he dutifully began to return the books to their shelves.

I said, 'You never really did say who sent you.'

'Well, we never really know.'

'Oh. Right. Okay. Fair enough.'

'Though for all we're being paid, don't see what difference it makes. I mean, thirty quid, and ten per cent of that goes to our agent.'

'Your *agent*?'

'Aye well, you need someone a bit organised, bit of a talker, to bring in the business. Bit like a taxi service: you call in for a job or they call you and give you the address. If we weren't available, they'd go down the list to the next pair.'

'You always work in pairs?'

'Yep. One to hold you down, and one to do the bashin'.'

'And do you take turn-abouts?'

'Nah. Yer man enjoys the bashin, I don't mind the holdin'. We just get sent to do a job.'

'Do you think you could find out who wanted me dealt with?'

He finished placing an armful of books on a high shelf before turning to study me. 'You serious?'

'Yep. Absolutely. I'll match what you were paid.'

'For both of us?'

'Will it take both of you?'

'Like I say, one to hold him down, one to do the bashin'.'

'Okay. Both of you. Deal?'

'Deal.'

I am *so* good at this.

Rolo helped me to my feet. 'Still bleeding?'

'Slowing,' I said.

Still holding the towel to my face, I went behind the counter and took out one of my own business cards this time and handed it to him. 'Give me a call when you find anything out.'

He flicked it between his fingers. 'Sure thing.'

'And take this.' I handed him a copy of *The Godwulf Manuscript* by Robert B. Parker. Funny, tense, complex without being forbiddingly wordy. A perfect way to start. 'I think you'll enjoy it.'

'I can't really afford . . .'

'It's on the house. Go on.'

He took it. For a moment I thought he might well up. But it wasn't an act of kindness or some sort of philanthropic gesture. He would read it and he would come back for another. And then another. He wouldn't be able to help himself. Parker wrote nearly sixty novels before his recent untimely demise, and I would make sure that after this first one, Rolo paid for them all. I would be in profit in a matter of *weeks*. And then, once he was addicted, I would move him on to the harder stuff.

Spider-web rapped on the window and gave him an impatient *let's go* gesture.

I nodded at Rolo.

He nodded back.

He opened the door. He hesitated. He looked down at the nunchucks.

He said, 'Are you really featherweight nunchuck champion of Ireland?'

'No,' I said.

22

I told Alison about trying to convert Rolo to mystery fiction. I said it was just like *Pygmalion*, except interesting. She responded with: 'You can't polish a turd.' To be fair, that response only came after a lot of screaming and crying when she saw the state of my nose, although even during that she stopped long enough to snap: 'I thought you said you were a haemophiliac?' and I took time out to study my reflection in the shop toilet mirror, and the relatively small quantity of blood on the towel, and then punched the air and shouted, 'It's a miracle!'

'You could have been killed!'

'Nah,' I said.

I started in on my theory about their reasonably light beating, but she cut in with:

'Never mind that, what are we going to do about your nose?'

'Is it that bad?'

'Man dear, it looks like someone tried to open it with a can-opener.' She shook her head. Then she kissed me on the forehead. 'I saw them go in from across the road, but I was in the middle of this hard sell and couldn't get away. I thought there was something suspicious about you having two customers in a day, but I just couldn't get rid, and then the wrinkled old bag didn't buy anything. I came as quick as I could, a bit like you.'

I gave her a look. She gave it to me back.

'Is it very sore?' she asked.

'Yes.'

'Have you taken a painkiller?'

I gave her another look. I had been addicted to Nurofen, Anadin, generic paracetamol, Night Nurse, Sleepeaze, co-codamol, Kapake and Vicks since 1992. My senses are so dulled that if I was caught in a flood, I would be able to cut off my own arms for use as paddles without flinching, although I wouldn't be able to hold them.

'What do you think it means?' Alison asked.

'What what means?'

'Presuming for the moment that they were sent by Dr Yes, what do you think it means?'

'I'm not sure we can presume. I have a lot of enemies, and not just in retail. But *if* it's Dr Yeschenkov, and if we're thinking that he hired Buddy Wailer to whack Augustine, then he must either think we're not worth the whack treatment, or Buddy Wailer isn't available right now. Which is probably good either way. Rolo will go back and report that I've been dealt with; that takes the spotlight off for a little bit, gives us time to manoeuvre.'

'And how are we going to manoeuvre? Bearing in mind that I'm with child and if I'd been in the shop they would probably have beaten me as well?'

'We just have to be careful.'

'Careful would be leaving it alone.'

I nodded. She nodded.

'But we won't do that,' said Alison.

'Probably not.'

I went home via the Sunny D. I gave Mother a stern talking-to. She pretended not to hear. But when I casually mentioned that I'd forgotten her illicit supply of vodka, her head snapped round like a demon.

'Gotcha,' I said.

'You are an evil child,' she said. 'I like you least of all my children.'

'I'm an only child, Mother.'

'That's what you think. What child would lock his own mother up in a prison like this?'

'It's for your own protection, Mother. And if you behave like *that* again, they *will* throw you out.'

'Then I'll come home.'

'No you won't. You're living here, and you will conform, or I will stop bringing you your drink.'

'You're as bad as they are. Nazis.'

Despite her numerous complaints about the regime

at Sunny D, it was clear they were doing *something* right. Previously she would have said *Nathis*. Since her stroke Mother had had some trouble talking clearly, but she'd been undergoing speech therapy in her new home and her diction was definitely improving. Where before *Youfthinweakthwistedfud-headth* would have left most listeners baffled, it was now clear for her fellow patients and caring support staff to hear that she was referring to her son as a 'fucking weak-wristed fudd-head'.

She referred to her lady-bits as her *fudd*. I'm not sure why. She just always had. She wasn't the least bit sheepish about it either. As a child I clearly remember her screaming at me one Sunday afternoon, 'You look like a slapped fudd, you pathetic little cretin!' Needless to say, her membership of the Plymouth Brethren was swiftly revoked.

Now she was staring at me.

'Well?' she snapped.

'Well what?'

'What happened to your beak?'

'I told you, Mother, what I do is dangerous, that's why you're safer here.'

'Yeah. Being poisoned and screamed at. Who did it?'

'It's a long story. Don't worry about it.'

'I do worry about it. You're my son.' She nodded to herself. She didn't meet my eyes. She stared off into the distance. 'Such a disappointment.'

To fill the awkward silence that followed, I decided

to tell her about the case. She closed her eyes as I spoke. I wasn't sure if she was treating it as a good-night story and was slowly drifting off, until I came to the end, with Rolo and Spider-web in the shop, and her eyes snapped open. 'Is that it?' she barked.

'That's it.'

'I don't understand.'

'Well, it's complicated.'

'No, I don't understand why you don't just go straight to the horse's mouth instead of dilly-dallying with the support staff. Why don't you just go up to this Dr Yeswhatever and ask him about it?'

'Because . . . because he's an important man. People wait months and months for an appointment with him.'

'He's only an important man to people who want him to operate on them. When he's at the garage, getting petrol, he is not an important man, he is just a man who wants petrol for his car. Take him out of his environment and he is no longer an important man, but a shit, like all men.'

For the first time in a long, long time, I smiled at her. 'You know something, Mother, you may have a point.'

'Of course I have a point. I'm your mother, you should listen to me more often. And stop smiling, it makes you look like an imbecile.'

'Yes, Mother,' I said.

I hadn't been home for ten minutes when the phone rang. It was the manager from the Sunny Delight saying that Mother had done it again and she would have to go. I told her she had a wrong number. She said she recognised my voice and I said that was impossible. I hung up. The phone rang again and I picked it up and said, 'It's still not me.' I clearly hadn't thought it through properly, but fortunately it wasn't the Sunny D, but Alison.

'My hormones are up the left,' she said. 'I have a craving.'

'You're pregnant, not disabled. If you want something to eat, go down to the shop.'

'I was talking about sex.'

'I'm on my way.'

'Don't bother if . . .'

I didn't hear the rest. I had dropped the phone and grabbed my keys.

When Alison let me into her apartment, the first thing she said was, 'Craving's gone.'

23

We were in bed. It was after midnight. She wanted to be held. I wasn't in the holding business. She huffed.

She said, 'You pay more attention to your mother than you do to me.'

I said, 'Well, my mother talks sense.'

This did not help.

She said, 'I'm not some kind of sex machine.'

I said, 'It appears not.'

She elbowed me in the stomach. She almost dislodged my gastric band.

It was darkish. The curtains were open, street lamps providing a faint glow. It was unsettling. Alison maintained a bizarre ambition to make it as a comic-book artist, but had yet to win any professional commissions. She had a Facebook page to promote her work that had so far attracted seven members, of whom I wasn't one. This lack of an outlet for her debatable talents meant that she inflicted them not only on herself but on her occasional guests by hanging completed pages and panels unframed on the walls. All her characters and creatures had horrible bug eyes. If she had a style, or a theme, it was a bug-eyed style, or theme. And now they were all looking at me, plotting. With my glasses, with lenses stronger than the Hubble telescope, making my eyes look so big, I wondered if that was what had first attracted her to me.

'No,' she said.

'I said that out loud, didn't I?'

'You did.'

'I'll have to stop that.'

'It's quite endearing. I'd hang on to it. Do you think absence makes the heart grow fonder?'

'No. Why do you ask?'

'You and your mother, getting on well.'

'I wouldn't go that far. She's still a nightmare, just with occasional outbursts of clarity.'

'You can't just abandon her there.'

'Yes I can. At least until they reconsider. They should learn to deal with their problems, not be handing out ultimatums.'

'You think she has a point, about confronting Dr Yes?'

'I don't know about confronting, but certainly getting closer to him. As you know, I prefer to examine the evidence and draw my conclusions; I'm not big on interaction . . .'

'Or holding.'

'. . . but sometimes there's no escaping it. I think we should stay clear of Pearl, she . . .'

'Scares you . . .'

'. . . is too much of a player . . .'

'. . . scares you . . .'

'. . . and tackle Dr Yes outside of his natural environment. Let's build up a picture of him based on our own observations, not from Augustine's ramblings or what we've picked up on the internet. Let's see if he doesn't somehow give himself away.'

'Staking him out? Following him? Doing this how? Me with my job and you with the shop.'

'I can do nights.'

'Lurker extraordinaire.'

'He's going to be in the clinic most of the day, but we still need to watch him, see if he pops out, or what he does on his time off.'

'I'll do my share, but it won't be enough. We need Jeff.'

'Jeff ran off, calling me a mentalist.'

'I thought he paper-cutted himself?'

'He did, but I shouted at him and he didn't take it well.'

'Did you fire him again?'

'Nope. Though I don't believe he'll be back.'

'He has a nerve, after everything you've done for him.'

'Stood by him through thick and thin.'

'He owes you big time. You took him back when he sold you down the river.'

'The *Case of the Cock-headed Man*.'

'You let him use the phone for all that Amnesty International wank.'

'Exactly.'

'You didn't say a word when he tried it on with me.'

'He tried it on with you?'

'Yes! Remember we all got pizza and you said you were allergic to it and went to bed. We rented out *Hotel Rwanda* and I started to cry and he tried to comfort me by fondling my breast.'

'You never told me that.'

She was silent for a little bit. Then she said: 'I thought you were dealing with it rather too well. Forget about it. He was drunk.'

'And you let him?'

'No, I removed his hand and poked him in the throat with a fork.'

'He said that was a love bite.'

'He would.'

We were silent for another bit. Then I said, 'You have to be a weirdo to eat pizza with a fork.'

She said, 'You have to be a weirdo to pretend to be allergic to it to get out of paying for it.'

We lay quietly, assailed only by bug eyes.

After a bit I said, 'I have cravings too.'

She didn't respond. Her breathing became light, regular. After ten minutes of it, I put my hand on her breast.

'Weirdo,' she said.

24

A Belfast dawn, with a shepherd's-warning sky.

I was staring out of the window, thinking about the good old days when I could spend the night standing in the bushes in Alison's garden watching her watching TV or getting changed for bed. It is such a joy to watch somebody sleep peacefully through their slightly steamy window, like love in soft focus, and to not have to listen to her alternately snoring and farting her way towards daybreak.

They say if you want to stop somebody from snoring you should gently pinch their nose, but it wasn't having much effect. I think to be sure you should block all airways, forcefully, and hold them down until they stop moving. What is a death rattle but a final snore? Sometimes the temptation is *overwhelming*. But then common sense prevails and sanity is restored. I would be caught, and then how would I survive prison with my claustrophobia? And she lies there, unaware that her lives are in the balance, every night we stay together.

There was a knock on the front door, unexpected and heavy. Alison mumbled, 'Brian?' and I immediately regretted allowing her to survive.

Who could be calling for her at this time of the morning but a lover? Or a postman with a parcel that would not fit through the letter box. Or a lover. The knocking came again. It could be a lost traveller seeking directions, or a relative in distress, or a fireman saying the building is burning and for God's sake get out while you still can, or the ghost of Christmas to come with special offers, or Mother, tracking me down, or a lover, or a lover, or a love—

Alison jabbed me with her elbow. 'Will you just frickin' get it? I've nothing on!'

Oh yes, I remembered now. She did, after all, have a craving.

I stumbled out of bed, pulled on underpants, trousers, socks, shoes, T-shirt. I wasn't sure what was louder, the repeated knocking or the clicking of my joints.

'Will you hurry up?'

She was face down in her pillow, and snarling out of the side of her mouth. I should have finished the job while I had the chance.

'I'm going, I'm going!'

I moved along the hall. By the time I reached the door, most of the grogginess was gone and I was thinking clearly. This normally doesn't last for long, as my meds dull me right down again. But such was my rush to crave last night that I had left them behind. I would have to go home for them before work. But now I *really was* thinking about who would call at this time, bearing in mind the dangerous line we were in, and that perhaps I shouldn't just open the door in case it was Buddy Wailer with a silencer. *Knock loudly, kill quietly.* The moment it was wide enough he'd shoot me in the eye. I was wondering which eye would be better to get shot in. You have to give way to traffic from the right at a roundabout, so surely the left eye would be better, but what if I was to go on holiday to France, where they go round the roundabouts the wrong way, or at least they don't think they're going round them the wrong way, but I, as a visitor, would find it strange, and would need the use of my left eye, not that I was ever going to go to France, what with their French cows, or on holiday, because I get violently ill if I move outside of a three-mile radius of Belfast and . . .

'Answer the frickin' thing!'

I stood behind the door and called, 'Not today, thank you!' before stepping smartly to the side in case they, he or she, shot right through it.

There was an audible sigh, and a familiar voice said, 'Just open it.'

So I opened it, and DI Robinson was standing there, shaking his head.

'Does your mother know you're out?' he asked.

I gave him my wiseacre smile and said, 'What is it?'

'Can I come in?'

'Do you have a . . . ?'

But he had already brushed past me and was moving down the hall into the kitchen. When I reached the kitchen he was filling the kettle.

'Make yourself at . . .'

'Tea or coffee?'

'No, I don't . . .'

'Is she in?'

'Is who in?'

'Don't play funny buggers. Get her up, I need to speak to the pair of you.'

'You talk as if we are a pair.'

'Just get her.'

I went and told her who was there, and that he wanted to see her, and she grumbled a bit but wouldn't get out of bed until I left the room. She was funny about me seeing her naked, despite the fact that I had just recently performed the procreative act with her, even though she was already seeded. I returned to the kitchen.

'How does she like her coffee?' Robinson asked.

'Black.'

'Like her men.'

'What do you mean?'

'I was only joking.'

'No, what do you mean?'

'Relax, Sherlock. Take a seat.'

I stood where I was. He leant against the sink while

the kettle boiled. He was in early middle age. He had the wan, unshaven and lightly crumpled look of someone who had not been to bed. That he felt the need to visit Alison's home *before* he went home was not a good sign. Or proof that he was her lover, and had a habit of calling unannounced when the notion took him, that he was actually the father of her child but had refused to take responsibility, and that she hated him but loved him at the same time, and welcomed him into her bed for lusty sex while knowing that they would argue violently later, and perhaps that was part of the attraction. I looked at him and wondered if any of that had come out in the form of actual speech, and he looked back at me with a face so unreadable that I would probably never know. Alison appeared in the doorway, still buttoning a pink dressing gown with a bunny embroidered on it, but with a stain on his nose that might have been morning sickness or curry. She stood beside me with her arms folded.

'Need help with a case?' she asked.

'Yes, matter of fact. Look, I made you a coffee. Black.'

'Just like your men,' I said.

Her brow wrinkled.

'Show some respect,' said DI Robinson.

I looked at Alison. 'Do you feel disrespected?'

'Usually. If Jeff was alive, he'd insist on calling it an Afro-Caribbean coffee.'

'Lattes totally confuse him,' I added.

'Same old Punch and Judy,' said Robinson. 'And in

case you're trying to get my knickers in a twist, I saw Jeff last night, down at a poetry launch, and he appeared to still be alive.'

'You're writing poetry now?' I asked. 'You should try writing about what you know.'

'Not writing poetry, no; there was a bit of a rumble had to be sorted out. Anyway, I'm sticking to crime.'

'You should try writing about what you know.'

He smiled without meaning it; we smiled meaning it for each other, but not for Robinson, though it was probably difficult to tell, although we could tell, because we knew each other so well.

Robinson put the two mugs on the table and pulled back a chair. 'Join me,' he said.

'Is that an order?' Alison asked. 'In my own house, at six in the morning?'

'I'm just saying, take the weight off your feet.'

'I'm not fat, I'm pregnant.'

The jury was out on that one. He held his hand out and indicated the chairs. We exchanged glances and shrugs, and sat.

'So,' he said, 'what have you kids been up to?'

'Nothing,' I said.

'Nothing much,' said Alison.

'Out last night? Say between nine and one?'

'I was here,' I said.

'So was I,' said Alison.

'Doing it,' I said. I looked at Alison and said: 'Your brow will stay like that if you keep frowning.'

Before she could respond, DI Robinson said: 'Know anyone by the name of Liam Benson?'

'Has he been murdered?' I asked.

I just blurted it out. Sometimes I can't help myself.

Robinson sat back and clasped his hands. 'Here we go again,' he said wearily.

Of course I tried to claw it back by saying it was a natural assumption, seeing as how he investigated murders all the time, and why else would he be here with us so early in the morning unless it was something as serious as murder.

I said, 'We're still on the Augustine Wogan case.'

'Still?'

'Yeah. Still.'

'Why?'

'We believe he was murdered.'

'Why?'

'We have our reasons.'

'So how does Liam Benson come into it?'

'He works freelance for Dr Yeschenkov. We called by yesterday to ask him some questions. He wouldn't tell us anything. End of story.'

'Did you think he had something to tell you?'

'Yes. But he was more scared of Dr Yes than he was of us.'

'Go figure,' said DI Robinson.

'Is he really dead?' Alison asked. Robinson nodded. 'Murdered?'

'Don't know yet. We fished him out of the Lagan

about midnight. Crack on the back of his head, but he may have collected that on the way in. They're checking out if he was dead before or after. I can't think of any sane reason why anyone would choose to dump a body on that particular stretch – too many people passing – so he was either attacked there or he went in of his own accord. He had this in his trouser pocket.'

DI Robinson produced an evidence bag from his jacket and pushed it across the table towards us, before turning it round so that we could read what it said on the damp-looking business card it contained. It had Alison's name, home address, work and home phone numbers, mobile number, plus her Facebook, Bebo, MySpace, Twitter and e-mail contacts. It described her as a comic-book artist. I pushed it closer to her.

'You have a lot of explaining to do,' I said.

She gave me an upper-lip sneer and pushed it back. 'It was the only card we had with us at the time,' she said to Robinson. 'What would he be doing by the Lagan anyway, if he wasn't intent on jumping in? I mean, there's a tourist path, but not at that time of night.'

'Unless you're gay,' I said.

'Gay?' said Alison.

'It's a well-known rendezvous spot. You didn't know that?'

'I didn't know that.' She was studying me. When I looked round, so was Robinson.

'You're both funny,' I said.

'You see anyone laughing?' said Robinson. 'And of course, we have *this*.'

He produced a second evidence bag. It contained a mobile phone.

'His clothes protected it pretty well from the water; a bit damp, dried out in half an hour sitting on a radiator. The boys lifted prints, but only his. We checked his texts; most recent was an hour before we think he went in, to and from a pay-as-you-go phone, so untraceable.' Robinson called up the messages, pushing the buttons through the plastic of the bag, even though, with the prints lifted, there was no need. He slanted it so we could read it and said, 'This was from Liam.'

We nd to tk, mt usual 9?

'And this was sent back.'
He called it up.

See u then buddy.

Robinson was fixing me with one of his fixing looks. He said, 'The question is, do you have a pay-as-you-go phone, *buddy*?'

25

And the answer was no.

If Robinson expected his early-morning visit to spook us, he was sorely mistaken. We were old hands at this, veterans, battle-hardened by close hand-to-hand combat on the war-torn streets of Belfast. If it did anything, it renewed our resolve to find out exactly who had murdered Augustine and why. And possibly make some money from it while we were there.

We had been down some murky roads since we'd taken on this investigating lark, and DI Robinson was usually there or thereabouts. I didn't really think of him as a detective. He was more like a traffic cop, pointing us down one road, or closing off another, or giving us a severe warning for going too fast. He didn't seem very adept at anything apart from insinuation. In the beginning we were a little scared of him, but that faded with each case we solved and his role in their solution became smaller and more insignificant. He gave us titbits of information and prayed that we could make sense of them, because he couldn't. He knew that we paid no heed to paperwork or warrants or forensics, and that therefore we would never physically be required to give evidence at a trial, which meant that he could step in and try to make a provable case from what we had discovered, and in the process claim the glory for himself.

He left us with a warning not to get involved, not to interfere with the official police investigation, and to get a deadbolt for the front door because the current locking mechanism was useless; what he had actually done was present us with the little evidence he had and basically told us to see what we could do with it because he didn't have a clue.

When he had gone, Alison sat over her coffee, and I sat over my Coke and Twix. It was a balanced diet, in its own way.

She said, 'Liam Benson. A crack on the back of his head? If he smacked his head while throwing himself in, wouldn't it be to the front?'

I nodded, but I was thinking, not necessarily. I had tried to commit suicide during a swimming lesson in primary school by putting inflated armbands on my feet and throwing myself into the pool. There were many ways to do it.

I said, 'He meets with Buddy, Buddy whacks him.'

'If they wanted him whacked, shouldn't it have been

the other way round? Buddy texts him and arranges a meet?'

'Not necessarily. Liam is worried, thinks for whatever reason that he can trust Bud. Bud lets his handlers know Liam wants the meet; he's told to find out what Liam's worried about, and if he needs to whack him, whack him.'

'Liam gay?'

'Maybe. He had a ponytail.'

'Buddy gay?'

'Maybe, they'd obviously met there before. Cigars are quite phallic. The cigar cutter could represent circumcision and be a code for a preference for cut penises.'

Alison studied me. 'I'm not even going to ask.'

'I just know stuff. I know ten million things about murder, but I've never killed anyone.'

'You're killing me.' I smiled. She said: 'Do you think we need to penetrate the gay community, or that section of it that would hang out along the Lagan on a dark night on the off chance of a quickie; see if they know anything about Liam or Buddy?'

'Maybe. Although I can't. I'm allergic.'

'To gays?'

'To towpaths. Moss, mostly.'

'Well not me. Not in my condition, and anyway, a man would have more chance, surely?'

'It's another one for you-know-who, isn't it? I'll call him as soon as I get into work. We should be getting ready, unless, of course, you have a craving?'

Alison shook her head. 'Someone has just been murdered, we're trying to track down a killer and expose a conspiracy, and you're still interested in getting your end away. Man dear, before I met you, you wouldn't go within twenty paces of a woman, and now you're rampant.'

'Is that a no?'

'Yes, that's a no. But if you're that desperate, why don't you pop down to Boots?'

'Boots.'

'Boots. Ask them if they have something for a moss allergy.'

She winked. She left. I stewed. She was so stupid. There was *nothing* for a moss allergy. I was destined never to tread a towpath in search of illicit homosexual sex.

We drove. I stopped off at home to pick up my medication.

Alison said again, 'One day I'm going to get you off all that shit.'

Inside I checked my messages. There was a succession of increasingly frantic ones from the Sunny D. The final one said, 'There's only so much shit we can take,' which could be interpreted in several ways.

Alison went into work, and I opened up the shop. She was already sitting looking out of the window with a fresh coffee in her hand by the time I opened the shutters and undid all the locks. I waved back. I'd barely taken up my position when the door opened and Jeff came in. He had an ugly swelling on the side of his face, right about where I'd struck him with Jim Thompson's *Pop. 1280*.

I said, 'I knew you'd come crawling back.'

He said, 'I'm not crawling anywhere. I came for my nunchucks.'

I took them from under the counter and held them out. 'Take them. Frankly I'm embarrassed to even have them in the shop. Bruce Lee is so 1970s.'

'Who's Bruce Lee?'

'You're serious? How old are you?'

'Twenty-three.'

'And you've never heard of Bruce Lee? I presumed that's why you had them. You were emulating Bruce in *Fist of Fury*.'

'No, I'm emulating Michelangelo in *Teenage Mutant Ninja Turtles*.'

'Ah. Right. That makes more sense.'

I nodded. He nodded.

I said, 'That eye looks sore.'

He said, 'What happened to your nose?'

'A couple of heavies did me over. Usually you'd be here to protect me.'

'Yes, I would. But you attacked me for no reason.'

'I didn't attack you for no reason. I attacked you because you were being an idiot.'

'Violence is the last resort of the scoundrel.'

'That's blatantly bollocks,' I said. 'If you're here to apologise, you're going the wrong way about it.'

'I'm not here to apologise. I'm here for my nunchucks.'

'Well you appear to have them.'

'Yes, I do.'

'Okay then.'

'Okay then. See you around.'

'See you.'

He went to the door. It was still open.

I said, 'I suppose we could both apologise.'

He hesitated. 'I suppose.'

'Okay.'

'Okay.'

'Okay. You go first.'

He sighed. 'Okay. I'm sorry for being an idiot.'

'All right. Apology accepted.'

'And?'

'And?'

'Your apology?'

'What have I got to apologise for? You've just admitted to being an idiot.'

'Fucking hell! You're impossible!'

'Do you want your job back or not?'

'Yes!'

'Okay, then come in and shut your face. There's books need shifting.'

He came in.

I'm good.

I'm *damn* good.

26

Every ten minutes or so, Jeff would pull down the passenger-side mirror and examine his reflection. 'I'm scarred for life,' he'd say, then repeat it over, and over, and over. He was such a moaner, particularly when it was *obvious* that I was the one with the much more serious injury. My nose was swollen, it was split, I had difficulty breathing, if I had ever been able to sleep it would have affected my sleeping, my looks were ruined, I couldn't wash what was left of my hair for fear of the chemicals in the shampoo infecting my injury, my sense of smell was compromised and when I sneezed, due to my allergy to unleaded petrol, blood corpuscles peppered the windscreen because it was too sore to use a handkerchief.

'It's not a competition, you know,' Jeff said, and I became aware that I had said all of it out loud. 'But now that you mention it, my eye is *throbbing*, it's full of pus, I think I have blood poisoning. If I die from this it will all be your fault.'

'Yeah,' I said.

We were in the No Alibis van, parked down a bit from the Yeschenkov Clinic. We weren't exactly inconspicuous, but it was the only vehicle we had access to. Alison's Volkswagen Beetle was in for its MOT and she felt the need to babysit it despite her favourite mechanic volunteering to take it through for her. Anyone would think she didn't want to sit in a car alone with me. It was dark and the engine was off and neither Jeff nor I smoked, so there were no lights. I had filled him in on much of what had happened since his bizarre flight from my shop, and then we had moved on to discussing current trends in crime fiction.

'Stop lecturing me,' said Jeff, after forty-three minutes. 'Can we not turn the radio on or something?'

'It's stuff you need to know, Jeff. I'm educating you, free of charge.'

'I know enough.'

'You don't know shite from Shinola.'

He nodded in the darkness. Then said: 'I've no idea what that means.'

'Shite from Shinola?'

'From what?'

'Shinola. It's an old American brand of shoe polish. People would say it when—'

'I get it,' he snapped, and gingerly touched his swollen eye.

'Okay. Never mind. I'm only trying to help. It's always good to know about the books, Jeff. *Prose*.'

'Yeah.'

'I hear you've been hanging out with poets again.'

'Who told you that?'

'Little birdie.'

'What of it?'

'I warned you about that. You'll be led astray.'

'I'm old enough to look after myself.'

'You think you are, but you've a lot to learn. You hang around with them, you'll be sucked into stuff you can't handle.'

'I can handle it.'

'You think that. They suck you in with easy rhymes, but pretty soon that's not enough, you're into it harder and harder; you'll hear talk of villanelle, you'll want to try it, and then you'll be able to think about nothing else. Take my word for it, once you go down the v-road, you'll be hanging from the rafters. I know I was.'

'Hanging from the rafters?'

'Yup. And do you know what I learned from it, Jeff?'

'No. What did you learn from it?'

'Use rope, not string.'

I drummed my fingers on the wheel. Up ahead, the coming and goings at the Yeschenkov Clinic had slowed and a number of lights had winked off, although it was still, very obviously, a twenty-four-hour facility. Time doesn't stand still. Although it can bend, in certain dimensions. Alison and I had taken up position in the early afternoon and had been rewarded with our first glimpse of Dr Yes himself at around three p.m., rolling up in a black Porsche convertible, top down and teeth bright. It had personalised number plates. *DOC 1*. It was now nine fifteen and his car was still in position in the small private car park for which the front garden had clearly been sacrificed. The plan, insofar as we had one, was to follow him. We were trying to establish his habits and his haunts, and from there decide on the best place to isolate and confront him, that is when we had something to confront him with. Evidence of any wrongdoing remained very thin on the ground. I had invested a lot of faith in Rolo, but I'd heard nothing; in retrospect I realised it was a mistake to give him the Parker; he was probably so engrossed in it that he had forgotten his mission. My e-mail appeal to my database of customers had yielded nothing *at all*. I had contacted a fellow collector who ran a mystery bookstore in Denver, Colorado, and asked him to check what his FBI contacts had on Buddy Wailer. He got back to me pretty quick and said that they'd never heard of Buddy Wailer, or any Wailer for that matter. I wasn't unduly surprised. If Buddy was as good as people seemed to think he was, then he would have a whole string of identities and multiple bank accounts. He could only operate efficiently if he remained below the radar. He was an international assassin, anonymous, faceless, free to travel without fear of being hauled in at passport control. That or my contact in Denver was a bullshit artist who wouldn't know an FBI agent from a plumber.

Jeff said, 'What's villanelle?'

'Jeff, I'd really rather not . . .'

'Just tell me.'

'Okay. But don't try to take it all in at once, all right? The villanelle has nineteen lines, five triplets with a closing quatrain. Two refrains, used in the first and third lines of the first stanza, and then alternately at the close of each stanza until the final quatrain, which ends with the two refrains. There's also an a-b alternating rhyme to think about in the closing lines.'

Jeff was silent for a long time. Then he blew air out of his cheeks and said, 'Fuck.'

I nodded sympathetically. 'I think the reason I chose string instead of rope was that subconsciously I wanted to have another go at the villanelle. It's a real mind-fucker, Jeff.'

'I didn't figure you for a poet.'

'I'm not. I wasn't. I just don't like being defeated by things.'

Eventually he said, 'Thanks, I appreciate the advice. They're not bad people.'

'Most of them are gay,' I said.

He nodded along, but it was as if he wasn't really listening, lost in his own thoughts, at least until his head suddenly jerked towards me. 'Gay?'

'Kind of goes with the territory.'

'Oh. I hadn't really . . .'

'But you're comfortable enough with . . . gay.'

'Yes, of course.'

'You mix quite freely with them.'

'Them?'

'I don't mean it in a derogatory way. I mean as a social group.'

'Yes, of course.'

'But you're not yourself.'

'I'm not myself? I'm not myself gay? No, I'm not, although it shouldn't matter. It doesn't matter.'

'Absolutely not. Where I grew up, Catholics were treated the way Jews were treated in Nazi Germany. Times have changed. It's a good thing. But human nature doesn't change, and the lower orders always need someone to blame and hate, and as we don't hate Catholics any longer, gays are the new Jews, as Jews were the local Catholics.'

'You lost me somewhere around Germany.'

'Belfast is not a forgiving place. We have tidied it up with bells and whistles, but it's still as hard as nails. Gay men congregate on the Lagan towpath at night for sexual congress.'

'They do?'

'They do. Now, there are two of us in the van, watching a building. It should, technically speaking, only take one of us. So although I appreciate the company, you're not helping in the slightest.'

'Oh. I thought I was. I went and got Starbursts.'

'Opal Fruits,' I said.

'Starbursts.'

'Opal Fruits. They were created as Opal Fruits; just because some marketeer changes their name, it doesn't mean that they aren't still Opal Fruits. Same with Marathon and Snickers.'

'I went and queued in Starbucks, and that's about half a mile away. And I went back for your muffin.'

'You forgot the muffin, that's why you went back.'

'I *went back* is the point.'

'And it's appreciated. But do you want to know how you could really help? You could really help by popping along the towpath and talking to some of the men you'll find there.'

'You mean where Liam was found?'

'Where Liam was murdered. There are questions that need to be asked.'

'You want me to go along there in the dark, and start talking to complete strangers, about a murder, when one of them could quite easily be the murderer, and I myself might get murdered.'

'Nobody said crime-fighting was easy.'

'It's easy enough sitting in a van.'

'Jeff, we all have our jobs to do. I'm watching the building, I'm watching for Dr Yeschenkov; you should be happy to be off pursuing other lines of enquiry, fresh leads, part of the team again, but all you can do is complain about your eye and try to hide your homophobia.'

'*What?*'

'It's quite clear to me, *Jeff*, that despite all your protestations, despite your claiming to be open-minded by working for Amnesty International and hanging around with poets, you are actually rampantly homophobic . . .'

'That's just ridic—'

'Soon as I mentioned the towpath, you just bristled . . .'

'Because a murderer . . .'

'. . . with disgust, and now you're saying that they're all potential murderers . . .'

'I never . . .'

'. . . tarring them all with the same brush, just because the murder happened in a notorious cruising spot. Where does Amnesty International stand on the persecution of gays, Jeff? What would they think of you going around daubing *unclean, unclean* on their houses, or deriding their life-style choice as corrupt and dysfunctional and nauseating . . .'

'I didn't . . .'

'I need you to go down, Jeff, down along the river bank, and ask the questions that need to be asked.'

'I didn't say I wouldn't go, I just said it's dark, and dangerous . . .'

'It's dark and dangerous for them too, Jeff. Yet they're there every night. Don't you think it's hard for them? A murder has been committed, and yet they can't help themselves, slaves to their abhorrent compulsions.'

'Abhorrent?'

'Isn't that what you're thinking? You have to

conquer this, Jeff. Get down there. They are perfect witnesses; what they do, and where they choose
to do it, means they do it with their eyes open. They
are watchful, fearful of discovery, their eyes are accus-
tomed to the dark; they are bats, Jeff, they have radar,
they are homosexual bats with radar. Gaydar.'

'But I don't even know what I'm asking them.'

'Them?'

'I didn't mean . . .'

'You know what to ask . . . did anyone there see
anything unusual? Did they see or know Liam Benson?
Was he a regular? If he was, did they also know or
see Buddy Wailer? He's a harder call. All we know
about him is that Manuel Gerardo Ramiro Alfonzo
Aurelio Enrique Zapata Quetzalcoatl says he's thin,
real thin, and tall, real tall. He smokes cigars.'

'Tall, thin, smokes cigars.'

'Yep.'

'Tall, thin, smokes cigars.'

'Yes.'

'Tall, thin, smokes cigars.'

'Jeff, for Jesus' . . .'

'Tall . . .' Jeff nodded forward. 'Thin.' He nodded
again. 'Smokes cigars.' I was about to snap at him again,
but he snapped first. 'Will you fucking look over there?'

I looked, at the really tall, really thin man carrying
a large circular box just approaching the Yeschenkov
Clinic. He hesitated by the door and took a final puff
on his cigar, before throwing it down and grinding it
out with his foot.

27

There are a lot of very tall, very thin men about. Otherwise there probably wouldn't be a need for a shop in downtown Belfast called Very Tall, Very Thin Men. The market for very tall, very thin men who smoked cigars was somewhat smaller. The market for very tall, very thin men who smoked cigars and carried boxes like the one this very tall, very thin cigar-smoking man carried, round like a hatbox with a ribbon on top, was probably minuscule.

Buddy Wailer, for it was almost certainly he, entered the Yeschenkov Clinic, and the moment he was through the door I had Jeff scampering across the road to retrieve the remains of his cigar. I would have done it myself, but my scampering days are long gone.

He had it bagged and back to the van in less than a minute. I do not routinely carry evidence bags with me. I had tried to order them over the internet, and the internet had tried to overcharge me. Yes, proper bags come with tamper seals, sequential numbering, security stitching and usage logs, but they are £75 for two hundred, *plus* VAT, whereas freezer bags from Asda cost only £1.65 for eighty plus 93p for a magic marker. And people wonder why the police are always whining about being over budget.

Jeff closed the door, secured his seat belt as I prefer him to do, even when stationary, and handed me the bag. I squinted around the bold Asda lettering to examine the cigar, and more importantly the tip of it. Yes, indeed. Somewhat squashed, but definitely a V-cut, and with the DNA of a killer attached. I didn't need an expert to tell me it would be a match for that found on the cigar rammed into Augustine Wogan's mouth *after* he had been murdered.

Well, yes, I did need an expert to tell me that, but really, he would just be confirming what I already knew. He might have his degrees and his banks of sophisticated scientific equipment, but I had my incredible powers of deduction, all based on the knowledge gleaned from reading ten thousand volumes of crime fiction. Agatha didn't need DNA to tell her who the killer was in *Ten Little Niggers*. I had a copy of the book under lock and key. A Collins Crime Club first edition from 1939. She had been forced to change the title to *Ten Little Indians* because of political correctness. And then the next PC wave had forced her to change *that* to *And Then There Were None*. It was and is a crazy, mixed-up world.

I hadn't told Jeff about the hatbox in my summation of the case to date, but now I did, and the colour drained from his face.

'A head? A human head?'

'No, Jeff, a giraffe's head. *Yes*. Of course.'

'But why?'

'Giraffes are harder to come by. I *don't know*. But serial killers quite often take souvenirs from their victims. Usually it's a piece of clothing, or maybe a lock of hair. A whole head is a bit extreme, but not unheard of.'

'Is that what he is, a serial killer? I thought he was like a hit man?'

'Well what's a hit man but a serial killer with an agenda?'

'But what's he doing going in there with his hatbox thingy?'

'Because his killing spree isn't over.'

'But . . .'

'There's always a but with you, Jeff.'

'Yes, but . . . he didn't take Augustine's head, or Liam's head.'

'Perhaps he didn't have the time or opportunity. Maybe he only takes heads he finds aesthetically pleasing. Maybe the head thing is a red herring, or an urban myth. It might just be a hatbox with a hat in it. Perhaps we should ask him.'

'He creeps me out.'

'He's just a man.'

I was only saying that to keep Jeff's spirits up. Fact

was, Buddy Wailer scared the Shinola out of me too.

What kind of a sick individual would carry his victim's head about in a hatbox? Was he collecting, or delivering? And after ignoring the warning to keep our noses out of Yeschenkov business, were we next on his hit list? Was he going to need extra boxes, one of them slightly larger than average? Would he preserve our heads in formaldehyde or pickle them in vinegar? Would he suck the brains out of the nostrils or remove the crown and eat them? A shiver ran through me. And at that exact moment there was a sudden hammering on my window.

I yelled.

If Jeff hadn't been restrained by his seat belt, he would have jumped clean through the window in his attempt to escape.

Behind me the back door was flung open.

I yelled, 'NOOOOOOOOOOOOOOOOOOO . . . !'

And Alison's face beamed in. 'Guess what! Passed my MOT!'

Jeff buried his head in his hands. 'Fuck, fuck, fuck, fuck, fucking hell! Don't do that!'

Alison climbed in. 'Don't do what?'

'THAT!' I shouted.

She laughed. 'Jesus, man, take a chill pill.'

I took a deep breath. When I had recovered sufficiently, I explained to her *why* we were so upset. She said, 'Oh. Well, I still think your reaction was a bit extreme. You screamed like a couple of schoolgirls.'

Jeff and I fumed, united.

Up ahead, Dr Yeschenkov emerged from the clinic. He paused on the top step while he answered his mobile phone. Even from a distance, he had a lot of bright teeth. Passing cars were flashing at him to turn them down a bit.

'Okay,' I said, 'here's where it gets interesting.' It was time to take command, show them exactly why I was the boss and they the munchkins. 'Jeff, head for the towpath; it's dark enough now for incognito fumbling. Alison, back to your car, wait for Buddy to emerge, then follow him back to his lair. I'm going after Dr Yes. Understood?'

'Swell,' said Alison, 'leave me to the murderer why don't you?'

'I don't want you to rugby-tackle him, I just want you to tail him. You can do that, can't you?'

'I *suppose.*'

'And when I say tail, I don't mean right *into* his house. Agreed?'

'*Agreed.*'

'Alison, I'm serious. We've all watched the same movies, and we've all groaned at the same point when she sees him leave his digs and decides to break in and nose around. Everyone but the stupid cow knows he's just gone round the corner for a pint of milk and a Topic, and that he'll be on his way back in a minute and then she's going to get trapped in there with him. So do me a favour, just follow. You're three months pregnant; don't do anything you'll regret later.'

'Like sleeping with you?'

'Just *go*.'

Dr Yeschenkov was in his car now, and reversing out of his space.

'You all know the drill. If there's anything interesting going down . . .'

'Be wary of that on the towpath, Jeff,' said Alison.

'. . . call me, keep the line open, wear your earpiece. Stay safe.'

Jeff got out, grumbling. 'It's a long walk from here to the towpath.'

'Then run.'

Alison leant forward. She put a hand on my shoulder. I stiffened. I don't like human contact at the best of times.

Her mouth moved to my ear. She whispered: 'Honey?'

'*What?*'

I don't like anyone whispering in my ear. The ear is like an express tunnel into the brain. And the mouth contains more bacteria than any other part of the body. Whispering is tantamount to spitting a disease into the cerebral cortex.

But I was prepared to make an exception for sweet nothings.

Her voice was husky. She said, 'I don't mind you treating Jeff like an idiot, but if you keep it up with me, I'll fucking brain ye.'

She smiled pleasantly and exited the vehicle.

28

You're probably thinking, Dr Yeschenkov in his sleek Porsche, capable of nought to sixty in five seconds, or six seconds, or seven seconds, or eight seconds, or nine seconds, and me in the Mystery Machine, capable of very little; how was I ever going to keep pace with him? But I had several things in my favour that allowed me to follow at a respectable distance and not once lose sight of him. One was the fact that he drove dead slowly. Another was that he was still on the call he'd started on the steps of the clinic. A third was the common knowledge, even to an American interloper, that post-Troubles Belfast cops have little to do with their time and are always on the lookout for boys and their fast toys.

There was a light spring rain. Neon reflected off the tarmac on Great Victoria Street. The Grand Opera House gleamed. The National Trust's Crown Bar invited in the gullible. Dr Yeschenkov turned down a side street and emerged on to Bedford Street, opposite the Ulster Hall. Three doors up, the glass-fronted Forum International. He pulled into the set-down-only area and got out. He smiled at a doorman in a top hat and beige livery and breezed into the foyer. He was carrying what looked like a medical bag.

I parked a little further down Bedford. I checked in with Alison. No sign of Buddy. I called Jeff. He was out of breath. He complained about the rain. I locked the car and walked towards the hotel. The doorman gave me a look and I said, 'Wet night.' He grunted. I walked into the foyer. No sign of Dr Yeschenkov. Plush carpets. Muzak. Reception straight ahead, elevators to the right, restaurant also to the right, plush sofas and chairs on the left, a twirlygig stuffed with leaflets promoting shows and tours, concierge at a desk beside it.

I walked over and sat down opposite him. He looked to be about thirty, black suit, black poloneck, and goatee beard. He said good evening and how could he help me, Belfast accent, working class but on the make. It was a big hotel. He had no way of knowing if I was a resident or not, short of asking.

I said, 'Is it true what they say about concierges?'

'Sir?'

'You want something, anything, twenty-four hours a day, you're the man to see.'

'Within reason, sir.'

'What kind of reason?'

He had been sitting back; now he leant forward, elbows on his desk, hands clasped. 'Why don't you tell me what you're looking for and I'll see what I can do?'

'You can be discreet?'

'The soul of.'

'The soul of discreet?'

'Of discretion.'

'Concert tickets?'

'Absolutely.'

'At a premium?'

'At a discount.'

'Dodgy seats behind the mixing desk?'

'Front row.'

'VIP party afterwards?'

'If humanly possible.'

'At a premium?'

'At your discretion. Who do you want to see?'

'No one, just establishing the boundaries. Quiet night.'

'It is a quiet night.'

'Not much to do.'

'No, there's not.'

'What if I want to take someone up to my room?'

'A visitor?'

'A visitor, yes.'

'That's not a problem, sir.'

'It's a single room.'

'That's not a problem, sir.'

'A friend up to my room, for a couple of hours.'

'Soul of.'

'What if I don't have any friends?'

'I'm sure you do.'

'Yes, I do, but not right here, right now. Could you recommend a friend?'

'Yes, I could do that.'

'A blonde friend?'

'Yes, sir.'

'Premium?'

'Discount.'

'If I wanted two?'

'Two friends?'

'It's a quiet night.'

'Yes, it is. Two won't be a problem.'

'How does it work?'

'How does what work?'

'Finding me friends deserves a reward.'

'At your discretion.'

'Have you ever met Dan Starkey?'

'Dan . . . ?'

'He's a reporter on *Belfast Confidential*; he goes about exposing hotels and how they work hand in hand with escort agencies supplying sex-trafficked call girls to their clientele.'

'No, I haven't.'

'You have now.'

I took out my mobile and pushed a button, as if I was switching off a tape. To his credit, he did not flicker or flinch. He remained as cool as his clothes.

'Nice one,' he said. 'Walked into that.'

'Yeah, you should have asked what room I was in.'

'Noted.'

'But I don't have to write anything. A little info is all I'm looking for.'

'Really?'

'Yeah. Doing a piece on yer man. Dr Yes.'

'Dr Yeschenkov?'

'That's the one. He came in a minute ago.'

'Yes, he did.'

'Visiting his patients.'

'Yes, he is. He's here most nights.'

'Have much to do with him?'

'He's always pleasant. He tips well. His patients are from the needy end of the spectrum.'

'Does he ever have company?'

'Sometimes, other doctors, nurses. There's an arrangement with the hotel.'

'Does he ever stay over?'

For the first time the concierge hesitated. It was only for a fraction of a second, but it was enough.

'How do you mean?' he asked.

'The clinic block-books rooms?'

'Yes, it does.'

'But not all of those rooms are going to be used all of the time. I'm guessing the hotel doesn't want those rooms let out to ordinary guests, because the guests don't want to be seeing patients in all states of disrepair roaming the corridors screaming in pain. So there are certain rooms that stand empty, and I'm asking if Dr Yes ever stays over.'

The concierge cleared his throat. 'Occasionally.'

'He have company?'

'Occasionally.'

'Mrs Yeschenkov?'

'Occasionally.'

'This woman?'

I turned my phone to show him the photo of Pearl I'd lifted from the Yeschenkov Clinic website.

'Occasionally.'

'It doesn't do her justice,' I said.

'Nope.'

'She's bigger than that.'

He looked me dead in the eye. 'She's the most beautiful woman I've ever seen. She sat where you're sitting one night and talked to me for twenty-three minutes.'

'What about?'

'Absolutely no idea, but at the end of it if she'd asked for my pin code I would gladly have given it to her.'

'Do you know Buddy Wailer?'

'Buddy . . . ?'

'Very tall, very thin, might be with Dr Yes from time to time.'

'Can't say I . . .'

'Carries a hatbox.'

The concierge smiled. 'The Mad Hatter? Sure. We've all seen him.'

'Frequently?'

'Hard to say.'

'You know what he does?'

'Isn't it obvious?'

'Is it?'

'Hats? The hatbox?'

'Right,' I said.

'I mean, we don't know, that's just what we guessed. Those women have more money than sense, and time to kill. They have the shopping channel piped in, but it's not the same. There's designers coming in here all day, can't believe their luck: a captive audience, and a captive audience on painkillers and champagne.'

'Good job you're discreet.'

'The soul of.'

Across the way, the elevator doors opened and Dr Yeschenkov emerged. He walked straight for the exit. I stood up.

'Thanks for the help,' I said.

'That's what I'm here for.'

'Tipping is . . . ?'

'Discretionary.'

'Bear that in mind,' I said.

29

The Blackheath Driving Range is a floodlit facility on the outskirts of Holywood, County Down. I only know that because that's where I was, and it was floodlit and on the outskirts of Holywood, County Down. There was now a stiff, cold breeze, and a mean rain, but that wasn't going to stop Dr Yeschenkov getting some practice in. It was ten-thirty when he arrived, and there were only two other cars in the car park. A bearded man in orange waterproofs was just in the process of closing up the garden shed that served as his office when the Porsche pulled in right beside him; the window slid down, something was said, and the man began to reverse the process. I guess you don't say no to Dr Yes.

I parked on the other side of a BMW, switched off, and considered my options. Sure, it was a splendid opportunity to confront him. Or if not confront him, talk to him. Or if not talk to him, observe him. But it was cold, and wet, and from what I had read of the sport, it usually wasn't a good idea to disturb anyone attempting to play it. Someone famous had once summed up the frustrations of golf as 'a good walk, spoiled', but I thought it was simpler than that. It was just shit.

Confrontation for the sake of confrontation was pointless. I had no proof of any wrongdoing, merely suspicions. Equally, he had no proof that I knew anything of his deeds, yet he had surely been behind the visit of Rolo and Spider-web to my shop, the warning to mind my own business and the shocking damage to my nose. Rolo had yet to come back to me on that one, but there wasn't any doubt in my mind. Dr Yes was rich, good-looking and a social mover. He was used to getting his own way. He liked power, and when people rubbed him up the wrong way, he wiped them out. But here he was, on a rain-swept spring night, all by himself. There would never be a better opportunity to introduce myself. He was just getting his clubs out of the back of his car.

I had to do it *now*. I had to ignore the rain, and the pneumonia that would surely follow; I had to try and blot out the fact that we were almost in the country, that there were fields not too far away, featuring the cows of night and sheep that could fly when no one was looking.

I got out of the van and approached the chap now standing morosely in the shed doorway.

I said, 'I want a go.'

'A go? We're just closing up.'

'Oh.'

Dr Yeschenkov came walking past us, his golf bag over his shoulder. He nodded at the man. The man nodded back. He looked at me.

'He was the last one,' he said.

'I was here before him.'

'He's a member; that has certain privileges.'

'But your sign says open to the public.'

'And we are, except when we're closed.'

'I just want a quick game. I'll finish the same time as him.'

'Read my lips: n . . . o . . . spells . . .'

'Hey.' It was Dr Yeschenkov, standing on the slatted wooden path leading to the sheltered range. 'Why don't you let the guy play? What difference does one more make?'

'I'm not supposed to . . .'

'Just say he's with me.'

The man blew air out of his cheeks. 'Right,' he said. 'Whatever.'

Dr Yeschenkov winked at me. I would have winked back, but once I start, I find it difficult to stop. As Dr Yes continued on to the range, the man in charge muttered something under his breath. The only word I picked up began with 'a' and ended with 'hole'. It was probably a golfing term.

'It's ten quid for an hour,' he snapped.

'How much for half an hour?'

'We don't do half-hours.'

'How much for fifteen minutes?'

'We don't ...' He took a deep breath. 'A tenner. You need balls?' I nodded. 'That's another fiver. Clubs?' I nodded again. He kept looking at me. 'How many?'

'Just one.'

'*Which* one?'

'I don't mind.'

'Whaddya mean, you don't mind? Which one do you want?'

'A good one. You pick.'

He rolled his eyes. He crossed the interior of the shed and brought me a plastic bag full of golf balls and a club. I examined it as if I knew what it was.

'Yes,' I said, 'that will do the trick. Is it supposed to have this big thick bit on the end?'

'Funny,' he said.

'No, really, is it supposed—'

'Just *go and play*. I'm closing in fifty minutes come hell or high water.'

I took the bag, and walked with the club over my shoulder, like one of the Seven Dwarves going to work with his pickaxe, except with a golf club, and balls, and going to the driving range. The rain was made huge and eternal by the floodlights; the range was peppered with balls, like abnormally large hailstones.

My mobile phone vibrated. I checked it: a text from Alison.

Followed Buddy. House on Tennyson. Eyes peeled. Love you, cheeky chops.

I texted back:

Okay.

There were maybe thirty tee-off positions; there were two other practitioners, and then Dr Yes, already in full flow. So far as I could judge, his swing was as smooth as he was. I stood at the tee to his left. My swing would not be smooth. I had never previously swung. If I swung, he would know that. If I swung, I would tear many ligaments, much muscle and several pounds of gristle. Bones would creak and snap. My hand/eye coordination was off the scale, but not in a good way.

I said, 'Thanks for that,' as he swung back.

He completed his swing, unfazed. There was a crack, as club head met ball. Ball launched. Rose high.

'Oh,' he said. 'No problem.'

He lined up another ball. As he swung back I said, 'Jobsworth.'

He struck it cleanly once again. He followed its trajectory before nodding, satisfied.

'Get them everywhere,' he said. He looked at me, standing over my ball. 'But understandable. It's a dreadful night. Do I know you?'

'I don't know.'

'Where do you play?'

'Malone.'

'That'll be it.'

'Good spot.'

'Yes, it is. Nice people. What do you play off?'

The club continued to rest over my shoulder. I looked down at my ball. I knew that I wasn't going to even attempt to strike it. There was no point. I am allergic to golf. I had once almost played Arnold Palmer's Pro-Shot Golf as a child; it featured an action figure of the apparently legendary golfer at the end of a pretend golf stick, with an assortment of toy clubs you could fit into a hole in him and operate mechanically, a square of green polyester material to act as a green, a variety of small polystyrene balls for the Axminster fairway and small marble ones for putting. However, before I could take my first swing, my pet gerbil appeared from nowhere and made off with the poly-styrene ball. In chasing after her I accidentally knelt on her and broke her neck. I cried and wailed so hard that Mother locked me in my cupboard for three hours.

So I instead of swinging at it, I picked the ball up. I held it up to the floodlights, so that it appeared dark, and larger than it deserved to be.

'You're a little sphere of doom,' I told it, before nodding at Dr Yes. 'My handicap is the knowledge that I will never achieve perfection,' I said. 'Some-times you don't need to hit the ball. Holding the club, and being in the moment, is as good as it gets. Actu-ally striking it is like peeing on your dreams.'

He studied me for what felt like a long time. 'You know something, sir?' he said eventually. 'You are absolutely right.'

I nodded. He nodded. He moved his club between his legs, and leaned on the shaft. We both looked out at the slow-motion rain.

'Tell you something?' he asked.

'Absolutely.'

'I once stood at the first tee for nineteen minutes, debating whether to take the first shot and risk ruining my day, or leave it, stay happy. For what I do, and the volume at which I do it, I have to be calm, settled, in control, completely stress-free. Nineteen minutes, and it felt like ninety.'

'Nobody complained?'

'I was in my front room. It was the Nintendo Wii. Tiger Woods PGA Tour 10.'

'Gets you,' I said.

'Gets you,' he concurred.

We nodded. We stared out at the rain some more.

'What business you in, you have to be so steady?' I asked.

'Medicine.' He smiled. The night got a little brighter. He stepped across with his hand out. 'Yeschenkov, of the Yeschenkov Clinic.' He took my hand. He had a firm grip. It grew firmer. I was trying to match him on the grip, but it was useless. I have brittle bones. I was trying not to scream. His eyes held steady on mine. 'And I know what business you're in.'

All I could manage was, 'Uhuh?'

'Murder.'

All I could still manage was, 'Uhuh.'

Finally he let go. I was determined not to show how

much he had hurt me, and just hoped he would mistake the tears for raindrops.

'Catchy. *Murder is Our Business*. Nice van,' he said. 'No Alibis, that's in Botanic, isn't it?'

Like you don't know.

I nodded. He was so up himself he hadn't even asked for my name.

'If you don't mind me asking, what happened to your nose?'

Like you don't know.

'Book trade's tough, and getting tougher.'

'I could do something about that.'

'It's beyond saving.'

'The nose, I mean. You should call by.'

'The clinic? I've heard of you. Aren't you the surgeon to the stars?'

'I take on mere mortals as well.'

'Six-month waiting list, I heard.'

He was lining up for another shot. He stopped and looked across at me. 'Yep, that's the story I put out. Then people feel very important when I agree to see them in a matter of days.' He smiled. He reached into his back pocket and produced a business card. He handed it over. 'Give me a call. That's my private line. I'm sure I'll be able to sort out a fellow swinger.' He winked.

I said, 'Is it going to cost me an arm and a leg?'

'Only if something goes tragically wrong.'

Smart.

As he swung I said, 'There's a first time for every-thing.'

It did not affect him at all. Straight and true and high.

I left him to it. He was good. He was charming. He was pleasant. He was warm. As a doctor, he would instil confidence in you. As a friend, loyalty. He had to know who I was, yet he had come across like I was his best bud. Or *Buddy*.

It was still bucketing down when he finished his practice. He must have cracked off two hundred balls, and there wasn't a hair out of place. When he emerged from the covered area, the rain seemed to avoid him. His cream trousers remained pristine. He smiled at the man, and his tip appeared big enough to ensure a wide grin and a grovel in return. I was a hundred metres away, parked up in the van, lights off, watching through binoculars. Dr Yeschenkov wasn't quite so calm and collected when he saw that someone had scratched *Tosser* into his passenger-side door. And *Knob* into the driver's door.

My nail for the scratching of cars with personalised number plates hadn't had an outing for months.

It felt good to be back.

30

I wasn't unduly worried when I couldn't raise Alison. I was more concerned for my own well-being. I had followed Dr Yeschenkov home to his mansion high up in the Craigantlet Hills. He disappeared behind security gates and a high wall, leaving me on a lonely country road, alone but for ten billion insects. It was close to midnight, the lights of Belfast were twinkling below and there was a half-moon above, providing just enough light for me to mistake trees for monsters and hedges for ghastly spice sucking *Dune*-worms. If he had lived in town I would have thought nothing of donning the night-vision glasses and slipping over his wall to stand staring in at his windows; God knows I did it most nights around the city anyway. But this was different; he had dogs that barked, and I am allergic to dogs, and cats, and hamsters, and wheat, and gravel, and daffodils. I could not physically bring myself to get out of the car for fear of the Bogey Man. Mother had instilled in me a lifelong dread of the BM. Once, when I was very young, and Father was away on business, the BM had climbed into bed beside me and tried to remove my pyjamas. He had smelled of Old Spice. When I protested he had apologised and gone to look for Mother's room. She told me over breakfast that she had wrestled with him all night, and ultimately triumphed. I now suspect that she was lying, but that did not negate my fear of the Bogey Man, who contributed still to my lack of sleep. Out here, in the wilds, he did not have to be a Bogey Man; he could be a Bogey Cow or a Bogey Goat. It was Bogey Land, and I was uncomfortable. Also, night pollen.

I tried calling Alison, but it went to her answer machine. Jeff picked up but said he couldn't talk. I went home. I called Alison again, but nothing. I took my medication and went to bed. Obviously I did not sleep, but went jogging in the Land of Nod, and opened my eyes again at six, exhausted. There was still no message from Alison. I presumed she was being both dozy and dizzy. I drove to work. There were three messages, all from the Sunny D. Mother had locked herself in the toilets. Then she had emerged from the toilets and taken refuge in an airing cupboard. Finally she had broken down in tears and confessed to being a Communist. Could I *please* come and pick her up?

I wiped the messages and took up position. At nine fifteen the shop door opened and Rolo came in. He was wearing jeans and a denim jacket. They didn't match. He had *The Godwulf Manuscript* in his hand. He placed it face down on the counter. He tapped the back of it and said:

'I want another.'

I smiled.

'My wife couldn't believe it. She'd never seen me even pick up a book, let alone read it straight through, one sitting. I was up till all hours. It was just . . . that Spenser, man, he's good. Is he in all the others?'

'Not all.'

'Oh.'

'Just thirty-five of them.'

'Really . . . ? That's . . . fuckin' brilliant! Are they all as good as this?'

'Some are better.'

'I want them all, I really want them all.'

'And you can get them all, but not all at once. Maybe one a week.'

'I don't think I can wait that long.'

'If you want to find another dealer, that's fine, but I can only let you have one a week. I've had too many clients who tried too many too soon, and it burned them out. One a week, max. The *Godwulf* was a gift from me, an introductory offer, but I don't give credit. So don't ask. I have *Looking for Rachel Wallace* here, you want?'

'You know I do!'

'It's an American edition, he's never really taken off over here; it's expensive. But I can do you a deal.'

'Fine, mate, absolutely fine. Gimme.'

'Not so fast, Rolo. Gimme the skinny.'

'The what?'

'Who wanted me warned off, who wanted me beaten up?'

'I did my best, honest to God, but he didn't know.'

'Your agent? How could he not know?'

'It was done by phone; cash arrived in an envelope.'

'That's convenient.'

'I swear. Look at my knuckles. See, they're skinned? I don't normally do the bashin', but this time me mate held him down and I beat the livin' daylights out of him, and that's the best I got. He's telling the truth.'

'You're sure?'

'I'm certain. He swallowed three of his own teeth.'

I hesitated. I drummed my fingers on the counter. Then I turned to the shelves behind me and pulled out *Looking for Rachel Wallace*. I set it down and said, 'That's a fiver.'

He handed it over before I could draw breath. I gave him the book. He was delighted.

'Thank you so much,' he said. 'I can't wait . . .'

'Take your time. Savour it.'

He nodded. He looked up at me, and then around the shelves. 'These are all . . . like this?'

'Rolo, you have no idea what's waiting for you. It will rock your world.'

'Do you think . . .' He hesitated. He even looked quite bashful. 'I don't like to . . . like . . .'

'Just ask, Rolo.'

'Do you think you could . . . y'know . . . show me . . . or guide me . . . just I never . . . went to school much . . . This is just like . . . being blind . . . and then suddenly you can see, but there's too many colours . . .'

'You're dazzled.'

'Yeah. God, like, imagine . . . you get to work in somewhere like this all day.'

'It's my dream job.'

'I never had a proper job. Just doing *stuff*. Thieving and beating and threatening. I thought that was all there was, but there's more, so much more. Now I get to read about thieving and beating and threatening, it's so much more satisfying.'

'Any time you want to come and look through the books, Rolo, you just come ahead.'

'Really?'

'You want to read a few pages, I'll make you a cup of coffee and you sit there at the back, put your feet up and enjoy. More than a few pages, you're going to have to pay, you understand?'

'Yes, of course . . .'

'Odd time, you want to help me shift some boxes, do some rearranging, maybe you could lend a hand.'

'Love to!'

'Can't pay you anything . . .'

'Man, I would pay you, place like this, all these books.'

'Well,' I said.

The door opened and Jeff came in. He looked Rolo

up and down, clocked the beatific look on his face and mine, and said, 'All right?'

'We're fine, yes,' I said.

He took his jacket off, hung it up, then joined me behind the counter.

'You work here?' Rolo asked.

I snorted.

Jeff said, 'Clearly. Do you want me to take for that?' He indicated Rolo's book.

'I got it already,' I said.

Rolo smiled. He held the book up. 'Can't wait,' he said. 'I'll be back.'

'Leave it for a week, Rolo, you'll appreciate it in the long run.'

'Sure thing. And, uh, you want a hand shifting those books, you know where I am.'

He gave me the thumbs-up. His gaze lingered on Jeff for a moment. Then he left. Jeff watched him closely as he passed in front of the window.

'You see, Jeff,' I said, 'no one is indispensable.'

It's good to keep the staff on their toes, even though I did not, in fact, know how to contact Rolo.

Jeff was staring at me. I said, *'What?'*

'I've spent most of the night standing soaked on the river bank letting damp men feel my arse just so I could ask them questions about your shitty case, and you pull that on me?'

He was quite serious. I said, 'Would you ever wise up? I was only raking you.'

'Who is he?'

'Rolo? He's my latest project. Did you ever see *Pygmalion*?'

'No.'

'Did you ever see *My Fair Lady*?'

'No.'

'*Educating Rita*?'

'No.'

'Ever heard of Henry Higgins?'

'No.'

'Eliza Dolittle?'

'No.'

'Okay. Let me explain. He'd never read a book until last night. Now I'm going to turn him into a crime-fiction aficionado, and I'm going to do it in six weeks.'

'Why six weeks?'

'Because I have a short attention span. But never mind him; how did it go? Was it awful?'

'Yes, it was. So I don't need this shit.'

'Hey, relax. C'mon. Spill them, spill them beans. Did you have to kiss a few frogs before you found a stool pigeon?'

'It isn't funny. There were hundreds of them! Their hands were everywhere!'

'It's a little bit funny,' I said.

The tiniest smile appeared. 'No it *wasn't* . . . Next time, screw your moss allergy, *you're* going . . .' He sighed. 'The short answer is, and bearing in mind the whole point of them going down there in the dark *is* the anonymity thing, both Buddy Wailer and Liam Benson stood out sufficiently for several of them to say they

257

were regulars. But nobody admitted hooking up with them or recalled seeing them with anyone else or on the night Liam died.'

'So either they're a couple who fancied a bit of strange or they're using the cruising spot as cover for clandestine meetings.'

'That's about it. So?'

'So?'

Jeff cupped his hand to his ear. 'Do I hear anything?'

'Do you . . . ? Oh. Well. Cheers. Much appreciated.'

'Huh,' he said.

'You weren't, you know . . . tempted?'

'No.'

'Not even a wee bit?'

'No.'

'Is that a love bite . . . ?'

His hand shot to his neck. 'Where?'

We were enjoying Starbucks in the shop. We were talking about a newly delivered box of books. Amongst the highlights were a repackaged Chandler collection and a children's book by Patricia Cornwell called *Slice & Dice*. Jeff was talking his usual crap, eulogising *The Wire*, but every once in a while he would break off, and he would look perplexed for a bit and kind of far away, and then he would shake himself and pick up where he'd left off.

Jeff had done a brave thing, putting himself out there, and I would probably never know what part of his soul he had sacrificed to gain what was, it was generally agreed, completely useless information. Nobody had witnessed Liam's murder, nor recalled seeing anything suspicious. It was just too dark. That was the attraction of the towpath.

There was something nagging at me as well, but I couldn't quite put my finger on it. I stared into my Starbucks. The books needed to be shelved. I was desperate to dip into the Chandler, but some of my customers were particular about their books; they could tell if the pages had been turned, and did not appreciate even casual perusal. If I, the owner, read a book first, before putting it out on display, did that render it second-hand? A car surely did not become second-hand if test-driven by a showroom owner. Licking a plum and then putting it back up for sale was a whole different kettle of fish. But if you bought a mackerel and the fishmonger removed the bones for you, and he went on to make a fish soup from the bones, were you within your rights to claim ownership of the soup? And who kept fish in a kettle? And who would drink tea from water boiled in a kettle that had held fish?

Jeff said, 'So how did Alison get on?'

'FUCK!'

'What?'

'I knew I'd forgotten something! Alison! Christ!'

I grabbed my phone. No messages. I stood and pressed my face to the window. Across the road the jeweller's looked as busy as ever. But no sign of Alison.

'You spoke to her this morning, right?'

'I didn't see her this morning!'

'She left for work early, you mean?'

'No! We all split up outside the clinic last night, remember?'

'I thought you guys were more or less living to—'

'Yes! No! Sometimes! I spent half the night watching Yeschenkov's house, I was knackered, I just went on home. She sent a text at about ten saying she was outside Buddy's house, but I presumed if there was anything else to report she'd call. She didn't; I thought she must have gone on home.'

'Without checking in?'

'You know what she's like, she's a law unto herself, she has mood swings!'

'So let me get this straight. You left your pregnant girlfriend outside a suspected serial killer's house, fourteen hours ago, and you haven't heard from her since, knowing full well that she's the sort to go and find things out by herself, no matter how many times you warn her, and the guy she was following has a habit of killing people and keeping their heads in a hatbox?'

I cleared my throat.

'She's not my girlfriend,' I said.

31

I had warned her about going into caves or a haunted houses or the lair of a beast, knowing full well that given the opportunity she would ignore me. I almost expected her to do it. And better her than me. This is exactly why I don't form attachments. You give people advice and the benefit of your experience, yet they almost always let you down. People are a disaster. I should have just stayed in the shop and let her, perhaps literally, stew. God knows I had plenty of other things to be doing rather than racing across the city to rescue her. I had a new project now. Rolo. A blank canvas. When I retired, he could take over. Jeff was an idiot. Rolo I could shape.

'Just coming into Tennyson,' said Jeff. 'You can open your eyes.'

'I have a migraine coming on.'

'We haven't time for a migraine!'

Who did he think he was? He wasn't even insured for the Mystery Machine. If they pulled him in, it would serve him right. Amnesty International would deny knowing him.

Tennyson. East Belfast. Edwardian semis. Showing their age.

'There's her car.'

No trouble parking behind. Most people were at work, or parked in their drives.

'Check her car,' I said.

Jeff went. I studied the gardens. Untidy. Early daffodils. Doorbells. Sellotape, a legacy of Christmas lights. Shrink-wrapped Yellow Pages leaning against doors. Stone cladding. Leaf-stuffed drains. Jeff came back. Got in.

'Locked, no sign of her, her mobile's sitting on the passenger seat.' I could feel his eyes on me. He said, 'You okay?'

I nodded. And then I asked quietly: 'What have I done?'

'What?'

'Nothing.'

I knew she never listened, I knew she was impetuous, I knew she would poke her nose in, I knew everything, and yet I had quite happily sent her on her way. Well. There was nothing I could do about it now. What was done was done. Now all I could do was find out where she was, if she was still living, and if somehow the bookseller and the idiot could pool their talents and work out how to save her.

Okay, okay, okay, okay, okay, okay, okay: THINK.

I scanned the houses on both sides of the road. I pointed. 'It's that one.'

Three doors up from where we were, opposite side of the street.

'How . . . ?'

'She's not going to park right outside, but somewhere that gives her a good view. That narrows it down to three on either side. Whacking is not a full-time job, he doesn't rush out to work in the morning. The Yellow Pages against every door but one. They must have been delivered after people go to work. That house is the only one of the six where the directory has already been lifted in.'

'Is that it?'

I nodded.

'So what do we . . . ?'

'We wait.'

'Wait for what? We call the police, we raid, we rescue!'

'No. If she's dead already, then we're too late.'

'And what if he's caught her, and he's torturing her or worse?'

I stared at the house. It was unremarkable. As opposed to having a flashing neon sign on the roof advertising the fact that *Buddy Wailer, International Assassin and Serial Killer, lives here*. There was a car in the driveway. A Vauxhall estate. I made a mental note of the number. It wasn't personalised. A gravel driveway. Crunchy. Difficult to approach quietly.

Curtains closed downstairs and up. Small garden at the rear, another house immediately behind and overlooking.

'We wait.'

'That's all you have to say? Well I'm not sitting here. I'm going to find out.'

He clawed at the door handle.

'No!' He hesitated. 'Okay. Listen. Go next door, lift their Yellow Pages, then knock on his. If he answers just say you're delivering and wanted to check if he has one already.'

'And then what?'

'Then you walk away. We know he's in there.'

'I can't just walk away. If he answers, I'm going in. If he doesn't answer, I'm going in. The short and tall of it is, I'm going in. Man, don't you care?'

There was no simple answer.

Instead I said, 'He's a killer. If you try anything, he will kill you. Even if you had your nunchucks, he would still kill you, and disappear. That's what he does. Storming in there will not help Alison. If she's not already dead, it will speed her demise.'

'Well what, then?'

'One step at a time. Baby steps. Keep your line open and your earpiece in.'

Jeff took a deep breath. Then he got out of the car. He gave a surreptitious glance around before hurrying down the drive of the house right beside us. He lifted their Yellow Pages, stuffed it inside his jacket and retraced his steps. He nodded at me as he passed the van, then continued three doors up, crossed the road and approached the front door of the house I had identified as the lair of the Wailer.

He rang the bell. I slipped further down in my seat. I was determined to preserve the integrity of the crime-fighting service I provide. Sometimes I have to be like an army general, organising, planning and inspiring, rather than actually leading the charge. As attractive as the front line must be, there is not much sense in recklessly exposing yourself to danger or ridicule, because if you are injured or somehow incapacitated it is not merely you that suffers, but the troops, who find themselves rudderless and confused, dejected and demoralised. This is why it was important that I didn't confront Buddy Wailer myself. I didn't yet know if he was merely my enemy, or would become my lifelong nemesis. It would have been foolhardy indeed to have revealed my hand or identity so soon.

When he got no response, Jeff looked back at me and shrugged. I pushed myself up in the seat in order to shrug back.

'Okay then,' he said down the line.

'Jeff, don't do anything rash. Just . . .'

He kicked the door in. One blow. After a pause, I heard, 'Aow.'

Then: 'Going in.'

Then: 'Hall. Nothing. Lounge. Nothing. Kitchen. Table set for three. Stairs. Bedroom, double, unmade. Dresser, make-up, women's clothes, pants, scattered around. Bathroom. Bath. Mirror partially steamed up.

Second bedroom. Bed made, cold, radiator off, guest room.'

I could see him now, looking across at me from the bedroom.

'It's the wrong house, Sherlock,' he said.

Alison was in the habit of calling me Sherlock. I didn't mind her doing it. I objected to Jeff. It didn't set the right tone for an employer–employee relationship.

'It can't be,' I said. 'Check under the beds.'

He tutted. He disappeared from view. 'Nope, nothing. No . . . wait a minute. I've found them.'

'You've . . .'

'Slippers.'

'Jeff, I don't think . . .'

'FUCK!'

He had just reappeared at the window, but he suddenly threw himself down.

'What . . . *what*?'

'I saw him! The house opposite! He just passed the upstairs window . . . He's gone . . . he's in the hall. He's coming out, man, he's coming out!'

'Okay, Jeff . . . stay calm . . . I can't see . . . there's a hedge in the way . . . Do you see Alison?'

'No, just him, zipping up his jacket. He has car keys, going to his garage . . . he's leaving . . . what do we do, what do we do?'

'I'm thinking . . .'

'THINK! The garage doors are opening!'

'Okay . . . okay . . . get back here, get back here and you take the van and follow him . . .'

'Me? But you're . . .'

'Listen to me! You have to do it! You can drive fast, you have eyesight, it needs to be you. I'll search his house. If Alison's alive, we'll follow in her car; if she's dead, we'll bring in the cops and we'll know where he is.'

'And if she's in the van?'

'Jeff, for fuck's sake, use your initiative!'

'You're always telling me not to . . .'

'This is different! Now get out here!'

Buddy Wailer drove past. He was focused on the road. His white van had plenty of room in the back for furniture, bricks, wood, tyres, concrete, vases, books, agricultural machinery, livestock, mirrors, telescopes, water features, national costumes, irrigation equipment, curtains, legal documents, photocopiers, computers, lentils, lintels, lemons, lubricants and lepers. Or Alison and my baby. Two for the price of one.

Jeff was across the road. I jumped out, he jumped in, he took off, I stood there. I was a leader, not a follower. I gave commands. I wasn't being a coward. My instinct told me she was in the house. My instinct is never wrong.

Except when it is.

Buddy Wailer had locked the doors. Just because he was a psychotic killer didn't mean he wasn't security-conscious. People talk a lot about the old days when you could leave your back door open, as if there weren't mad people roaming the world back then. The difference then was that people would leave the back door open, get raped and pillaged, and then just not talk about it, thus propagating the myth that you really could leave your door open.

I looked around the outside of the house. There were no handy windows open. I would have to kick the back door in, but with my wasting disease, brittle bones, and the metal from the screws of the Latham device they had inserted in my face to offset my cleft palate still playing havoc with my taste buds, it was easier said than done.

I kicked at it three times, but the door didn't seem to notice.

Then I lifted the doormat and picked up the back-door key.

The kitchen was gloomy, blocked from direct sunlight by the house behind. It was spotless.

I stood listening.

Complete silence.

Nothing.

I moved into the hall. There was a lounge to the left. Neat. Tidy. Walk-through into dining room. Pristine.

I paused at the bottom of the stairs.

'Hello?'

I listened.

Everything about the house felt menacing.

In a movie, the music sets the tone.

No music sets its own tone.

There was probably no need for me to go upstairs. If she was around, she would have answered.

I would be better off getting back to the shop. There were probably customers waiting. Rolo, maybe. What if he returned eager to try something else and I wasn't there and he gave up and returned to a life of crime? I should be there. I had a responsibility.

There was an odd smell.

I couldn't place it. It wasn't horrible. But it could easily be something you spray to cover up something horrible.

Upstairs: gloomier still. Doors closed.

I had wasted my breath warning Alison not to enter a cave, and now here I was, in the cave. I should get out and call for help. This wasn't my game. I solve puzzles. I don't confront. I suffer from arachnophobia. I am also scared of people who suffer from arachnophobia. They haven't invented a name for that yet.

I stood on the first step. Light switch. Flipped on. Brighter, but didn't help much. Buddy could return at any moment. He probably had slippers for walking on gravel so that he could sneak up unawares. He would shoot me and cut off my head.

Second step. Three, four, five, six. I peered between the banister slats. Landing, another flight, hall, four doors off. I made the landing. Three of the four doors were closed. The half-open one was at the end of the hall; the room beyond was sunlit.

I was drawn towards the light. Sunlight ought to be good and pure.

It isn't always.

I recognised the smell. Alison's perfume.

No. Not her perfume. Her deodorant.

I was almost overcome by dread. I wasn't even aware of moving my legs. I was on castors and being inexorably pulled towards the room by a demon's string balls. The half-open door showed me a wardrobe and the corner of a bed.

I pushed the door fully open.

At the foot of the neatly made double bed: a hatbox.

Ribbon on top.

'No,' I said.

I dropped to my knees.

Buddy Wailer had left me a present.

32

Open the box. Don't open the box. Open the box. Don't open the box. Open the box. Don't open the box. Open the box. Don't open the box. Open the box. Don't open the box. Open the box. Don't open the box. Don't open the box. Don't open the box. Don't open the box. Don't open the box.

Open the box.

I opened the box, and I screamed.

Not because of what was in it. It was empty. But because of the hand that was brought down firmly on my shoulder just as the top came off.

And when I'd finished screaming and hurling myself across the room, trying to hide in a sock drawer, I was stopped in my tracks by:

'Where THE FUCK were you?'

Alison, glaring at me.

'I was . . .'

'I was stuck in that cupboard all night! All night with that monster in the same room!'

'I'm sorry, I . . .'

'I had to pee in his slippers!'

'I'm sorry, I . . .'

'You're a complete waste of space!'

And then, thankfully, she broke down. She began to cry and shudder and I hesitantly took her in my arms. She still managed to raise her fist and beat it weakly against my chest, which was, frankly, rather ungrateful of her, seeing as how I was there now, and also, just as frankly, rather dangerous, given the paper-thinness of my chest and the combustible nature of my ribs.

I said, 'It's okay,' and patted her back.

She said, 'Where were you? I was so scared . . .'

'I did my best . . .'

'All night . . . all night . . . I saw her . . . oh God, I saw her . . .'

'Saw . . . ?'

'Arabella . . .'

'Arabella! Where?' She pointed. 'On the bed? In . . . the box?'

She nodded. 'It was horrible, horrible . . . I know I shouldn't have come in, but when I saw him leave, I couldn't help myself . . . I just couldn't . . . He left his back-door key under the mat, if it hadn't been there I wouldn't have . . . but I went in, and it was just like a normal house . . . until I came upstairs . . .

and I came in here . . . and the box was on the bed . . . and I couldn't resist it and . . . Jesus . . . I opened it, and her head was in there, smiling up at me . . . and I screamed and I remember . . . staggering back . . . and then knowing I had to get out of there . . . but in my panic I missed the stairs, I ran into the other bedroom . . . and the rest of her, fucking hell . . . the rest of her was lying on the bed . . .'

'The rest of . . . ?'

'Headless!'

She cried against me, big, heaving, snottery sobs. I held her as tightly as my weak arms would allow.

I've read enough crime fiction to know what Buddy was up to. Arabella had been dead for some considerable time, yet there was no smell beyond Alison's deodorant. Although I knew it offered twenty-four-hour protection, the smell of death is not one that can so easily be covered up. Buddy had murdered Augustine and Liam because he had been professionally engaged to do so. He may or may not have murdered Arabella, but he had indisputably come into the possession of her body. Perhaps he had been ordered to dispose of it and couldn't because he had a thing for women's corpses. For Arabella not to have become a rotting, glutinous, maggot-ridden mess by now meant that he was using chemicals to preserve her. Either he had some training as an undertaker or he had developed an interest in their methods.

As I rubbed Alison's back gently, I became aware that my fingers felt quite sticky. When I examined them over her shoulder, I saw that they were partially coated in some kind of residue. I looked across at the empty box on the bed and saw that there was a similar-looking smear on the lip of the lid. It was, I feared, essence of Arabella. It was all I could do to stop myself from throwing up down Alison's back. Instead I quietly rubbed it off on her blouse and forced myself to focus on the case.

'Which room is Arabella's . . . torso in?' I asked softly.

Alison snorted up. 'She isn't. He was sleeping in here . . . all night I was trying not to breathe . . . There was a phone call about half an hour ago . . . I couldn't hear what was said, but it seemed to panic him . . . and I could see a tiny bit out of the hinges . . . He took her head out . . . Jesus, I saw him carrying Arabella by her hair . . . and then I could hear him dragging something, and the front door slammed and I took the chance to get out and I saw him drive off. I just wanted out . . . but I couldn't help but look in the other room, and she's gone, he's taken her with him, and then I heard the key in the door again and I thought he'd forgotten something and I'd blown my chance to escape . . . but it was you, thank God it was you . . . He's away now, he's escaped and maybe we'll never . . .'

'No,' I said confidently, 'he hasn't escaped. We have him.'

'Have' was, of course, a little wide of the mark. We had a rough idea of where he was because Jeff had followed him, but being in the Mystery Machine meant that he couldn't get too close, particularly when Buddy's route took him out of the city and into the country. Jeff had to drop back, and he almost lost him on several occasions, but now he was back on track. *Literally* on track.

'You're where?' I asked.

'Tollymore.'

'The forest park?'

'The very one. He paid his fiver to get in, but he's gone off the roads open to tourists; he's on tracks the park keepers and woodsmen must use. I don't know whether to follow or what?'

We were in Alison's VW. She was still badly shaken, but preferred to drive rather than meander along with me in control. Tollymore was about thirty minutes away – with a normal person driving – just outside of Newcastle at the foot of the majestic Mourne Mountains. I say majestic because it says that on the internet, but in reality they're just dark and brooding lumps of rock, and they terrify me. It is mostly their height, but also their past life as volcanoes, and the knowledge that they could, despite what the so-called experts say, erupt at any moment, drowning me in lava. Tollymore itself has hundreds of thousands of pine trees standing so densely that sunlight cannot penetrate, which, together with the plentiful water running off the *majestic* mountains, encourages the growth of vast carpets of moss on the forest floor. There are also countless billions of twigs. Twigs can put your eye out, and do. A forest with moss and twigs and mountains looming over is my idea of hell.

But home from home for a demon like Buddy Wailer.

We would follow him into that hell, though I might wait in the car.

'Hello?' Jeff shouted. 'Anyone at home?'

'What does he want?' Alison asked.

'He wants to know if he should follow Buddy into the forest.'

'And what do we think?'

'We think you should keep your eye on the road. This isn't one of those movies where we can have a conversation where you look at me the whole time and traffic just magically avoids you. Keep your eyes . . .'

'All right!'

'Will you make your minds up!' Jeff yelled. I held the phone away from my ear, both to protect my fragile drum and to allow Alison to hear. 'Oh, wait – he's stopping. Hold on. Let me just pull in . . . here . . . Okay, don't think he can see me . . . He's getting out . . . looking around . . . Nope, he can't see me . . . He's going to the back of his van, opening up . . . pulling out . . . two black bin bags . . . I think . . . something heavy anyway . . . dragging them into the trees . . . He's . . . he's . . . he's disappeared now. Seems like a long way to come fly-tipping.'

'It's Arabella, Jeff,' said Alison.

'What's Arabella?'

'In the bags.'

'Oh. *Both* the bags?'

'Both the bags.'

We could hear him inhaling deeply. 'Oh lordy. What am I supposed to do now?'

'In an ideal world,' I said, 'you would catch him red-handed, subdue him, get him to confess, and keep him there until the police arrive.'

'Unfortunately,' said Alison, and left it at that. She looked at me. 'Well, MacGyver, you're the expert, what do you think? He's burying the evidence, right?'

'Yeah,' I said. And then: 'Jeff, stay where you are, we'll call you back in five.'

'But . . .'

I cut the line. I began to punch in numbers.

Alison said, 'What are you . . . ? Are you chickening out and calling Robinson?'

I shook my head. Before I pushed the call button I said: 'What did I do before we left Buddy's house?'

She began to shake her head, but then it came to her. 'You went to the bathroom to wash your hands, and then when I told you to hurry up, you said you couldn't, you had to use the toilet, your irritable bowel was playing up. How the hell does that . . . ?'

'While I was sitting on the throne I noticed that he had a phone extension in there. I remembered you said he got a call that panicked him. So having nothing better to do while waiting for plop, I called 1471 and got the number of the last person who called. And now I'm about to find out who it was. You see, you think I'm just having a poo, but I'm always working something out.'

I pushed the button. It rang five times. Then it went to answerphone. The message, delivered in a familiar voice, said, 'Hi, you're through to Pearl. I can't talk to you right now, but please leave me your number and I'll get right back to you.'

I chose not to. I cut the line.

'Pearl,' I said.

'As in Knecklass? The trampy vampy?'

'The very one. She calls Buddy, tells him to bury the evidence. Buddy's American. We know he's a professional, he's surely buried bodies before, but he can't know over here that well, so how come he drives straight to Tollymore?'

'Because she told him where to go.'

'Exactly.'

My phone rang. I answered with: 'Jeff, I said give us five . . .'

'Hey, I recognise that voice.'

It was Pearl, with the same trick as mine. It wasn't much of a trick. In fact, it was no trick at all. People did it all the time, every day. It was a useful service provided by a forward-thinking telecommunications company. Useful things can fuck you up pretty easily.

'Is that Pearl?' I said. I made big eyes at Alison. She made them back. Pearl was in a car, somewhere; I could hear traffic, her indicators, a radio. 'Funny, I was just calling you.'

'Yes, I know. You didn't leave a message.'

'Well I hate those things. How's it going?'

'Yeah, great. I haven't heard from you in ages; are we still friends?'

'Yes, of course,' I said.

'Special friends?' she purred.

'Definitely.'

Alison's ear couldn't have been any closer.

'You calling about the case?' Pearl asked.

'What case?'

'Hey, stop messing! *The* case. Augustine!'

'Oh, that, no, I wasn't calling about that. Just wondering how you were.'

'Aw, isn't that sweet? You know me, busy as ever, out on the road. Clinic business.'

'Really? I thought you were just the receptionist.'

'Oh, you're so cheeky. I am, but I do sales, and give talks to women's groups. Times are hard, sometimes you gotta drum up business. They even call me a director, but do you think I have shares? Not a chance. What about you? You sound like you're driving too.'

'Yeah, out on the road, looking through some book collections down Newcastle way.'

Alison looked at me. She could look all she wanted. I was immune.

'Newcastle . . . really? A long way to go for books.'

'Yeah, I know. There's thousands of them to go through. Sometimes you can't see the wood for the trees, but if you stick with it, usually you find exactly what you're looking for.'

Her voice had lost a little of its chirpiness. She said,

'I thought we were going to work together on this case.'

'So did I,' I said. 'Been kind of busy.'

'I get the feeling you're avoiding me.'

'Me? Never. Didn't we just agree we were special friends? You know I'd give you my last Rolo.'

Under her breath Alison said, 'Jesus, subtle as a brick.'

'Anyway,' I said before Pearl could come back, 'gotta go, traffic's a bit mad, not even out of Belfast yet. Sure, call in and see me some time; now I know the type of books you like, I can keep you well supplied.'

She was just starting to say: 'Maybe we could meet . . .' when I hung up.

I looked at Alison. She gave me her disgusted eyes, which were just like her normal eyes, but disgusted.

'You got rid of her pretty quick,' she snapped.

'Yes, I . . .'

'Something to hide?'

'What?'

'She's the one you really want.'

'What are you talking about?'

'I see the way you go all gloopy when you speak to her, and your cheeks go all red.'

'Would you ever wise up?'

'Don't tell me to wise up!'

'Okay, okay! I wasn't . . . she isn't . . .'

Alison took a deep breath. We picked up speed.

'It's just the case,' I said.

'Uhuh. Whatever you say. So why did you have to

tip her off? The first thing she's going to do is phone Buddy and warn him we're in the area. It sounds to me like you're in league together.'

'She's not going to warn Buddy about anything.'

'You know her that well, do you?'

'Yes. No. Just think about it, Alison, would you? Buddy could bury the evidence anywhere, but she's directed him to the most out-of-the-way place you can imagine. Why?'

'*Because* it's out of the way, knucklehead; nobody will ever find the body!'

'Yes, granted, partly. But there's *more* to it than that. As soon as I mentioned Newcastle, you could hear it in her voice. She's on her way to meet him, and I don't think he's digging a hole for just one body; I think he's digging it for two.'

'For *Pearl*?'

'No! For himself, though he doesn't know it yet. He's killed Augustine, he's killed Liam, but he didn't kill Arabella. Instead of getting rid of her, he's *preserved* her, and worse than that, he's left her lying around the house. They must know he's a liability and they know we're closing in and the police are sniffing around, so they're having to act fast. They've sent him down to Tollymore to bury Arabella, and Pearl comes down to supervise and pay him off, maybe lull him into a false sense of security by throwing in a little action as well. She's a femme fatale, Alison, that's what they do. One minute she'll be puckering up, thanking him for a job well done, next she'll be sliding a blade between his ribs.'

'You're always thinking about her and sex.'

'I'm just saying . . .'

My phone rang. Before I could answer it, Alison let go of the steering wheel, grabbed my hand and bent my fingers back until I screamed and released it. She swapped it to her right hand, but as I lunged after it, she pushed her left hand into my face. I peeled her fingers away from my eyes and twisted them back until she yelped. I made another grab for the phone but she slapped my hand aside and elbowed me in the face. As I cradled my already damaged nose, Alison answered the still ringing phone by yelling: 'Keep away from my man, sugar tits!'

I could just about hear Jeff shouting, 'What the fu . . . ?' in response as we mounted the kerb and slammed straight into a bright red Royal Mail postbox.

Our airbags erupted.

From somewhere south of consciousness I heard Alison cry, 'I'm hormonal!' before everything went dark.

33

We were fortunate, in a way, that the police no longer send patrols out into the countryside. Out there, it's the law of the meadow.

The only witness to our collision with a Royal Mail postbox was an elderly woman who lived in one of a row of cottages opposite it. She came scurrying out as best she could and helped us out of Alison's car. Or so I'm told. I was unconscious. Together, the old woman with the one leg – did I mention that? – and the moderately pregnant Alison dragged me out and laid me on the side of the road. Alison, knowing me too well, refused to give me the kiss of life, so the old woman knelt over me and pressed her lips to mine, which meant that not only did I get a lungful of old woman's breath, but also several crumbs of slightly stale short-bread. No one can say country folk aren't generous.

Her affections, for there was certainly a little tongue

action, absolutely brought me round, enough to appreciate that I was in considerable pain, having been elbowed on my broken nose by Alison and then assaulted by an airbag. Alison curled her lip up at me and said, 'It wasn't that bad, lightweight.'

I growled at her that it was entirely her fault, and she snapped back, 'So? What's your point?'

'That's my point!'

'So? What's your point in making that point?'

'That's just . . . stupid talk.'

'Oh, I'm stupid now?'

The old woman looked from Alison to me and shook her head. She rolled her eyes, though I'm not sure if that was voluntary or not. She said, 'Ah, I remember young love.' She must have had a good memory. She shepherded us into her cottage. It was full of china. She made us a cup of tea. While she was in the kitchen, I said, 'Is the baby all right?'

'For all you care.'

I sighed. 'And the car?'

'Oh, get your priorities right!'

'I did!'

'Yeah, right.'

She was fuming.

I said, 'I know you're upset with yourself.'

'Oh, fuck off.'

The woman came back in with a tray. There was shortbread. I felt sick. She said, 'They collect the post in about half an hour. If you want to make a clean getaway, you'd better get moving soon.'

I looked at Alison. 'We better. We have things to do.'

She nodded. She was settling down. She came over and gave me a hug.

'Sorry,' she said.

The old woman looked moist-eyed. She probably always looked moist-eyed.

The front of the VW was badly staved in. But it started first time.

Alison reversed, then got out and we examined the damage to the postbox together. 'There's not a scratch on it! It's a miracle!'

'Not really,' I said. 'It's a Jubilee pillar box dating from 1887. When the IRA bombed the Arndale shopping centre in Manchester in 1996, just about the only thing that survived unscathed was a Victorian box exactly like this. They're built to last.'

'You,' Alison said, 'know far too much crap.'

'It's why you love me,' I said.

I was slowly learning that like the worst kind of soap-opera actor, Alison had a limited range of looks. The same expression seemed to cover love, loss, tragedy, elation and hatred, and so was always open to misinterpretation. Often no reaction was the best policy, so I ignored her and got into the car and waved goodbye to the old woman whose tongue I had so recently played host to.

All told, between the crash, the aftermath and the tea in china cups, we had lost about an hour, and we were still twenty minutes away from Tollymore. Besides my fractured skull and internal injuries, and the staved-in front and the cracked window, the only other damage was to my mobile phone. It looked perfectly fine, but, like Sophia Loren, was otherwise dead.

'Effing brilliant,' I said as we drove. I had already taken the SIM card out and rubbed it like an expert, and replaced it to absolutely no effect. 'What are we supposed to do now? How're we meant to find Jeff? What if he's been trying to call us and . . .'

Alison's hand snaked into her handbag. Thankfully her lesson was learned and her eyes did not once deviate from the road ahead. She still managed to produce her own phone and hand it to me with a theatrical '*Duh!*'

I examined it. 'There are no messages from Jeff,' I said, 'but there are dozens of texts from Brian.'

Her face coloured slightly. 'Why don't you mind your own beeswax and just call him?'

'Brian?'

'Jeff! Honest to God . . .'

I called him. There was no response. It gave me the option of leaving a message. I chose not to, in case his phone now lay in enemy hands.

'What do we do now?' Alison asked. 'Drive around Tollymore looking for him? It's huge, and he was supposed to be hiding, and it'll be getting dark soon.'

'I don't see what else we can do.'

So that's what we did. It wasn't much of a plan.

We drove for the next ten minutes in silence. Then I asked Alison how come all the texts from Brian.

'He's my ex, and we're not enemies, and he has issues.'

'What kind of issues?'

'Hating you issues.'

'He can't handle that you chose the better man.'

'I didn't choose the better man. I chose a different man.'

'Same difference,' I said.

'I can easily change my mind,' she said.

I snorted. 'Yeah, right.'

She looked at me. I looked back.

I said, 'When I was unconscious, I dreamt that I was trapped on the golf driving range at Blackheath, and Dr Yes was firing giant balls at me, and they were exploding, and getting closer and closer, and he kept shouting *four!* and *four!* and *four!* until the very last one came right at me and it was about to blow me into little pieces, and he shouted *five!* What do you think that means?'

'Baby's fine,' said Alison.

We stopped at the gate leading into Tollymore. It was a National Trust forest park. I didn't trust them. They were do-gooders and jobsworths and holier-than-thousers. Places should be allowed to fall into disrepair. Forests should burn. God created woodworm and arsonists. The man in the yellow jacket said, 'It's a fiver and we're closing in half an hour.'

'That's fine,' Alison said, handing over the money out of her window.

We drove the official roads within the park until we came to the end of them. There were locked gates, supposedly to stop you going further, but you could drive around them. So we did. The fiver also gave us a map, and the tracks, ostensibly for walking, were clearly marked upon them. I had it open on my lap. I told Alison there were dozens of tracks covering hundreds of miles, if you added them all up. She asked where we should start. I said at the very beginning. She said that was a very good place to start. By the end of the first stretch we were well into *The Sound of Music* soundtrack. She had a voice that could pickle eggs. But together we sounded like Sonny and Cher, if someone had taken a mallet to Cher. We were looking for killers, and our silent friend, in hostile country full of moss and twigs. The singing was a way to mask our fear. We knew that. And sang louder.

The tracks were rough and strewn with boulders, and the VW rattled and clanked. We crissed and we crossed. The trees were dense and the sun was blocked out by the mountains, so it was dark and getting darker. The last few walkers were making their way back to the entrance; any we saw we stopped and asked if they'd seen the Mystery Machine, but no luck, at least until some superannuated Scout, all kitted out for an assault on Everest, appeared suddenly out of the murk and nearly paid for it with his life. As he dragged himself out of the brambles, Alison repeated the question, prefacing it with a lazy 'sorry', and he surprised us by saying yes, he had seen it, parked about half a mile further up, partially hidden amongst the trees. We asked if there'd been any signs of life about it and he said he had been reluctant to approach in case the occupants were, you know . . .

'Screwing,' said Alison.

'Making love,' said the Scout.

'That's what I said,' said Alison.

We drove on. After *exactly* half a mile, we stopped. I'm good with distances. It comes with thirty years of counting footsteps, and recording them in my ledger. The problem was that the Scout didn't have my talent for it, so his observation was just a guesstimate. It was now pitch black. We couldn't see the van. We couldn't see *anything*.

'What now?' I said.

'Spare keys for the Mystery Machine?'

'Don't call it that,' I said, though I did myself, in secret. 'And of course.'

I had three spare sets about my person, because you can't be too careful. I gave her a set, and she got out, and I got out and stood beside her, and she pointed them into the trees and moved them across 180 degrees, pushing the unlock button repeatedly.

Nothing.

I said, 'Give them here.'

'I've already . . . please don't click your fingers at me.'

'Then hand them over.'

Alison did her eye-rolling thing before dumping them into the palm of my hand. I selected the right key, before raising it and pointing it at my head. I pushed the button, and two hundred yards away the lights of the Mystery Machine automatically switched on as it unlocked itself.

Alison's mouth dropped open. 'How *the fuck* did you do that?'

I smiled. 'It's quite simple, on my planet.'

It is good to keep some mystery. It literally isn't rocket science. The key fob is basically a low-power transmitter that functions on a line-of-sight basis. As with any transmitter, the higher the antenna is, the further the signal travels. Thus pointing it at my head might have seemed like I had a mechanical brain capable of amazing technological feats, but I was just using common sense.

Alison said, 'Yeah, right.'

She went to her boot and rummaged around before producing a flashlight. She locked the car and started walking towards the Mystery Machine. I followed, but stayed well behind. If there was going to be any shooting, they would go for the light first.

With the lights of the van on, we could tell from some distance that it was empty. When we got there, we checked the back just in case Jeff had taken refuge there or his body had been dumped inside.

Nothing.

'Now what?' Alison asked. 'It's not like there's even trampled grass or anything to follow his tracks.'

No tracks, but ample moss. I had already sneezed a dozen times. The moss was soft but spongy. You would make an impression if you stepped on it, but it would quickly spring back into shape, like a community of travellers ejecting a truancy officer.

I clicked my fingers again. She gave me the torch, and another warning. I did a 360-degree sweep. Jeff was my assistant, my helper, he was the sorcerer's apprentice; he would know better than to desert the Mystery Machine in the middle of nowhere without leaving some kind of message. Quite possibly he *had* left one, on my dead phone. But equally, when he couldn't get through to speak to me, he should have surmised that something untoward had happened, and therefore sought another means to convey his intentions. That is, if they were *his* intentions, and he hadn't been forced away.

Alison was just saying, 'There's no point, we'll never . . .' when my third sweep found it, and I signalled for her to follow. It was sitting roughly eleven point seven metres into the trees, at thirty-eight degrees from the manufacturer's trademark in the centre of the MM bonnet.

Alison stared down at it. 'It's just a sweetie paper.'
'No, it's an Opal Fruit wrapper . . . an orange one . . .'
'You mean Star—'
'And if I'm not mistaken . . .'
The flashlight beam picked up a second, a lime-green one, twenty metres further into the trees.
'This way,' I said.

There was a third and a fourth, and before very long we'd left the track and the MM far behind. The paper trail was smart thinking on Jeff's part, thinking no doubt enabled by the sweets themselves, a splendid source of vitamin C.

Alison caught up with me where I'd stopped, and asked why I had.

'This is the last one.' It was another orange paper.

'How do you . . . ? Oh – I get it, six, that's all there is in the packet? I thought there was more . . . ?'

'There's nine. But I make him take the blackcurrant ones out and throw them away; they're not one of the original flavours and I won't have them in the shop.'

'Because . . . ? Oh, bugger *because*. Whatever you say. So what do we do now that we're in the middle of . . . what's that smell?'

I normally have a very acute sense of smell. I have to, with my allergies. But repeated bashings of my nose, with the resultant swelling and bleeding, had impaired my smellbuds. Alison was getting something I wasn't.

'Smoke,' she said, answering her own question. She knocked off the flashlight and we both peered ahead. There was a wavering pinprick of light just visible through the trees.

'Keep it off,' I said.

We advanced. The only way I could avoid sneezing was by holding my nose. My nose hurt. I was a martyr to the cause. We drew closer. Spring had not yet advanced sufficiently towards summer to render the twigs dry enough to snap underfoot, while the moss acted as an efficient muffler. We got close enough to establish that there was a bonfire, and that there was a figure sitting on a log beside it. As we drew further in, we realised that that figure was Jeff.

We stopped.

Alison whispered, 'What if it's a trap?'

Jeff laughed abruptly. 'I can hear you!'

It might have been the cool, crisp mountain air carrying Alison's words to him with such clarity. Most likely, though, it was the higher state of enlightenment that came with the huge joint he was smoking.

I called: 'Is it safe?'

'Is what safe?'

'To approach!'

'Yes!'

'You're sure?'

'Yes!'

'If it was a trap, you would say that!'

'Good point!'

If it was a trap, they would have us anyway. I couldn't run for toffee, and gasping for air would only lead to me inhaling even more moss molecules, which would cause me to expand to the size of a Zeppelin.

Alison went forward first. When she failed to be shot, stabbed or pounced upon, I emerged into the firelight.

Jeff waved us closer. 'Pull up a log,' he said.

We stood, warily. He was very relaxed. We were not. We peered into the darkness.

'Jeff,' said Alison, 'what's going on? Where are they?'

'They? Oh, here, there, everywhere. They buzz, but they're not mosquitoes.'

I took a step towards him. 'Jeff . . .'

Jeff suddenly pulled his hands up to guard his face. 'Don't hit me!' he cried. 'You're always hitting me!'

'Jeff, for goodness' . . .'

Alison swept past me and put a protective arm around him. When he had settled sufficiently, she gently peeled his fingers back. 'Jeff, baby,' she purred, 'he's not going to hit you.' And then she snapped the joint out of his hand and tossed it into the fire. 'But I fucking will if you don't wise up. Do you hear?'

Jeff cowered down. 'I hear! Okay! Sorry! There was no need to . . .' He looked wistfully after the joint. His eyes flitted up to me. 'Where were you? I waited and waited . . .'

'Jeff,' said Alison, lowering herself on to the log beside him, 'tell us what happened.'

He nodded. He looked at me again.

Alison snapped: 'Do you think you could sit? You're making him nervous.'

There was another log. I rolled it closer with my foot, and then positioned it more carefully with my hands. I wanted the heat from the fire, but I didn't want to be so close that a spark could set my hair alight. I have precious little of it as it is. When I took my hands away they were smeared with gunk. Being short of my usual packet of baby wipes, I wiped them on my trousers. The countryside is *disgusting*.

Jeff stared into the fire. As I sat, I said, 'Jeff . . .

Jeff?' His eyes didn't move. 'Did you see Pearl? Was Pearl here?' I was aware of Alison's eyes upon me, but the question had to be asked. It was no time for jealousy. I had a case to crack.

'Pearl?' Jeff answered vaguely. 'Pearl the singer?'

'No . . . Pearl from the clinic . . .' I was trying to remember if he had ever actually laid eyes on her. 'Pearl . . . she's like a model, really good-looking.'

'Will you just let him tell us what happened?' Alison snapped.

'I'm trying to . . .'

'Then shut up and let him do it in his own words. Jeff? Do you want to tell us? Was Buddy here? Buddy Wailer?'

'The long tall thin man . . . yeah . . . Bunny was here . . .'

'Buddy,' said Alison.

'Yeah, Bunny. I followed Bunny.'

'Buddy,' I said.

'Shhhhh,' scolded Alison. 'You followed . . . ?'

'I followed Bunny. He was dragging the bags, I followed him into the trees. The trees. Like giant Ents, but . . . *trees*. I couldn't get too close . . . He was gathering wood . . . wood for a fire . . . wood for *this* fire . . . and I had to hide 'cos he couldn't get it lit and he went back to his car for petrol . . . and he nearly saw me . . . the big, tall, thin man nearly stepped on me . . . but he didn't and he came back and he lit his fire and he threw the bags on it and some more petrol and up they whooshed . . . and the sparks just . . .

fizzled up into the trees and the branches . . . and the hair of the Ents . . . but then, but then there was someone else there . . .'

'Pearl?' I said.

'No . . . no . . . not the singer . . . a fella, a man . . . I couldn't really see . . . I knew it was the big tall thin fella because I'd followed him, but in here, in the dark, but with the fire, it was all kind of brighty-dark so it was hard to tell . . .'

'Silhouettes,' suggested Alison.

'That's the one . . .'

'Was it Dr Yeschenkov?' I asked.

'Didn't you just hear him say he couldn't see because of the brighty-dark?'

'Okay, keep your hair on. Go on, Jeff, before you were so rudely . . .'

'She wasn't rude, she means well; she's really quite lovely, aren't you?'

'Yes, Jeff . . . you were saying . . . ?'

'Oh yeah, the fight . . .'

'What fight?' I asked.

'Between him and him. The longy tally fella and the newy fella . . . I wasn't close enough to hear . . . but they were arguing . . . and then there was . . . it . . . you know . . . *it* . . . and I knew I had to get out of there . . .'

'*It*, Jeff?' I said.

'Yes, exactly, a gunshot . . . so I went back to the van and waited there . . . and after a bit I saw lights coming towards me, so I keep my head down and a car drives past . . . but I don't see who it is . . . and then everything's dead quiet, and kind of spooky, and so I light up my gear just to chill a bit, you know, and then when I'm chilled enough I wander back over here, and sit by the fire, and have another one, and think about things, you know, and how pointless it all is and how we should all just love each other, you know? I might have had an E as well.'

He began to look around his feet, thinking that he'd dropped his spliff. Alison prodded him and said, 'Jeff . . . if someone was shot . . . and someone drove off . . . was there not a body?'

'What . . . ?'

'Was there no body when you got back here?'

'Oh, body, yeah . . . there's one kind of over there a bit . . .' He waved his hand somewhere behind him.

'Jeff! Who is it?'

'Did I drop . . . ?'

He was, as they say, away with the fairies. And as far as I was concerned, they could keep him.

Alison flicked the flashlight back on. I pointed down. There were drag marks through the moss and twigs, leading up a short rise, and then down the other side. At the bottom, someone, the killer, had made a half-arsed attempt to cover up the body with fallen pine branches, but even without the torchlight, the size and shape of his ad hoc burial mound would have made it stand out from its surroundings.

Alison said, 'We should leave it to Forensics.'

'Yep, or we'll be contaminating a crime scene.'

'Poor Bunny,' said Alison.

'Don't you start. Anyway, it might not be him.'

'Who is it then, Pearl in man drag?'

'Stranger things.'

'It's Buddy all right; look at the length of him.'

'Lived by the gun, died by the gun.'

'If he has a phone on him, it may contain vital evidence. Who set him up. Who the killer was.'

'All sorts of shit,' agreed Alison.

'And meanwhile the killer is getting away.'

'Time is of the essence.'

'So we'd be within our rights.'

'And we'll only contaminate it a little tiny bit.'

We were in agreement. We looked down at the branches.

Alison said, 'So?'

I looked at her. 'With these allergies?'

She sighed. She crouched down and began to remove the covering. In a few moments there was only one branch remaining, the one obscuring his face.

'Well, are you ready for your big reveal?' Alison asked.

'Just do it,' I said.

She did it.

We gazed at his still, pale face.

And then Alison said, 'Who the fuck's that?'

'Rolo,' I said.

34

Alison led, and sped, and I brought up the very distant rear. I had to cope with the oncoming lights and an inability to go above thirty. Jeff lay snoring in the back of the van, only emerging from his dope sleep on particularly sharp bends for long enough to tell me how much he loved me. We had decided to get out of Tollymore fast and thus reduce the risk of being framed, blamed, seized or ambushed. We agreed to leave the metaphorical post-mortem until we got back to my place.

By the time I arrived, Alison had been pacing about in front of the house for some considerable time. *Obviously* I have not given her a key, but the front door was *already open* and there were lights on within.

I joined her. 'Did you . . . ?'

'No! I've learned my lesson. This one you can do by yourself.'

Jeff clambered out of the back of the van and stumbled across to us. He put his head on my shoulder and went back to sleep. I moved to one side and let him slump to the footpath.

The door did not look as if it had been forced. Equally, nobody else has access to the nineteen keys required to gain entrance. The lights were on upstairs *and* downstairs, something I would never be guilty of.

'If it's a trap,' I said, 'they, he or she wouldn't have left the door open. Or maybe that's what they, he or she want us to think.'

'A double bluff.'

'No, just a bluff.'

Alison nodded. 'You're right. We use double bluff too easily. It's just a bluff. But we can argue semantics all night; they don't get us in there to find out.'

'They're not semantics,' I said.

There was, of course, an obvious solution, and it was so apparent that we didn't even have to say it; we only had to look at each other and nod.

We hauled Jeff to his feet.

'Jeff, honey,' said Alison, 'go on in and have a wee lie-down.'

He mumbled, 'Okay . . . okay . . . thank you . . . just a wee . . .' and made his way groggily up the steps and through the open door.

He disappeared from view. No shot rang out. There were no obvious sounds of a struggle, though a squirrel with a peashooter could have felled him without much of a problem.

'What now?' Alison asked. 'Could still be a bluff. They, she or he might be holding him down, covering his mouth, or they, she or he could have just slit his throat.'

'We could call Robinson.'

'It might *be* Robinson.'

'Could be Buddy.'

'Maybe Buddy wasn't the problem; maybe your mate Rolo was the problem, and they decided to kill two birds with one stone. Burn Arabella and shoot Rolo.'

'Then why not bury them both? Or burn them both?'

'I don't know.'

'There's something we're not getting.'

'There's a lot we're not getting.'

'Maybe the answer's waiting in there.'

'Maybe it is.'

We both stared at the house.

Alison said, 'I'm not going in, I'm pregnant.'

'It's not a disability, you know. You lot spend long enough whining for equality, but when it's presented to you on a plate, you complain about the plate.'

'You're such a coward.'

'It's my heart.'

'Your heart will still be beating long after I'm gone.'

'That would be the pacemaker.'

But then there was a blood-curdling scream.

And all the more blood-curdling for being from a familiar source.

'GET OUT OF MY BED, YOU FUCKING RAPIST!'
Mother was home.

She said she'd escaped from the Sunny D, but I
thought it was altogether more likely that they had
dumped her back whence she came. Her clothes
were in bin bags in the hall beside her wheelchair.
She had dragged herself up three flights of stairs to
climb into her bed, she claimed, though I thought it
more likely that she had walked up quite normally,
as I knew she was capable of it. Judging from the ash
and butts, she had stopped on each of the landings for a cigarette. Beside her bed was a half-drunk
bottle of sherry, and on the floor, out cold, was
Jeff.

'I didn't push him,' she said unconvincingly. 'He
fell. Is he another one of your sex partners?'

'Mother, I don't have any . . .'

'And what sort of a state have you left my house
in? Everything's everywhere. It's disgusting.'

Mother knew all about disgusting, but this time she
was wrong. 'Mother, you know I have ASD; everything is the opposite of everywhere.'

'That's you all over, always contrary. Look at the
state of you: dirty stains everywhere, tramping them
into my lovely house . . .'

She had a point. I'd wiped my hands on my trousers
out in the forest but not noticed in the dark the mess
I was making. The gunk had dried into a waxy substance
that I could have scraped off with my fingernail, if I'd

had any. I would have to burn the trousers. They were infected now.

'Mother, how did you even get into the house?'

'With keys, how the hell do you think?'

'But where did you get them from?'

'What do you mean? I have my own keys.'

'Mother, I took them off you, and I changed the locks.'

'Well I borrowed yours and had copies made, didn't I, you dozy kipper? What sort of a son takes the keys to her own house off his own mother, and then changes the locks? I ought to throw you out, and then where would you go, you little shit? Move in with that scrubber?'

'That would be me?' Alison asked from the door.

Mother had never, to the best of my knowledge, been taken by surprise in her whole life before, but this was the second occasion in a matter of minutes. She hardly blinked.

'When are you going to stop abusing my son and marry him?' she snapped out.

'Soon as he asks,' she snapped back.

Alison and I sat at the kitchen table, sipping Slim a Soup. Mother was in a sherry-induced coma and Jeff was in between precarious columns of books in one of the spare rooms throwing up into a plastic basin.

'This is exactly why no really good fictional detective ever has a family,' I said, although I knew that wasn't strictly true. I could get away with saying it because Alison wasn't and never would be as well read as I was, but it was my way of saying that we were never going to get married.

'Your mother is like a salmon, swimming upriver, determined to get home to spawn, no matter what.'

'Devil spawn,' I said.

'But she made a fair point. I would hate to bring shame on the family.'

She smiled, and hugged her mug.

I hugged mine and said, 'Let's talk about the case.'

She said, 'You can't keep sweeping it under the carpet.'

I said, 'There's two bodies out in the woods and a killer at large. Let's focus.'

'What*ever*.' She sighed. 'Okay. Do we go to Robinson?'

'He's useless.'

'What if Buddy's at the airport, fleeing the country?'

'We don't want the monkey, we want the organ-grinder.'

'We want both. Robinson could stop him, Buddy could spill the beans on Dr Yes, case closed.'

'Buddy is a contract killer; he's professional, he's cool, he's not going to spill any beans. He won't be at the airport. Or at least not at George Best or the International. He'll be at a small airstrip somewhere, or across the border. He's no mug. And we have these . . .'

I took out the mobile phone and wallet we'd recovered from Rolo's jacket. Two calls had come in from

Pearl since we'd taken possession of the phone; his ringtone was the theme from *Captain Pugwash*. She had left two messages, each asking Rolo to call, the second shorter and more urgent than the first. A check of the call history showed that Pearl and Rolo were the only ones using the phone, which suggested that it had been purchased purely for that purpose. The wallet contained two twenty-pound notes, and nothing else. A phone that could be thrown away, and a wallet without identification. Rolo probably wasn't his real name.

'Dr Yes is no mug,' I said. 'Everything comes through Pearl, and in the end he'll sacrifice her as well. For the moment we don't know for sure who was being set up in Tollymore.'

'If Buddy is as cool and professional as you say, he wouldn't have fled the way he did, leaving Rolo half buried and the fire still going. He would have tidied up. But he was taken by surprise, he was betrayed. So what would you do in that case?'

'Me?'

'No, I know what you would do: you would hide under the quilt. Buddy, what would he do, what would he really do, bearing in mind what he does for a living?'

'He'd be angry, so angry that he's gotten sloppy with the murder scene.'

'And if he's angry, he's not going to go gently into the night, is he?'

'You're right. He'll be looking for whoever set him up.'

'Pearl.'

We looked at each other. I was noticing how cool and calculating Alison's eyes were.

'Maybe we'll be doing the world a favour if we let him sort her out,' she said. 'She's rotten to the core.'

'Just sit back and let her be murdered?'

'One less bad guy to worry about.'

'You wouldn't really, would you? Just because you don't like her.'

'That has nothing to do with it.'

Her gaze did not waver. Mine did, obviously, but only because of my dysfunctional tear ducts.

'No, Alison.'

She drummed her fingers on the table. Then she pushed Rolo's pay-as-you-go phone across to me. 'Maybe we should establish if she's still alive?'

I picked up the phone. 'And if she answers?'

'Do what your heart tells you.'

'*That's* . . .'

'I'm only winding you up. Call her. Do what you think is best.'

'There you go again!'

'I mean it! Do the right thing *for the case*, Sherlock.'

'With no comeback?'

'We'll see.'

I sighed. She winked. I shook my head. I dialled. It was answered on the third ring.

'Rolo! Where the . . . ?'

'Rolo's dead.'

'What? Who . . . ?'

'It's me.'

There was a few seconds of silence. And then: 'How did you get his phone?'

'It's a long story, Pearl, you wouldn't believe it . . .'

'Tell me.'

'I can't . . . there's no way of knowing who's listening . . .'

'You think someone is?'

'I don't know! This is way out of my league! I don't know what's going on exactly, and I'm not sure I want to know, but there are dangerous people out there and I don't think you know what you're involved in . . . I think I was right all along, Pearl, it's Dr Yeschenkov, I think he's a killer, he's using a hit man called Buddy Wailer . . .'

'Buddy!'

'Yes!'

'But that's impossible, Buddy's . . .'

'I have the evidence, Pearl. Come and see for yourself. We need to talk this through. I said we were partners, and we are. I trust you, and we can work this out together, but you have to tell me the truth.'

'Yes. Of course. You're right. I've been sucked in to this and I don't know how to get out. You're a good man, Mr No Alibis, I do trust you. I have to see you. Will I come now?'

'No, it's not safe. They're watching. Tomorrow, come to the shop tomorrow, tomorrow at noon. I'm having a little get-together, book stuff, but we can talk after, find somewhere private, yeah? Will you trust me on this?'

'Of course I will. And thank you. I had no idea . . .'

'Just come.'

'Slick,' said Alison. 'But I don't follow. What gathering? Why bring her to the shop?'

'Because it's that time again.'

'That time?' She studied me. 'Oh. *That* time. The time when all the cogs begin to turn and you sit up all night until the solution comes spewing out of you. Does that mean you have an inkling already, and if you do, is it roughly in line with what we've been thinking?'

'Yes and no.'

'Is that all I'm getting?'

'Things will be clearer in the morning.'

'And if they're not?'

'They will be. Trust me.'

'I do trust you. But not with Pearl. Not going somewhere private with her. Wherever she goes, I go too.'

'That's fine, absolutely. I'm not the slightest bit interested in her.'

'Man dear, that doesn't matter. If she wanted, she could have you for breakfast and you wouldn't have any choice in the matter.'

'I don't think so.'

'She walks through a room, men stand to attention. And I don't mean they stand to attention.'

'Not me.'

'Yes you.'

'I have erectile dysfunction.'

Alison patted her tummy. 'I think otherwise.'

'I'm not convinced it was me.'

She put her hands on her hips and sighed. 'Well, when he comes out looking like a twerp, we'll know for sure.'

'You're sure it's a he?'

'No, I'm sure it's a twerp.'

'You're funny.'

She came to me and kissed me. Then she whispered in my ear, 'So's your face.'

35

Alison was still coming up with questions as I ushered her out of the house. I told her to go home and get some rest; she was eating for two, she might as well sleep for two as well. That didn't go down well. She called me names and I called her them back. When she saw that I was serious about being left alone, she offered to make sandwiches and bring them in the middle of the night. I declined. She offered roast beef. I declined. She offered cottage pie. I declined. She offered chicken casserole. I declined. Obviously she could have continued until the end of time. Finally I just shoved her out of the door and told her to leave me alone. Two minutes later she banged on the front window and bellowed: 'Spaghetti bolognese?'

I pulled the blinds, I bolted the door. The house was quiet. Mother and Jeff were both asleep. I looked at my watch. It was ten p.m. I got a can of Coke from the fridge and a bag of Opal Fruits from the cupboard. I sat at the kitchen table with my laptop in front of me, Rolo's mobile phone, a notebook and pen. I opened the can and the bag. I emptied the sweets on to the table and threw the blackcurrant ones behind me. Then I sorted the greens, oranges and reds into three lines; they would be eaten in that order, at timed intervals, through the night.

At last I was ready to begin. You will know that I have a great facility for remembering figures. I had solved the *Case of the Musical Jew* by accurately remembering the numbers tattooed on the arms of two old people even though I had only observed them for a couple of seconds. Similarly, I now recalled the phone number that Buddy Wailer had texted from when responding to Liam Benson's request to meet on the towpath, which DI Robinson had very briefly shown me to me on Liam's mobile phone. I also knew his home number, following our visit to his house, but I thought it much more likely that he would be on the move.

I called him. I was not afraid. An hour ago I might have been.

I don't know if Rolo's name flashed up on his phone or even if he knew Rolo was the name of the man he had killed, but even his one word answer: 'Yes?' sounded strained.

I said, 'Buddy?'

'Yes.'

It was time for me to step up to the plate, take

control, be imposing. I could do that, at the end of a phone.

'I know you killed Rolo.'

'Excuse . . . ? You must have a wrong—'

'You shot him in the woods and now you're fleeing the country.'

'I don't know who you are or what you're talking about. Now if you don't mind I'm trying to get some work . . .'

He was interrupted by an amplified announcement: 'Will the last remaining passengers travelling to Alicante please report to Gate 12, which is now closing.'

'. . . and also I'm just picking someone up from the airport.'

'Buddy, I know who you are, and I know what you do and what you've done, so quit the act.'

'You don't know anything.' Pause. 'Who are you?'

'The name's Block, Lawrence Block,' I said, for I have a business and its reputation to protect.

'If you were on to me and had the power to do so, you'd be able to stop me going through security, and marching up to the gate the way I am now; you'd be able to stop me getting on my plane and getting the hell out of this shit-hole.'

'You're wrong,' I said. 'This isn't a shit-hole. It's just full of shitty people. I think you want a quiet life, you like to slip in, do your thing, and slip out, but you've been caught up in something here, and it has gotten out of hand, and it has to be sorted out. But you're also right. I can't stop you getting on that plane; only you and your conscience can do that. I'm asking you to do the right thing.'

There was a pause.

Then he started laughing and cut the line.

I was not unduly surprised. He didn't know who the hell I was, or who he could trust, so he was getting out. He'd probably heard all about Belfast justice. We have a tendency to shoot first and ask questions thirty years later at a public enquiry.

My next call was to Dr Yeschenkov. He had given me his mobile number on his business card at the Black-heath Driving Range. I didn't expect it to actually be his mobile, but some kind of service that vetted his calls, or at the very least a machine, but it was a chirpy Dr Yes himself who answered on the third ring.

'Hello there,' he said. 'Who's this?'

It was pleasantly informal and welcoming. He was probably used to cranky but rich patients calling him late into the evening.

'Hey,' I said, 'sorry to call so late . . .'

'Not a problem.'

'You won't remember me, but we met at Black-heath . . .'

'Yes, of course I do, the guy with the nose, and the van, and the bookshop, sure I remember you. Glad you called. You been giving it some thought?'

'Kind of,' I said.

'Yeah, well, it's a big decision. Why don't you drop by, let me take a proper look at . . . ?'

'Well I was rather hoping you might come and see me.'

'That . . . well, it's not really how I work. Lovely as I'm sure that would be, I have all the equipment right—'

'It's not about the nose.'

'Oh. Right. I understand. It's the ears, then. I can certainly sort those . . .'

'I'm having a little get-together tomorrow here in the shop; it's kind of a celebration of the life of Augustine Wogan. You remember Augustine?'

'Yes, of course I . . . but why would I possibly want to . . . ?'

'As part of my presentation I will be unveiling who was responsible for his murder.'

'His murder? But I understood he committed . . .'

'No, sir, he was murdered. In fact, he is one of four murder victims I can trace directly to the Yeschenkov Clinic.'

'The . . . what are you . . . ? The Yes . . . *my* clinic?'

'The very same.'

'But that's just . . . *nuts* . . .'

'Well you would say that.'

'But what possible . . . how can you . . . why . . . do the police . . . Sorry, but you have totally floored me. Is this some kind of a joke? Is this your zany British sense of humour?'

I had to give him some credit for recognising that we were forever British, not Irish.

'No, Dr Yeschenkov. I'm inviting you to come down

to the shop tomorrow, twelve noon, to listen to what I have to say about Augustine and what happened to him, and the others. I think it would be in your interests to be there.'

'Well, sir, I don't quite know what drugs you've been taking, but I'd appreciate it if you annoyed someone else with these . . . wild accusations. Now I've a busy day at the surgery tomorrow, and the very last place I intend to be is anywhere near your establishment. I'm warning you now that if the good name of the clinic or my own name is sullied in any way, I will not hesitate to instigate legal action.'

'Well you would have to be here to hear if it is,' I said.

I hung up before he could reply.

My third call wasn't a call at all, but a text. I hunted out DI Robinson's number and sent him a message on Rolo's phone detailing roughly where his body and the fire where Arabella had been cremated could be found in Tollymore Forest Park.

Everything had been set satisfactorily in motion.

All I had to do now was discover who really was responsible for the deaths of Augustine and Arabella Wogan, Liam Benson and Rolo. I had Opal Fruits, I had Coke, I had the brain of an alien super-being, and I had right on my side.

Easy-peasy.

36

Revelations are not half as interesting if they are delivered with only the accused and accusers present. Also I like to perform before an audience, and bask in the glory that comes with unmasking a killer. To this end I sent e-mail invitations to my vast database of crime-fiction fanatics, apologising for the late notice but hoping against hope that they could attend the next day's very special tribute to Augustine Wogan. In case they had never heard of him, because that's how much of a secret he was, I explained that he was Belfast born and bred, and an unsung hero responsible for some of the finest mystery novels ever written. I had no doubt that my customers would come out to support the event, but just in case, I added two considerable incentives – I promised two per cent off any purchase, and that there would be a mystery guest.

Alison and I were in the kitchen. I was taking off

my shirt and black tie and changing into something less formal; Alison was removing her smart suit and donning something a little roomier around the waist.

I said, 'You look lovely.'

She said, 'What do you want?'

'Nothing. Can't I pay you a compliment?'

'It would be a first. Ah – you're being nicey-nicey because you've solved the case.'

'Absolutely not,' I said. 'I haven't solved it yet.'

'But . . .' And she looked towards the door, and the shop floor beyond.

'Confidence, my love.'

She snorted. '*My love*. You *must* have solved it.'

I hadn't, but I firmly believed in Malcolm Gladwell's hypothesis that few people are born with genius, but many can attain it through practice, with ten thousand hours being the minimum required. I had put many more hours than that into my reading, and there was nothing about crime, or indeed human nature, that I did not know. I had every confidence that this high noon of mine would have a satisfactory outcome. The guilty would be unmasked, and if he, she or they tried to escape, Mother was in position by the door with a machete in her handbag. My only concern was that she would grow bored and begin to randomly butcher anyone she didn't like the look of.

Alison opened the kitchen door a fraction and pressed her eye to the crack. 'Starting to arrive now.

Dr Yeschenkov is looking at the books; there's a small, dumpy older woman pretending to look at them too, but she's really making big eyes at him. He *is* gorgeous. About half the seats are filled. Are they all really your customers?'

I moved her gently to one side and peered out. 'Most. The others . . . I sent Jeff out to the towpath last night to invite some of the regulars down. Thought they might like to see who tried to frame them for murder.'

'Are you sure you're not just going for the pink pound?'

'Show me something you can get in here for a pound and I might agree with you.'

As I watched, the shop door opened again and Pearl entered. She was in black leather boots with heels that could spike a thousand tabloid stories. She wore a tartan skirt short enough to corrupt shortbread, sheer black tights that did everything sheer black tights should do and a buttoned-up white blouse that was somehow more suggestive than buttoned down. Her hair was mussed. If she was surprised to see so many people, it didn't show. The only slight reaction was when she saw Dr Yeschenkov. 'Oh! I didn't know you were a fan!' she cried, before enveloping him in a hug that had every man in the place scowling with jealousy, including the gay contingent, who hadn't shifted their eyes from Dr Yes since he had arrived. The rotund woman beside him looked ready to clout Pearl with the book in her hands. Everyone was so busy watching the beautiful people embrace that hardly anyone noticed the door open again and Spider-web slip in. He had probably come with Dr Yes, or with Pearl, and just hung back.

'Ready to roll?' Alison asked.

'Not quite . . . Ah, here he comes . . .'

Finally DI Robinson entered the shop. He looked more musty than mussed. His eyes were tea-bag droopy and there was more than one pine needle in his hair. He leant back against the door and surveyed the audience.

It was time.

'Will you put Jeff on alert?'

'Calling him now,' said Alison. 'Man dear, you really like to turn these things into events, don't you?'

'It's lulling them into a false sense of security, and then I strike.'

Alison snorted. 'The very notion of you striking *anything* . . .'

'Just you watch,' I said, and pulled the kitchen door fully open.

It was another signal. Mother pressed a button on the CD player behind the counter, and immediately the sounds of pan pipes filled the air. They were from a pirated copy of the Muzak version of the title track from *The Mission*. I was avoiding paying for two separate music licences. I believe all music should be free to all people. Unlike books, which ought to be difficult to obtain and expensive. As the rich, hypnotic sounds of South America – albeit recorded in a garage

in Swindon by some itinerant jobbing musicians –
filled the air, all eyes turned towards Mother. Which
was not the intention. I cleared my throat loudly.
The eyes swung back. I was very happy, there and
then, about to take the stage and solve the case, and
could have milked that sense of expectation, but I
knew I had to get a move on because the next track
on the CD was 'Those Magnificent Men in Their
Flying Machines', and that wouldn't have set the
right tone at all.

'Ladies and gentlemen,' I began, 'I would like to thank
you all for coming here this afternoon to help cele-
brate the life and work of the finest crime novelist
ever to come from these shores, the great Augustine
Wogan. Though he never achieved best-seller status,
or ever became particularly well known, he was, to
students and aficionados of crime fiction, a master of
the genre who will forever be remembered for his
very wonderful *Barbed-Wire Love* trilogy. I think it is
only fitting, therefore, that our celebration should be
joined by a very special guest indeed ... Please
put your hands together for Augustine Wogan
himself!'

There were gasps of disbelief from all around the
shop floor. I nodded at Alison and she whispered into
her phone. A moment later the front door opened
and Jeff, in black suit and tie, entered, carrying against
his chest like an FA Cup about to be raised a hand-
somely decorated urn.

'Ladies and gentlemen, Augustine Wogan was cremated this morning at Roselawn. The brief, moving service was attended by myself, my sidekick Alison, my sidekick's sidekick Jeff and Augustine's solicitor.' I placed my hand on my heart and looked ceiling-ward. 'We were the only people present as Augustine passed from our world to the next.'

I nodded gravely.

A voice from my audience said, 'If we'd known it was happening, we would have gone.'

Several others nodded and grunted in agreement.

'Well that's not my—'

'And technically speaking,' said another, 'when he died, that was when he really passed from one world to the next. You were just cremating a husk.'

I fixed him with a look.

He said, 'I'm just making a point. In fact, I'm not convinced there is an afterlife.'

'Please, if you don't mind – whether he departed this mortal coil at the moment of his death or that of his cremation, it is indisputable that this *is* Augustine; his ashes are contained in this beautifully decorated urn . . .'

'You call it cloisonné, the design of the urn,' said one of the gay contingent. '*Cloisonné.*'

'Clossa what?' asked Spider-web, who was the closest to the urn, apart from Jeff.

The gay man said, 'It's an ancient technique for decorating metalwork. You solder silver or gold wires on to the outside, dividing it up into compartments, which are then filled in with different colours of enamel, and fire it in a kiln.'

'It looks like tat to me,' said Spider-web. 'Like something you'd pick up in the market for a fiver.'

I wasn't going to let that lie. 'It cost one hundred and twenty-five pounds,' I announced, 'and I'm hoping that at the end of our celebration you will each contribute a little something towards it. Say five pounds.'

There was some disgruntled murmuring as I signalled to Jeff to continue. He moved between two rows of chairs until he was facing one of our book-cases. I had cleared a space at just above head height, and it was here that he carefully placed Augustine's urn.

'This,' I announced, 'is going to be Augustine Wogan's final resting place, a place where he will forever be honoured, surrounded by the books he loved so much, and, in due course, by his own books, which, subject to an agreement with his solicitor, who seems like a very nice man, will appear in strictly limited lavishly illustrated special editions to be published by No Alibis Books next year.'

'How much will they be?' someone asked.

'That has yet to be established.'

'Will they be cheaper through your Christmas Club?'

'No,' I said.

'Is that all this is?' another of my regulars asked. 'One of your bloody sales pitches?'

Several heads nodded.

'No,' I said firmly, 'this isn't about me, it isn't about selling you books, and it isn't about cloisonné urns either.'

'Well what the hell is it about, then?'

'It's about the murder of Augustine Wogan!'

And that shut them up . . .

37

... for about five seconds, and then there was a lot
of jibber-jabber and finger-pointing, not least from
Dr Yeschenkov. Spider-web made a subtle move
towards the door, but found his way blocked by DI
Robinson. It wasn't necessarily a sign of guilt, more
of instinct.

I nodded around my audience. 'Yes,' I said, 'Augustine was murdered; as sure as I'm standing here today,
Augustine was murdered.'

'I thought it was suicide,' said someone.

'I heard he blew his head off,' said someone else.

Several others began to discuss it between themselves. The shop phone rang. For no reason whatsoever Mother pressed play on the CD and 'Those
Magnificent Men in Their Flying Machines' began to
boom through the speakers.

I was losing them before I'd properly found them.

And then, abruptly, the music stopped and Alison was standing with her finger on the stop button and shouting: 'Quiet! Please! Show some respect! Augustine Wogan in the house!'

It worked. All eyes turned to the urn. I moved to take up a fresh position immediately beside it.

I winked my thanks to Alison, but just as I started to launch into it again, Dr Yeschenkov stood up. 'This is just ridiculous, I won't be part of this charade; I didn't come here for some cockamamie murder-mystery weekend. I have work to do.'

He strode towards the door. The rotund woman who had cast loving glances towards him followed suit.

DI Robinson stopped him in his tracks by holding up a warrant card and saying: 'You're not going anywhere, skinnymalink melodian legs.'

Dr Yes looked at the DI as if the DI had taken leave of his senses.

'What?'

'Relax, it's a compliment. But I think you should stay. You might find it interesting.'

Dr Yeschenkov's teeth clouded over.

The rotund woman said, 'He can leave if he wants to.'

Dr Yes huffed and puffed, but some part of him could see that it wasn't making him look very good, with everyone staring at him. Image and appearance was everything. He jabbed a finger at Robinson and snapped, 'You, sir, have not heard the last of this!'

before retaking his seat. He had backed down, but issued a threat with it, thus saving a little bit of perfectly moisturised face.

The rotund woman shook her head at Robinson, snarled, and went after Dr Yes.

DI Robinson nodded around the shop. 'Now, folks, to tell you the truth, I'm not sure Augustine Wogan was murdered either, but I'm prepared to be convinced otherwise. This guy usually knows what he's talking about, even if he generally only gets to his conclusions via Biafra. But I'd appreciate it if you all just remained in your seats and listened to what he has to say. Apart from anything else, it's entertaining, someone usually ends up getting punched, and at the end of it all you might get to see a genuine murderer being arrested. Where else are you going to get all that for nothing? Plus I hear his Christmas Club is enrolling new members, and you wouldn't want to pass up that opportunity, would you?'

Laughter rippled around the room.

Even Alison was grinning.

It wasn't the tone I was looking for at all. This wasn't a joke, it wasn't entertainment; it was deadly serious.

Maybe they could tell I wasn't happy. Silence fell, smiles faded, laughter lines became disfiguring wrinkles.

'Augustine Wogan is dead,' I said, 'and somebody in this room murdered him. Liam Benson, a freelance photographer, is dead, and somebody in this room murdered him. Rolo, a thug whose real name I don't know, has been murdered. Even Arabella Wogan, Augustine's wife, whose only crime was wanting to look younger, which isn't a crime, is missing presumed dead. *Dead*, ladies and gentlemen, and this afternoon we are going to work out who did what to whom and why.'

Students of my methods will know that when it comes to the denouement, I favour the scattergun approach. It is the crime-solving equivalent of letting the fox loose in the chicken coop. There will be attempts at flight, and somewhere along the line eggs will be laid in blind panic. I wouldn't start at the beginning; I would start near the end and work backwards, forwards, sideways and into different dimensions, and after everything had been examined and dissected I would be left with the answers.

I thanked DI Robinson for his intervention. Then: 'And as we're already with you, maybe you could tell us where you have just spent the night?'

'I think you have a pretty good idea.'

'Why do you think that?'

'Because there aren't many tip-offs that come direct to my personal mobile phone. And also, this was found at the scene.' He reached into his inside jacket pocket and produced a paperback book. It was Rolo's copy of *Looking for Rachel Wallace*. 'He had it in his back pocket. You didn't find it when you searched him?'

'No,' I said, before quickly adding, 'We didn't search him. We weren't even there. And that isn't the point.

Tell us what you found at the murder scene, Detective Inspector.'

'We found the body of Raymond Buchannon, aka Rolo, a semi-notorious east Belfast bouncer and muscle for hire. He had been shot to death and partially buried.'

'And the other body?'

'Other body?'

I smiled knowingly. 'Come, Detective Inspector, we're not holding anything back here. Tell us about the other body.'

'There was no other body.'

'If you want to be pedantic, then, the *remains* of the other body.'

'Nope.'

'In the fire, the remains of Arabella Wogan!'

My audience murmured.

'Nope.'

'Detective Inspector, are you telling me that a man of your experience did not think to have the ashes of the fire examined?'

'Nope.'

'Nope you didn't?'

'Nope I did. And I'll tell you what was found. Ash from the wood that was burned and certain chemical residues that have yet to be analysed but that will probably turn out to be petrol or some other fuel used to ignite the fire.'

'No bones? No skull?'

'Nope.'

'You're certain?'

'Yes. No evidence of human remains whatsoever. In the vicinity of the fire, however, I did find evidence that marijuana had been smoked. I also found a bag of Ecstasy tablets. I found footprints that I believe I can trace directly to footwear belonging to you, to your sidekick and your sidekick's sidekick. And of course the aforementioned book, which again ties the deceased to you and to this shop, in particular the sticker featuring your logo that you affixed over the actual price, increasing it by two pounds.'

'It's a collector's item,' I said. 'And you deduce from this evidence?'

'One might easily deduce that a drug-fuelled party was taking place in the woods, an argument broke out, Rolo Buchannon was shot, and in your panic to get away, you failed to properly hide the body or remove the evidence of your presence at the scene or indeed of your use of illegal drugs.'

All eyes turned to me.

'And is that what *you* think?'

'I think there's a fair chance that I could get as far as a trial based on circumstantial evidence alone, and in days gone by I might have, but having dealt with you before, I know that things are rarely as they first appear and that you will most likely have some unlikely explanation up your sleeve. I will listen with interest.'

I regarded my audience. 'Do you hear that? Some *unlikely explanation*. That is what you are going to hear today, ladies and gentlemen, an unlikely, surreal, complex tale of deceit and fabrication that starts with the death of Arabella Wogan.'

Dr Yes was immediately on his feet. 'Arabella Wogan is not dead! She was alive when she left my clinic and there is nothing to suggest that she has since passed away!'

'She's in Brazil!' Pearl shouted. 'Or Portugal!'

'We have no evidence of that,' I said.

'You have no evidence she isn't!'

I shook my head. 'Well that's just where you're wrong. Ladies and gentlemen, for your information, this is Pearl, Pearl Knecklass . . .' Immediately there were sniggers from the back row. 'Pearl works with Dr Yeschenkov and is a director of his clinic. Pearl, I have very good contacts in the travel industry.' There was no need to tell anyone that it was one of my customers, Derek who worked in Co-op Travel. 'I am assured that no Arabella Wogan has travelled to Portugal or Brazil in the past six months.'

'That's because they weren't married.'

'*What?*'

'She was his common-law wife, and she used his name, but they were not married. She disclosed that when she provided her medical records prior to her treatment at the clinic. So if you were searching the travel records for Arabella Wogan, you were barking up the wrong tree. Her passport would have shown her under the name of Arabella Shaw.'

She looked smug and self-satisfied.

'See? He doesn't know what the hell he's talking about!'

It was Dr Yes, pointing at me.

They were working together, circling, throwing out jabs. There might be a few chinks in my armour of knowledge, but I knew more than they thought, and their arrogance would come back to bite them.

'Well, Doctor,' I said, 'if you're convinced I don't know what the hell I'm talking about, what's a busy man like you doing here at all? Why didn't you bring some high-powered solicitor to slap a writ for slander on me if I say something you don't like?'

'I did,' said Dr Yeschenkov. He indicated the rotund woman in the seat next to him, the woman I had mistaken for a groupie.

I am a master of self-control. I merely nodded serenely and said, 'You will not gag me. If I think you were responsible for the death of Arabella Wogan and the subsequent cover-up, I *will* say it.'

He was on his feet again. His solicitor was beside him. They were both shouting. They only desisted when DI Robinson strode through the audience and right up to me and said, 'Word in your ear?'

He drew closer. He whispered: 'I don't mind your little games, but let's get it moving, I can't keep these people here for ever.'

He was right. I didn't want Dr Yeschenkov storming out again if the detective inspector wasn't going to stop him.

DI Robinson returned to his place by the door. Dr

Yes and his legal eagle grumbled as they retook their seats. I glanced at Alison; she gave me the thumbs-up, but a hesitant smile.

'DI Robinson has asked me to get a move on,' I said. 'But I say to you, justice cannot be hurried, and the truth cannot be dictated by time! The truth will out, and it will out when it wants to come out!'

I had supposed it to be rousing. But they all looked at me like I was a halfwit, and several glanced at their watches.

I cleared my throat and said, 'Dr Yeschenkov, I understand your concerns, but whatever way you want to look at it, Arabella Wogan is missing. She *apparently* left her room at the Forum International Hotel, where she had been staying while she underwent her procedures, and then she vanished without trace. Dr Yeschenkov – did any problems arise during Arabella's treatment?'

'No, none, she was a model patient and I was very happy with her recovery. She was extremely pleased with her new look.'

'So when did you last see her?'

'On the afternoon of February the twenty-fifth, when I supervised the final removal of bandages.'

'And you discharged her then?'

'I signed off on her medical treatment, but I recommended, as I do with all of our patients, that she spend a further twenty-four hours resting before leaving the hotel. Unfortunately many patients choose not to follow my advice; they're so happy with their new appearance, they just want to show it off. I can't stop them. I believe Arabella discharged herself some time on the evening of the twenty-fifth.'

'And you haven't seen her since?'

'I have not.'

'So would you care to explain . . . this!'

As if by magic, but actually by PowerPoint, knowledgeably operated by Jeff, the photo of Dr Yeschenkov with Arabella taken by Liam Benson at the Xianth gallery in Dublin appeared on the ceiling.

Yes, the ceiling. All of the other walls were covered in books and the ceiling was the only uniformly flat surface. Everyone's head craned upwards. I would use this device sparingly, or be sued for cricked necks.

'Dr Yeschenkov with Arabella Wogan at the opening of the Xianth gallery as it appeared in the press. Were you not at this gallery?'

'Yes, I was.'

'Did you not insist on the freelance photographer Liam Benson accompanying you to the event for publicity purposes.'

'I did not *insist*. He was working for me.'

'Did he take this photograph?'

'Yes . . . and no.'

'Please explain.'

'It is clearly me, I remember it being taken, but this is not the woman I was standing next to. It must have been doctored.'

'It must have been doctored.'

'Yes, that's what I said. Did I not say it clearly?'

'I was repeating it for emphasis. If it was indeed doctored, the most likely explanation is that it was doctored by the photographer who took it, Liam Benson, who was employed by you. Now what other reason could there possibly be for doctoring this photograph, other than to show that Arabella was alive and well and in Dublin?'

'I don't know.'

'I spoke to Liam Benson shortly before he was murdered. He was a frightened man, Dr Yeschenkov, and mostly he seemed to be frightened of you.'

'That's just ridiculous. We had a perfectly cordial, professional relationship.'

'Is it not true that you were furious when this photograph appeared in the press?'

'I was upset, yes.'

'You're a wealthy man, Dr Yeschenkov, perhaps a powerful man. If you were completely certain that this photograph was doctored, why did you not find out how it came to be doctored? Why did you not bring down the full weight of your legal representative upon whoever was responsible?' I looked at his legal representative. 'I don't mean your full weight ... your weight is quite ... normal ... The only reasonable explanation I can come up with, Dr Yeschenkov, is that you were aware it was doctored, and you wanted it published so that you could point to it and say, look, Arabella was alive and in Dublin, so how can she have died as a result of one of my

operations? I put it to you, sir, that you knew that
she was dead and you were doing nothing short of
staging an elaborate sleight of hand! In short, a cover-
up!'

His legal representative was on her fat feet. She said,
'Sir, we are going to sue you for every penny you
have.'

38

By the look of her, every penny I had would not even begin to pay for Dr Yeschenkov's solicitor's usual breakfast. If she'd been worth her salt, she should probably have removed her client from No Alibis as soon as she issued her threat. That she did not was entirely down to my brilliance in immediately changing the subject through a simple nod in Jeff's direction. Another photograph appeared on the ceiling. *Everyone* looked up. This time it was of a very tall, very thin man, carrying a hatbox, and entering the Yeschenkov Clinic.

'Do you recognise him?' I asked.

Dr Yes's solicitor put a hand on his arm and shook her head. But he ignored her. 'No . . .' he said. 'What has he got to do with anything?'

'His name is Buddy Wailer. He's entering your clinic, but you don't recognise him?'

'No ... I ... it's a busy clinic, I can't account for all the comings and ... should I ... ?'

He was intrigued. Or he was stalling. Or he was lying. I glanced at Pearl. She was studying me intently.

I said, 'What he most certainly is is a murderer.'

There was a ripple, a murmur, a communal bleat from the audience. DI Robinson moved up and down on the balls of his feet, a sure sign of his interest.

'So let me tell you, let me tell you all about Buddy Wailer, and how we came by him.'

The only way to do that was to describe how we had become involved in the case in the first place. How the revered Augustine Wogan had come to my shop begging me to help him, having narrowly escaped being shot just outside. How he suspected Dr Yeschenkov of covering up his wife Arabella's death. I detailed my meeting with Pearl and how she came to be the only person outside of Alison and Jeff who knew where he was staying, and how there was something suspicious about his suicide. I repeated my theory about the V-cut on the cigar found in Augustine's mouth, which drew an eye-rolling *he's lost it now* reaction from Dr Yes and nothing at all from Pearl. (Later Alison would say, 'How could you tell? She's had so much Botox, she's half fucking Friesian.') They paid a little bit more attention when I related the discovery of the V-cutter in Arabella's room at the Forum Hotel, and this developed into at least a modicum of respect as I described how we had traced the V-cutter to the Las Vegas cigar stall operated by Manuel Gerardo

338

Ramiro Alfonzo Aurelio Enrique Zapata Quetzalcoatl and the fear that had come into his voice when he realised that it was Buddy Wailer who had purchased the device. When I had recounted how Manuel Gerardo Ramiro Alfonzo Aurelio Enrique Zapata Quetzalcoatl's friend had secretly entered Buddy's room and looked inside the hatbox, and what he had found, my audience looked suitably horrified.

'In the immortal words of Manuel Gerardo Ramiro Alfonzo Aurelio Enrique Zapata Quetzalcoatl: Buddy Wailer, he whacks people, that's what he does.'

Abruptly Pearl laughed. Everyone looked at her. She bowed her head and shook it. She wiped a tear away.

I said, 'Some people find this funny.' I gave it a Mexican twang. '*Buddy Wailer he whacks people*. You've seen enough movies, maybe you've read enough books to know what that means. Well, folks, we're private detectives; as you can imagine, the idea that we might be up against a killer for hire got us pretty excited, particularly when we spotted him entering the Yeschenkov Clinic, particularly when we followed him back to the house he had rented, particularly when we broke into that house and found Arabella's head in a hatbox!'

Dr Yes's solicitor was on her feet. 'That is outrageous! You are making these claims and you are not backing any of them up with evidence!' She swivelled in a way that only a fat girl in a too tight suit can, that is, with difficulty, and pointed a thick finger at

DI Robinson. 'If anyone ought to be arrested it's this man!' she shouted, pointing back at me.

'I hear you,' Robinson said.

His eyes fixed on me. An eyebrow rose.

'If you just let me finish,' I said, 'then you will understand. I mean, you may be a solicitor, but don't you want to *know*?'

She glared at me. She started to say something. Dr Yes tugged at her jacket. She sighed and sat down. 'Very well,' she snapped, 'but I'm warning you . . .'

'Okay. Where were we? Oh yes. Arabella's head was in a box – and the rest of her was in a different room, lying on a bed, *that's what we found*. It was horrific. But before we could report it to the proper authorities, Buddy spirited them away.'

'How convenient!'

'No, not really. Madam, Mrs, whoever you are, what *we* always strive to be is detached. We have to stand back and analyse the facts as we know them. And in this case we just couldn't figure out why Buddy Wailer would *want* to keep Arabella's head. If he was someone who liked to keep trophies from his victims, then why did he only keep some and not others? Our theory had it that this was a man hired in by Dr Yes to rid him of Augustine Wogan and anyone else who knew about the cover-up. Yet if he killed Augustine and Liam Benson and Rolo, why didn't he take *their* heads? Why take Arabella's *at all*, when our theory supposed that she wasn't murdered but died because of a medical problem? And why would a professional hit man like

Buddy Wailer fail to bury his last victim properly, out in the woods? Rolo might never have been found if the hole had been a few feet deep, rather than just a couple of inches. And if he brought Arabella's body out to Tollymore to burn it, why was there no evidence of her left in the ashes of the fire *at all*?'

'Because you're making this entire thing up and you are, in fact, a nut?' Dr Yeschenkov asked.

'Legally,' said his solicitor, 'you cannot refer to him as a nut, even if he shows all the characteristics of one.'

'If either of you call my son a nut again, I'll fucking brain you,' said Mother.

I glowed. Everyone else just looked at her, because with her fairly recent stroke her diction came and went. It was particularly bad when she was angry. So what everyone else heard was: 'If etheryoucallthmyson anuth again, I'll futhingbranoo.' It meant nothing to them, but everything to me.

I drew them back to me. I said, 'I don't blame you. It does sound mad. And actually, you're quite right. We were on completely the wrong path. I realised that only last night, and like the discovery of penicillin and photography, it was entirely an accident, yet completely fortuitous. You see, when I entered Buddy Wailer's house and examined the hatbox on his bed, my hands became stained with a sticky substance, which I quickly washed off. I believed it was some bodily fluid secreted by Arabella's head. But last night, in Tollymore Forest, I also found my hands covered in a similar fluid, but with nowhere to wash it off, I did what every mother would beat you with a bamboo cane for: I wiped my hand on my trousers. It was only much later, when I was sifting through the evidence of the case, looking for something I was sure I'd missed, that I idly began picking at the dried stain on my trousers, for it had hardened into a wax-like substance.' I made a point of looking down at Pearl. 'Except it wasn't a wax-like substance. It *was* wax. And with that the case was solved.'

Everyone was looking at me, and then, with furrowed brows, at each other.

When I had milked it for long enough, I raised my mobile phone. I made a call. It was answered on the first ring. I said, 'It's okay to come in now.'

All eyes turned to the door.

'Ladies and gentlemen,' I said, as the very tall, very thin man appeared in the doorway, a hatbox in his hands, 'I give you the one and only Buddy Wailer!'

39

Knowing that he was to be my star witness, I had borrowed a bar stool from Madison's Hotel a few doors down, and now Buddy Wailer was sitting on it, beside me, with Augustine Wogan looking down on him. Even sitting down, he was as tall as I was. He kept the hatbox in his lap, and his hands on either side of it, protectively. After briefly studying Buddy, his height, his thinness and his nervous disposition, my audience was now completely mesmerised by the box. *I* knew it wasn't empty. *They* had guessed it. They wanted to know, but at the same time, they didn't.

I said, 'Before we get into this, that box is going to be distracting, so the sooner we find out what's in it, the sooner we can move on. Do you want to tell us what you have there?'

'It contains a head.'

There were groans and little cries of disbelief and horror. They also craned their necks.

'Now I appreciate that some of you may be of a nervous disposition, so I'm going to put this to a vote. Before we hear what Buddy has to say, shall we open the box?'

'YES!'

Dr Yeschenkov said nothing. Neither did Pearl or Alison or Jeff or Robinson or Spider-web.

'Buddy, if you wouldn't mind?'

Buddy removed the lid and angled the box up. There were shouts and yells and *fucking hells!*

It was definitely a head.

Buddy Wailer's head. Staring blankly out.

My audience was stunned. They were mouthing:

But that's . . .

How in hell . . . ?

Fucking hell, that's creepy!

'Just to clear up any confusion,' I said, 'and particularly for the likes of my mother back there, who has just crossed herself, even though she's not a Catholic, will you please tell us whose this head is or was or belongs to.'

'It's my head.'

'Your head? But you are clearly alive. Did you have an identical twin brother?'

'No, this is a three-dimensional wax portrait of my head.'

There were gasps and whispers, and all around my shop, the sounds of pennies dropping.

I said, 'For the purposes of the webcam record of these proceedings, will you please tell our audience who you are and what you do for a living.'

Buddy cleared his throat. 'My name is Brian Wailer. Until 2005 I was Global Head of Wax Commissions at Madame Tussauds. Since then I have worked as a free-lance operative.'

'Which means . . . ?'

'I travel the world selling and making these 3-D portraits. They are, I hope you will agree, astonish-ingly lifelike.'

'And how much do they cost?'

'I will do a portrait for somewhere around eighty thousand pounds.'

'You're serious? Who's going to pay . . . ?'

'With power, wealth and success, there usually comes a degree of vanity that needs to be indulged, or exploited. I travel the world with this, my own head, and believe me, commissions are not in short supply.'

'And you make them yourself?'

'No, I employ a team of experts, many of whom worked for the Madame. It's a highly complex process. Hundreds of photographs are taken, colour trans-parencies of eyes and teeth are made. The teeth are accurately mapped and an exact set made; acrylic eyes are built from the iris outwards. I even use silk threads to reproduce the veins inside the eye. The whole process should take several months, but my service is not only cheaper, it's much, much quicker.'

'So how did you end up on these fair shores?'

'I was invited here by the Yeschenkov Clinic.'

I looked to Dr Yes. 'Is that right?'

'No. Yes. It is true that I invited this man to the clinic after hearing about his work, but on the day he visited I was unexpectedly called away. One of my fellow directors oversaw his visit and liked his work, but believed it was too expensive, and to tell you the truth, somewhat . . . unsettling. That is the extent of my dealings to date with Buddy Wailer and if he says otherwise, he is misrepresenting both himself and the clinic.'

'And we won't hesitate to take legal action,' said the rotund solicitor.

'Mr Wailer?' I said.

'It's true I have not met Dr Yeschenkov until today, but, nevertheless, I have completed seven portraits for clinic patients, and I've been paid for them.'

'That's impossible!' cried Dr Yes.

'As a hit man,' I said, 'you probably wouldn't have much in the way of paperwork, but as a creator of wax portraits, you probably do?'

'Yes. Of course. Not with me, but obtainable.'

'And you were paid directly by the clinic?'

'Yes.'

'And the director who you met when you visited, who lined up the clients, who paid you with money transfers from the Yeschenkov Clinic was . . . ?'

Buddy kept his eyes on me. But he said, 'Miss Kneck-lass.'

'This woman, in the front row?'

Buddy nodded. Eyes still on me.

Dr Yes turned to Pearl. They were separated by four chairs, three Augustine fans and a towpath regular. 'Pearl . . . this isn't true?'

She'd joined Buddy in staring at me.

'Pearl!'

Her eyes slowly moved towards him, like a sniper scoping no-man's-land.

'You made me promises you couldn't keep.'

Dr Yes looked at his solicitor. 'That's simply not . . .'

'I had to look out for myself. And you were too busy gazing at yourself in the mirror to notice.'

'It's simply not true!'

It was, of course. They'd been screwing in the Forum.

I said, 'Buddy, you didn't suspect something was amiss?'

'No – at least, not until Miss Knecklass called about Arabella Wogan. That's when it all started to come out.'

It had been weighing heavily on Buddy Wailer, so heavily that it had brought him back from the airport, brought him to my home in the middle of the night for a long, tearful confession. *Then* it had been rambling and panicked. *Now* he was calm and collected.

Arabella had been introduced to Buddy by Pearl as a potential client; they had discussed and agreed a fee and the work began. The photographs were taken by his regular local photographer, Liam Benson, as soon as the bandages came off her face. Arabella still had several medical procedures to undergo, but getting her face done first enabled the work on the portrait to get under way, with the idea being that it would be ready for her when she checked out of the Forum. But then Buddy received a call from Pearl in the middle of the night, ordering him to the hotel. She met him in the foyer and took him up to Arabella's room – where she was lying dead. Pearl said she'd suffered an extreme reaction to her medication; it was an accident, but if word got out, the clinic would not only be sued for millions, its reputation would be irredeemably tarnished.

'She already had it all worked out,' Buddy told me that night, him with his hand shaking as he held his glass of whiskey, mine with the shakes that come with the medication I take to stop me having seizures. 'She wanted me to complete work on the portrait, double-quick time, and also to provide a full torso so that we could mock up photographs to show that Arabella was still alive.'

'Did nobody else know that she was dead? Doctors? The staff at the hotel?'

'No. Several different doctors and surgeons were treating her, but if she had any problems, she had to go through Pearl to get to them. She called Pearl complaining that she wasn't well, but by the time Pearl arrived and let herself in, Arabella had passed away.'

'You didn't think at the time it was a rather extreme way of dealing with it? Patients die after surgery. It's a fact of life.'

'Sure I did, and I kick myself now for going along, but I was in a bind – Pearl controlled the money, and I needed it. All those trips to Vegas have turned what used to be a hobby into what you might call an addiction. I owe, big time.'

In the shop, Buddy looked out at the audience. They weren't a jury, but they were as good as one.

'She had two guys come in remove the body.'

'How did they do that?'

'Brazenly. They came in with a large cardboard box, loaded her into it, put it on a luggage cart, and I left with them via the service elevator.'

'Had you ever seen them before. Or since?'

'Sure. One of them's standing over there.' He raised a very long, very thin finger, and pointed towards the back of the store. 'That man, with the spider's-web tattoo.'

Spider-web gazed calmly back.

'And the other one?'

'I shot him dead last night.'

When the buzz died down, Buddy said he'd been out of the country for several weeks and only returned to his rented house the day before Augustine died. He immediately thought there was something suspicious about Augustine's death and confided his suspicions to his friend Liam Benson. Liam had already worked out that neither of them were actually working for Dr Yes, but for Pearl, and that she had made herself so essential to the running of the clinic, and had so much power vested in her, that she could run her scam right under Dr Yes's nose without fear of discovery.

'We know now why you felt you had to comply with her cover-up, but why did Liam? Presumably he wasn't making the kind of money you were? Did he have debts as well?'

'No, he didn't make much, and he didn't owe anyone a red cent. Problem with Liam was that he was in love.'

'Ah,' I said, nodding at Pearl. 'That's how she works.'

'He was in love with *me*.'

'Oh. You mean he was . . .'

'The feeling was mutual. He didn't think he could tell the police about what was going on because he knew about my financial difficulties and wanted to support me. And because he didn't tell, he died.'

Buddy swallowed hard. His eyes grew a little misty. He raised a finger and pointed at Pearl, in the process looking at her properly for the first time.

'You came to Liam's office and told him someone was asking questions and warned him not to say anything. But he had to tell someone, and who else but the love of his life? So we arranged to meet up, except he was followed, and he was murdered.' He looked back to me. 'I was scared, real scared. Then Pearl calls me, tells me there's a private detective has discovered all about the cover-up and is trying to blackmail the clinic; we have to get rid of whatever evidence there is, whatever happened to Arabella's wax head and torso? She nearly freaked when I told her they were still in the house. She wanted them melted down and Arabella's clothes we'd used to dress her burned.'

'Why Tollymore?'

'This isn't my country, and I know very little of it, but Tollymore was always special to Liam and me. It just seemed logical to go somewhere I was fairly familiar with.'

'And you told Pearl where you were going?'

'Yes, I had to. She wanted me out of the country, but she still owed me money and I said I wasn't going anywhere without it. So she said she would bring it down. Except it wasn't her that turned up, it was . . .'

'Rolo.'

'. . . Rolo. I recognised him from the hotel, I knew he was in the business of removing bodies, and I was convinced he wasn't there just to hand over the money.'

'So you grabbed his gun and shot him.'

'No! Yes. Sort of. It was more than just that. He was . . . *odd*. He was in no hurry. He sat down on a log beside the fire and said how lovely it was, it reminded him of camping with his dad when he was a boy, but they'd had no car, so they only ever camped in his back yard. He said he liked the trees. And the smell of pine. He had a hip flask, whiskey, he gave me a drink. He said he knew I was in a rush, but would I mind sitting with him for a while. So I sat with him. And we drank. He took out this book he was reading. He said it was great but he needed to finish it. Just one last chapter, he said. Don't worry, he said, they're really short chapters. I remember him saying, "That Spenser, he's some pup." I remember it because I didn't know what he was talking about. He asked me if I believed in God, and I said yes. He said he'd lived a terrible, evil life and was looking for salvation. He said he'd been sent down to murder me; that he had been murdering people since he was a teenager. He admitted killing Liam. He said he killed Augustine. He said they were the latest in a long list. Problem was he knew too much about where the bodies were buried, and that was fine as long as he continued killing, but once he stopped, once he went soft, they would rub him out, the people who employed him, some kind of agency he worked for. He said either he killed me, or I killed him. He had had enough. He didn't want to kill anyone else, but at the same time he couldn't let me escape. He took out his gun and handed it to me. There was no way I was going to shoot him, because he was drunk and would probably regret it in the morning, if he was alive, but he shouted at me to do it. When I wouldn't, he made a grab for the gun, but I wouldn't give it to him because that meant he might be shooting me instead, and so we wrestled for it, and he was stronger than me and he was getting it off me, but my finger was on the trigger and somehow it went off, and I killed him, and I might never be able to sleep again.'

You could hear a pin drop.

'I killed him, but I am not a murderer. I buried him as quickly as I could. I was just in a blind panic. I drove straight to the airport. But *this* man called me. His shop is called No Alibis and that suits me down to the ground. I have no alibi, but he convinced me that justice would look kindly upon me. So here I am.'

DI Robinson remained by the door. He studied Buddy, sitting there in despair, and said, 'We should talk. But first . . .' He nodded at me. 'You may as well see this through.'

I said, 'Pearl, would you take the stand?'

'It's not a stand, you moron. It's a bar stool. In this crappy little shop. I don't have to do anything.'

She was still lovely. And she was undoubtedly defiant. But then Dr Yes looked across the Augustine fans and the towpath regular and said, 'God knows it will sink us both, Pearl, but take the damn stand!'

40

Pearl's eyes narrowed.

It was a testament to Dr Yes's good work that they still could.

She stood up. She was three fifths stiletto. Buddy got out of the chair. He stepped away left as she came from the right. As she sat, she crossed her legs. In the crossing of them, everyone looked up her short skirt. It was a learned reaction. It wasn't just the men, or the impure of thought. If the Pope had been there, he would have looked. Mother Teresa would have taken a gander. The chances of two Catholic icons turning up in a mystery bookstore on Botanic Avenue were slim, particularly with one of them dead, but if they had, they would have eyeballed Pearl's nether regions just the same as everyone else. There was something about her. Even Alison was drawn in. Fact was there was nothing to see. With my eyesight I could see nothing anyway, so it was necessary for me to watch back the webcam coverage later, in high definition, and zoom.

She said, 'This means nothing; it's not a court, I've sworn nothing, my solicitor isn't here, it's not a confession or a denial or an admission. But I will tell you my story. My name is Pearl Knecklass and all I'm guilty of is falling in love.'

Dr Yes lowered his eyes. His rotund companion was shaking her chins.

I said, 'Pearl, maybe you could tell us if that is your real name?'

'Yes. Of course.'

'And how did you come to be working in the Yeschenkov Clinic?'

'I come from Estonia. There's no money in Tallinn. I know, because I was an accountant. I heard Belfast was nice. I came here. There's money here, but I'm not an accountant. My qualifications were not recognised. So I got a job as a cleaner with an agency, and they placed me in the clinic.'

'You have no accent.'

'I . . . lost it.' She looked pointedly at Dr Yes. 'He arranged it.'

'How do you mean?'

'He sent me for lessons, electrocution lessons Rolo used to call them.'

'So you knew Rolo for quite a while.'

'Sure. We were neighbours. Cleaners don't get to live in the Merchant.'

Dr. Yes

It was the best hotel in Belfast.

'Why would he send a cleaner for elocution lessons?'

'Because I was his little project.' She changed position in the chair, uncrossing and recrossing her legs. The shop window steamed up a little more. 'I was working night shifts. I was thirty years old but I looked forty. I was heavy. My teeth, stomach, tits . . . everything was wrong. I looked and felt like a pig. I saw women come in one way, go out another. I could only dream. I was depressed. One night Dr Yeschenkov was working late; he found me crying. He was so nice. Men tell you bullshit things, but he didn't. Or maybe he did, but in a different way. When I said I had bags under my eyes, he said yes, you have. When I showed him my fat tummy, he said yes, it is. Everything I hated about myself he agreed with. I wanted to smack his face. But he said he could help me. I asked him how and he said the best way for this clinic to promote itself was to show what it was capable of. Women came in for their breast lifts, or tummy tucks, or eye lifts, and they wanted it all done at once, but there was always a limit to how much could be achieved in a couple of weeks. He wanted a long-term project. He wanted to prove he could totally transform someone in every aspect of their life. He said I had the bone structure and the height for it, the economic and cultural background for it; if I wanted he could turn me into a goddess, his crowning achievement. I said I couldn't afford to have my hair combed in his clinic, never mind all that shit, but he said he would do it for free. Who could say no to that?'

'How long did all of this take?'

'Three years.'

'And what exactly did he do?'

'You really want to know?' The women in the audience nodded. 'Okay. I had liposuction, a tummy tuck, buttock implants, calf implants, arm lifts, thigh lifts, breast enlargement, breast uplift and nipple correction.'

'That's certainly . . .'

'I had a facelift, cheek implants, rhinoplasty, my ears were pinned back, the bags under my eyes removed, I had chin implants . . .'

'Is that . . . ?'

'I had dental implants, veneers, straightening. I had a gastric band. My vagina was tightened.'

'That, uhm, yes. It was, ahm, pretty thorough.'

'Then there was the elocution, the fitness programme, the studying for my accountancy exams, and at the end of it all, I was a new me, and I loved it.'

'But?'

'There was no but. I was a cleaner, I became a receptionist, then his PA, and then a director of the company. I was a director, but I still manned the front desk, I was the first point of contact for everyone who walked through our doors. From the day he put me there, business increased twenty-five per cent. We worked very well together. Dr Yeschenkov is a wonderful, talented man, and we fell in love.'

'You had an affair?'

'Yes.'

Dr Yes had bent forward, his elbows on his knees and his hands covering his face. His solicitor sat stiffly beside him, glaring at Pearl.

'So at what point did the waxman cometh?'

'Excuse me?'

'Why did you start ripping him off over the wax portraits?'

'I didn't.'

'So he knew about them?'

'No. But there are a lot of things he doesn't know about. Dr Yeschenkov is a remarkable surgeon, he likes to make love, he likes to play golf, he likes the finer things in life, but he is not interested in the day-to-day running of the clinic. I developed a number of services that to this day he is hardly aware of, but they all make money, and it all goes directly into the company. You can check the books.'

'As an accountant, you could fix them.'

'We have independent accountants.'

'Pearl, how did Arabella die?'

'Is she dead? You only have Buddy's word for it, a homosexual gambling addict and self-confessed murderer. His work has been going downhill for several months. I rejected his portrait of Arabella and he has obviously gone off the rails, whether it's his debts or the death of his pal. In his madness he took Arabella to their favourite spot and melted her down and got rid of anything that was left somewhere in that forest before concocting this entire story. He's trying to black-mail us.'

'Buddy is?'

'Yes. Isn't it obvious?'

Buddy sat shaking his head. He went to say something, but I held up my hand. 'You forget there's another witness.' I pointed. 'You. With the tattoo.'

Spider-web was trying to look small and insignificant, which was a pity, because he was large and significant. People around him shuffled sideways.

He said, 'What?'

'You helped remove Arabella's body from the Forum.'

'Nope. Not me.'

'You did it with your friend Rolo.'

'Nope. Not me.'

'So what are you doing here today?'

He shrugged. 'Just passin'.'

'You were Rolo's partner in crime; you came into this shop and roughed me up, you were with him when he killed Augustine and Liam.'

'I duffed you up right enough, mostly because you're a spaz. But I don't know anything about the other two. August who or what?'

He had probably sat in police stations a hundred times and pulled the same innocent face.

'You haven't a clue what you're doing, have you?' It was Pearl. She looked triumphant. 'You masquerade as a private detective, but it's all a big joke. You fumble around thinking you know something because you've read all these books, but actually it's all crap, it's all an act, it's all pretend. You've brought us here to face some kind of kangaroo court, and now you're falling flat on your face. You have no evidence, you have no credible witness, you're making wild accusations about anyone who happens to come into your line of sight. Why don't you admit it, say you're sorry and let us all get on with the business of suing you? Because I'm telling you, by the end of the week we're going to be knocking down that creepy old house of yours for apartments.'

As soon as she said it she knew it was a mistake.

My audience was confused. They were anxious to see my reaction to Pearl's tirade, but a smile was definitely not what they expected.

I had her on the house, and now I would slam the advantage home. I had a surprise up my sleeve. Two, in fact.

I said, 'You're right, of course. I mean, why would I put myself through this unless I was absolutely sure of the outcome? Yes, I can see how Buddy might be an unreliable witness. I can understand how a busy man like Dr Yes might not be aware of every detail of his business. But you're wrong on one point. These books, all around us, they're not crap, as you so crudely put it. They are important in a way that you will never understand. They not only teach me how to solve crimes, they show me how to do it in a dramatic fashion. For example, right now, just when you are thinking you are on top, and this wonderful jury might think that I've thrown the case away, these books tell me that it's always important to hold something back, always vital to save some crucial piece of evidence right for the very end, or perhaps some previously unheralded witness or expert in a particular field who can blow the whole thing wide open. Well, that's just exactly what I'm going to do, Pearl, and let's see how confident you are after they're finished with you.'

'Pathetic,' said Pearl.

'Alison,' I said.

She looked towards the door, thinking I meant her to fetch in these surprise witnesses.

'Alison, will you please take the stand.'

41

Alison climbed into the witness box. She whispered under her breath, 'I hope you know what you're doing. I know nothing about anything.'

I smiled reassuringly. At least it was meant to be reassuring. She might have thought I was grinning like an idiot. I knew what I was after, and it was very simple. I nodded at Jeff. All heads craned upwards again as the photograph of Arabella with Dr Yeschenkov at the Xianth gallery reappeared on the ceiling.

I said, 'We don't at this point know if this is actually Arabella with Dr Yeschenkov, or her wax double. But if it is her wax double, then she is dressed in Arabella's clothes, has hair like Arabella, earrings of Arabella . . . are we all agreed?'

I looked at Dr Yes, who indicated neither yay nor nay, and Pearl, who nodded slightly.

'Alison, will you tell the . . . shop . . . what you do for a living?'

'I work in a jeweller's.'

'You are a jeweller.'

'I work in a . . .'

'You are a jewellery expert.'

'Well I wouldn't . . .'

'Compared to everyone here, you are, without doubt, an expert in jewellery?'

'If you insist.'

'Okay then. I want you to study the photograph on the ceiling. And tell us what jewellery you can see.'

'There's quite a lot on Dr Yeschenkov. High-end stuff from the look of it, even though we don't see much in the way of high-end stuff in our little—

'Just Arabella, please.'

'Okay. Well, if she's wearing earrings, they're hidden by her hair, nothing on her neck, and only one arm in shot. There's a watch; I can't really . . .'

'Perhaps if I enhance the picture?'

Clearly I already had this worked out. I clicked to the next one. The watch was now much larger, big enough to make out the detail.

'Yep, that's more like it.'

'So what can you tell us about this watch?'

'It's a ladies' stainless-steel Citizen watch, uhm, expansion wristband, luminescent hands and hour marks outlined in black. It would be water-resistant to a hundred and fifty feet – I mean, it says that, but whoever goes to a hundred and fifty feet? Retails for about a hundred and twenty quid, though seeing as I know you I can probably do you a deal.'

She smiled. The audience tittered. I did not.

'What about the design on the face?'

'The snake?'

'Yes, the snake. Does it have any significance?'

'Yes, it does. We sell quite a lot of them. It's the signature of a company called Medic Alert. It provides a life-saving identification system for people with hidden medical conditions and allergies. The back of the watch would have been engraved with whatever medical condition Arabella happened to be suffering from.'

'Thank you, Alison, that will be all.'

She was clearly relieved to be out of the spotlight. I gave her the thumbs-up as she passed and switched it instead to Dr Yeschenkov.

I said, 'Doctor, you are aware of this system?'

'Yes, of course.'

'Are you also aware that Arabella was allergic to penicillin?'

'Yes, I was aware. I wrote it into her notes.'

'And who has access to those notes?'

'All of my medical staff, everyone who was involved in her procedures, doctors and nurses.'

'And if by some chance they failed to read the notes properly, they would be trained enough to look for the Medic Alert watch or locket or bracelet?'

'Yes, always.'

'And what would happen to someone like Arabella if she was inadvertently given penicillin?'

'Many people are allergic to it, but their reactions are relatively minor: a rash, perhaps, swollen lips or itchy eyes. Arabella suffered from a more serious form of allergy, and would have had an anaphylactic response, which would have been life-threatening – most notably causing a contraction of the airways. Blood pressure might also drop to a dangerous level. Either of these might render the patient unconscious. Her speech would have been slurred, her lips and nail beds would have turned blue. She would have thrown up. This, however, sir, is irrelevant. I was well aware of Arabella's allergy, and she was most certainly not given penicillin.'

I turned as quickly as my hips would allow and pointed.

'Is that right, Pearl?'

Her eyes were cold, her stare withering.

But before she could say anything, I pressed the button again and the next picture appeared on the ceiling.

Two prescription notes, side by side.

Both for penicillin.

Both issued by the Yeschenkov Clinic.

Both signed by Dr Yeschenkov.

But the two signatures quite clearly different.

'May I now introduce my handwriting expert?'

I looked to the door. All eyes looked where I looked.

He stood there with his side-swept hair and porcine cheeks, in his tweed jacket, and flannel trousers, and cream loafers, and with an unlit pipe in his mouth, smiling around it.

'May I present Professor Lowenbrau?'

He came into the shop. He gave a short, clipped bow, and nodded around the audience. In fact he wasn't a professor. In fact he wasn't called Lowenbrau. In fact he knew damn all about handwriting. His real name was Brendan Coyle. He was an acclaimed author of literary fiction, a much-despised part-time crime writer, an aesthete, an intellectual, a pain in the hole, and a friend of sorts.

Pearl had a very salient point, and one that I was already aware of. No Alibis wasn't a court of law, nobody was on trial or had taken an oath, so there was no responsibility on my part to adhere to those aspects of court procedure that one might normally take as sacrosanct. Everything I was doing was designed to wring a confession from the guilty, and if I had to perform a sleight of hand to get it, then I was quite happy too. The result was all-important. Others would have to prove it later; for the moment, all I wanted was the murderer cornered.

And so Professor Lowenbrau stood there, a pompous windbag if ever there was one, but he had the look of someone whose pomposity was based on the knowledge that he was the leader in his field. I was expecting Brendan Coyle to rise to the occasion, to perform, to bullshit mightily. He would point out the differences in the signatures, and produce samples of Pearl's own signature I had unearthed in the documents supplied by the clinic to Augustine's solicitor following Arabella's disappearance, and show the similarities in style, and hint at the fingerprint analysis that would shortly be carried out by one of his imaginary colleagues that would prove that Pearl had become so powerful within the clinic that she thought she knew enough to issue and sign prescriptions on Dr Yeschenkov's behalf, that she had decided herself what was wrong with Arabella and made the fatal mistake of not examining her medical records and failed to recognise the importance of her wristwatch before administering the penicillin that had killed her. These simple errors had precipitated everything that had followed, right up to the murder of Rolo in Tollymore Forest.

But in the event, the good professor uttered not a single word.

Pearl let out a sigh, and as the air issued from her she seemed to collapse in on herself. She came off her chair and on to her knees and bent over, and buried her head in her hands. Her shoulders heaved. Everyone stared at her, mesmerised. In the end it took a man of standing and authority to take hold of her, to pull her hands away from her face and say, 'Why?'

That, obviously, wasn't me, for I was as gobsmacked by her sudden collapse as everyone else.

It was Dr Yes peeling her hands away, revealing her make-up-run face, with one set of false eyelashes hanging down.

'*Why?*' she cried. 'I did it for you!'

'But that . . . doesn't make sense, Pearl . . . You wrote a prescription . . .'

'I wrote it for you! I was taking the weight off your shoulders!'

'But you can't do that . . .'

'It was a simple mistake! And I knew if you found out you wouldn't stand by me, because the clinic and its reputation means more to you than I do, so I had to cover it up, I had to. I couldn't tell you! What hope would there be for us then? You would never leave her, never leave that fat frump after this . . . !'

Pearl looked daggers at the woman I, and everyone else, had presumed merely to be his legal aid.

Pearl shook her head in despair. 'How could you, how could you choose her over me?'

Dr Yeschenkov finally let go of her hands and stood up. He shook his head sadly. 'Pearl, I created you . . . you were an experiment, a project, you were my Eliza . . . I fell, I fell in lust with you. But I did something wrong, I went too far. You weren't my Pygmalion, you were my . . . Frankenstein's monster. I could see it in you, but *this* . . . I never suspected you would go this far. I'm sorry, Pearl, I'm so sorry.' And then he looked at me. 'I'm truly sorry.'

I said, 'I always knew you couldn't judge a book by its cover.'

Alison stepped up beside me and hooked her arm through mine. 'And I always knew you couldn't polish a turd.' And then she whispered lovingly in my ear, 'Although I'm doing my best.'

42

When someone dies, all sorts of parasites emerge to feed on the mouldering corpse. It's disgusting. I was obviously only interested in securing Augustine's legacy, but once word got out about the murders, and Pearl's arrest, and Spider-web's arrest, and Brian Wailer's arrest, and Dr Yeschenkov being taken in for questioning, suddenly there were nephews, cousins and second cousins crawling all over Augustine's *oeuvre* and claiming rights. The prospect of No Alibis ever republishing his *Barbed-Wire Love* trilogy receded with each solicitor's letter. As for his fabled fourth book in the series, there was no evidence that it had ever existed. It was, it appeared, truly Augustine's final work of fiction.

Spring turned into a lengthy summer, with the sun high in the skies, and customers rarer than hen's teeth. I tried to spend as little time as possible with Alison, because she had grown from being just unpleasantly plump to the size of a Zeppelin. She said she understood, that she was happy with her few hours in the jewellery shop across the road, and with spending more time on her comic-book art, and I mean that in the disparaging sense, even though it was, literally, comic-book art. Jeff was on a ridiculously long break from college and had chosen to go travelling rather than help out in the shop, while Mother was now permanently back home and behaving, up to a point. I tried to get her to cover the till for me while I did essential stock-taking and reading, but ultimately I had to sack her from all duties in No Alibis. It wasn't just her insistence on continuing to smoke in the shop. It was her habit of using Augustine's urn as an ashtray. She had to mount stepladders and unscrew a lid in order to hide the evidence of her guilty habit, and was only discovered when she accidently knocked the urn off its shelf and spilled the contents over the floor. This, unhappily – or happily, depending on your point of view – coincided with the front door opening and one of those hen's teeth entering, bringing with him a draught of polluted summer breeze, which wafted essence of Augustine all over the shop, where it settled on books and shelves. One might look on it as the last macabre act of the *Case of the Pearl Necklace*, an ironic climax of fate, with Augustine moving from being Exhibit No. 1 to becoming part of the very fabric of No Alibis. I was naturally furious. One should never have to hoover up one of one's favourite authors.

Dr. Yes

*

On a late August morning, about five minutes after I opened up, Alison called and said, 'Guess what?'

'No,' I said.

'Waters broke. Driving to hospital.'

'Oh,' I said.

I didn't like the way I was suddenly feeling. Clammy.

I am allergic to hospitals. They are breeding grounds for *everything*.

'Well?'

At that moment the shop door opened and DI Robinson entered. I hadn't seen him in months. Not even my two per cent off summer sale had tempted him through my doors.

I said, 'I'm going to have to put you on hold.'

I put her on it before she could respond. I nodded at Robinson. He nodded back.

'How's business?' he asked.

'Slow,' I said.

'Thought you'd want to know, we found Arabella Wogan's body. Pretty bad state. Lenny McNulty led us to it, eventually.'

'Lenny . . . ?'

'The fella with the tattoo on his hand?'

'Oh yeah. So. What about Pearl?'

'She's changed her tune. Apparently the murders were all Rolo's idea. They were lovers. He was blackmailing her. She has a different version every week. But we'll nail her eventually.'

'And what about Buddy?'

'Buddy will be fine. Outside chance of a manslaughter charge, but I'm fighting it.'

'Well,' I said, 'everything turned out okay in the end.'

'Once again. You know, you're very lucky.'

'It's not luck.'

'You have your day in the sun, and you don't have to worry about the paperwork.'

'It's the way I like it.'

'Well I'm just telling you, you are very lucky, but one day your luck is going to run out. If I were you, I'd quit while you were ahead. You have a baby on the way, don't you?'

I glanced at the phone.

'Yeah,' I said.

'Well maybe now's the time to get out, leave it to the professionals.'

'Well maybe if you introduced me to one, I could hand over the reins.'

'You're funny,' he said.

'So's your face,' I said.

He left. I took out a Twix and a can of Coke. The morning was warming up. It felt good to be alive, although, obviously, all such feelings are temporary.

I am not entirely without feelings or consideration. Of *course* I went to the hospital. But it had to wait. I had customers. Three more that morning and two after lunch. In the early evening I took the phone off hold, and locked up the many locks that keep No Alibis safe and secure. I drove to the maternity wing at the Ulster Hospital. I took the stairs. One at a time. I lingered in the corridor until a nurse asked me what I wanted. She showed me to a private room. I looked through the glass in the door at Alison, pale, holding my son in her arms.

I entered the room. Alison smiled. There were tears in her eyes. She showed me our baby.

She held him up for me to take.

My arms would not move.

Instead I said, 'Where'd you get the monkey, love?'

With thanks to Richard Abbott of 3DTwin Ltd
for waxing lyrical